A James Acton Thriller

By
J. Robert Kennedy

James Acton Thrillers
The Protocol
Brass Monkey
Broken Dove
The Templar's Relic
Flags of Sin
The Arab Fall
The Circle of Eight
The Venice Code
Pompeii's Ghosts

Detective Shakespeare Mysteries
Depraved Difference
Tick Tock
The Redeemer

Special Agent Dylan Kane Thrillers
Rogue Operator
Containment Failure
Cold Warriors

Zander Varga, Vampire Detective
The Turned

POMPEII'S GHOSTS

A James Acton Thriller

J. ROBERT KENNEDY

Copyright © 2014 J. Robert Kennedy
CreateSpace

All rights reserved. No part of this publication may be reproduced, stored in or introduced into a retrieval system, or transmitted in any form, or by any means (electronic, mechanical, photocopying, recording or otherwise) without the prior written permission of the publisher.

This is a work of fiction. Names, characters, places, and incidents are products of the author's imagination. Any resemblance to actual persons, living or dead, is entirely coincidental.

ISBN-10: 1500324442
ISBN-13: 978-1500324445

First Edition

10 9 8 7 6 5 4 3 2 1

For the 276 who were kidnapped, and the over two million young girls estimated to have been taken against their will and forced into the global sex trade.

#BringBackOurGirls

POMPEII'S GHOSTS

A James Acton Thriller

"You could hear the shrieks of women, the wailing of infants, and the shouting of men; some were calling their parents, others their children or their wives, trying to recognize them by their voices. People bewailed their own fate or that of their relatives, and there were some who prayed for death in their terror of dying. Many besought the aid of the gods, but still more imagined there were no gods left, and that the universe was plunged into eternal darkness for evermore."

Gaius Plinius Caecilius Secundus, a.k.a. "Pliny the Younger", nephew of Gaius Plinius Secundus, a.k.a. "Pliny the Elder"
Letter to Tacitus, circa 100 AD

"Above all, we should acknowledge that the collapse of the Soviet Union was the greatest geopolitical catastrophe of the century. As for the Russian nation, it became a genuine drama. Tens of millions of our co-citizens and co-patriots found themselves outside Russian territory. Moreover, the epidemic of disintegration infected Russia itself."

Vladimir Putin, April 2005

PREFACE

To Roman historians, the name "Pliny the Elder" is well known. A prolific writer with an impressive résumé, much has been learned about life and public administration in Ancient Rome thanks to him. His nephew, known as "Pliny the Younger", is equally well known amongst volcanologists due to his detailed and horrific descriptions of the eruption of Mount Vesuvius, and the destruction it wrought upon Pompeii and other surrounding towns. His description was so memorable, he has been honored by history—forevermore shall the most violent of eruptions, such as that of Mount Vesuvius, be known as Plinian.

His descriptions have been used throughout this novel to lend realism to the horror that befell twenty thousand people, too many of their ghosts still haunting the nearly perfectly preserved streets of Pompeii to this day.

Though his letters to a friend years later are heavily relied upon, there is one glaring inaccuracy in his accounts that must be challenged.

If Pliny the Elder was overcome by the gasses from the volcano, why weren't the others with him as well? And if at least some of the others were able to breathe, what could possibly have been so urgent that they would abandon him, rather than take the few minutes to carry him to the waiting boats?

It is a two thousand year old mystery that is about to be resolved.

With tragic consequences.

"Pliny the Elder" Residence, Misenum, Roman Empire
August 24th, 79 AD

"What in the name of the gods is that?"

The ground shook with a rumble as if a beast contained under the marble floor was struggling to escape, its groan vibrating through the house as those lounging on the many cushions and silks jumped to their feet—some more spryly than others—and furtively glanced about, wondering what to do, fear evident in their eyes.

And immediately identifying them as foreign to the area.

For those who had lived near the Bay of Naples for some time, like Lucius Valerius Corvus, knew exactly what it was—just another tremor, the shaking of the ground a too often occurrence, though more frequent as of late. Instinctively he had placed himself in an archway with a hand gripping the stone for balance at the first hint, and now, as the ground beneath their feet settled, Valerius looked to his Lord and Prefect, Gaius Plinius Secundus, to make certain he was okay, then to their honored guest.

The man who had asked the question.

Emperor Titus.

Several of the Praetorian Guard burst into the room, the centurion leading them rushing to his Emperor's side, bowing—and looking more rattled than his charge. "Are you unharmed, Imperator?"

Emperor Titus waved the man off, having quickly recovered from the scare, he himself never thought of as a coward, having led many successful military campaigns, not the least of which was the defeat of the Jewish Rebellion. A man to show fear he was not, and in this case, all Valerius saw on his Emperor's face was curiosity.

And true to form, he ignored his guard and looked at Plinius. "Does this happen often?"

Plinius nodded as he motioned for everyone to sit back down. All waited for their Emperor to do so first. Emperor Titus dropped onto the large cushions with the difficulty age and a life in the military inevitably brought. Taking a long drink from his goblet, draining it of the sweet wine it contained, he held up his cup and a servant rushed from out of sight, filling it almost instantly.

Plinius sat, as did the rest of the guests. "Too often, I'm afraid, sire. I fear another earthquake as happened seventeen years ago. We continue to rebuild from it to this day. To have another one I fear would break the will of those who remained."

"And that mountain that continues to smoke?"

Plinius batted the words away as he swallowed a fat grape. "It has done nothing in my lifetime but threaten. It is like Helvidius. He rattled his saber but was harmless."

Laughter filled the room at the expense of the avowed enemy and critic of Emperor Vespasian, Titus' father who had died less than two months ago. The Emperor nodded, a smile on his face for but a moment, his visage suddenly becoming serious. He flicked his hand in the air in a dismissive manner. "Leave us. I wish to speak alone with my dear Plinius."

The room quickly emptied, no one daring say a word, and Valerius, after making certain all had left, turned to leave himself when his Emperor's voice stopped him.

"I would have you stay, as you are Plinius' trusted man, and are fully aware of what I want to speak to your master about."

Valerius bowed deeply but said nothing, instead sitting on the cushion pointed to by his Emperor, halfway between his Prefect and his Caesar. As he made himself comfortable, Emperor Titus' voice lowered.

"I have concerns, Plinius."

"Of?"

"These quakes. The safety of what is kept across the bay."

Plinius nodded, his face revealing little emotion, though Valerius knew he was about to dismiss the Emperor's fears but dared not trivialize them. "I understand your concern, sire, and I can assure you I share them. This is why everything has been stored underground, so should the walls collapse, nothing would be revealed. If another quake such as that which struck us over a decade ago should occur, the rubble would merely act to secure your concern even more until your own people would be able to salvage it." Plinius leaned forward slightly. "And I pledge my life to defend it."

"As do I, my Caesar," added Valerius.

Plinius nodded his appreciation to Valerius, then returned his attention to their Emperor whose face was creased with a frown.

"And your plan should something untoward occur?"

"I have over fifty ships and thousands of men at my command, safely anchored here. With a favorable wind, we can be in Pompeii within four hours, and secure the area within minutes of landing. As well, Valerius, my second-in-command and most trusted man, lives in Pompeii, atop the very vault in question, with a small contingent of our best men, and his primary duty is the protection and preservation of that which you have entrusted to me."

Emperor Titus' head bobbed slowly, his lips pursing as he looked from man to man. "Then I know it is in capable hands and I shall fret no longer." He chuckled. "If the Senate only knew what resided in a humble basement in Pompeii, I fear many daggers would hasten my union with Julius Caesar himself!"

He roared with laughter and Plinius joined him, Valerius smiling but not partaking as he knew full well that if anything were to happen to that now entrusted to his safekeeping, he would surely die.

As would his Prefect and friend.

For no one could resist the massive fortune now housed on his property overlooking the sea.

A war chest, taken from the Empire's treasury when Vespasian ruled, to put down any rival's bid to the throne.

"Have our guests return!" ordered Emperor Titus. "Let the feast continue!"

Within moments the others returned, none daring show any annoyance at having been unceremoniously ejected from the lunch, an earlier than planned gathering made necessary by the ever changing schedule of the Emperor. If it were Valerius, as it had been before, he knew he too would have shown no expression that might betray his inner anger and annoyance, as it would be of no use. He had served under Plinius for the better of fifteen years and thanks to his Lord's position had met his share of emperors, and he found they all had one trait in common—supreme arrogance. Having never met any before they had attained their position he couldn't say whether or not they had always been that way, or if it was an acquired skill learned upon gaining the highest office in the land.

All Valerius knew was that it pissed him off.

And he would never show it.

His Lord, Plinius, was different. Though of a far higher station than Valerius through birth, when Valerius had found himself under Plinius' command, a young officer fresh from the academy, Plinius had taken him under his wing like a son and treated him as close to an equal as was permitted in an empire obsessed with class and caste.

And through Plinius' tutelage and care, Valerius was now a wealthy man himself with a home in Rome and a summer home in Pompeii. *It is essential you pay as little in taxes as possible.* It was sage advice at any time, and coming from Plinius when he had gifted his old escape in Pompeii to his underling, he had explained the importance. *Hide your wealth outside of Rome, and the Senate cannot take what you have earned. Keep it in Rome, and they would soon have you parted from it.*

The advice, over a decade old, held true today more than ever. With the economy in recession, inflation then deflation wreaking havoc, Emperor Vespasian had tried to stimulate it through massive public works projects to keep the citizenry employed and distracted, his most ambitious a mighty coliseum that would dominate the Roman skyline for centuries to come. It hadn't worked, instead only draining the treasury, hence the late Emperor's desire to keep a large portion in reserve, outside of Rome, in the event of a challenge to his leadership.

And it was all kept in Valerius' basement.

Gold bars filled the newly excavated underground chambers on his property tucked into the mountainside. It was impressive, and terrifying. If word were to escape, every thief and marauder in the empire would descend upon his home and the treasury hidden away from the people of Rome.

It was a massive fortune worth dying for, either in pursuit of it, or defense.

The room shook again, this time harder than even Valerius remembered feeling, eliciting screams from the women and yelps even from some of the seasoned soldiers. The floor cracked at their feet as dust and plaster fell from the ceiling. Valerius leapt to his feet then pulled Plinius to his, ushering him out of the house and onto the lawn overlooking the Bay of Naples, the Praetorian Guard whisking the Emperor out at the same time.

The shaking soon stopped but no one noticed as they all looked across the bay at the sleeping giant that appeared to be awakening.

Valerius looked at Plinius. "I think I should check on our charge."

Plinius nodded. "Agreed. Send word immediately should you require assistance."

"I shall, my Lord."

Plinius gripped Valerius by the wrist, squeezing hard and looking deep into his eyes. "Good luck, old friend."

Valerius bowed slightly, then deeply to the Emperor who said nothing, this time betrayed by his eyes.

For fear was there, as it was in all of them.

Mount Vesuvius had awoken, and even in the darkest reaches of their souls, none could imagine the horrors that were about to befall them all.

Exiting Eritrean Airspace
Present Day

"We're descending."

Professor James Acton opened his eyes and glanced out the window then over at the source of the comment, Command Sergeant Major Burt "Big Dog" Dawson, BD to his friends. "How can you tell?"

Dawson shrugged. "Years of experience?" He pointed to a lone road that stretched across the landscape for as far as the eye could see. "We should be at least thirty thousand feet in the air. We're no better than twenty and falling. Slowly though."

"You can tell that from a road?"

"The width of it. That's a two lane road, which means a fairly standard width. There's a distinctly different look to a road from twenty thousand feet than there is from thirty."

Acton nodded, the explanation obvious once actually articulated. "Okay, so it was a stupid question," he said, smiling. "I'm sure there's a reason, though," he added, his Spidey senses starting to tingle, setting off a slight adrenaline rush at the thought of yet another thing going wrong in his life. He was an archeology professor at Saint Paul's, a small Maryland university where he had worked for much of his professional career. And his life now was far too "event driven" for him to remember what had attracted him to the damned profession in the first place.

Indiana Jones.

He had to admit that was the truth. He had loved those movies and even read the novels, voraciously devouring anything he could related to the character, and when he finished that, he chewed through the entire archeology and ancient history section of his limited school library.

He fell in love with history.

Especially ancient history.

Roman history was his favorite. The great empires. Greco, Roman, Egyptian, Mongol, Caliphate. Not to mention the more modern ones, British, French, Ottoman, Soviet, Nazi and American. He was fascinated by them all, and how similar they were in nature, no matter how old or new. Empires rose, thrived, and fell. It was inevitable, and he was convinced the empire he lived in now was collapsing. Would it take a thousand years like the Roman to fall, or would it be rapid like the British. World War Two essentially ended it for them. Would one good war end it for America? *Had one good war already ended it and we just didn't know it yet?*

He found himself preoccupied with that thought quite often, and he hoped that with today's knowledge of the past and our technology, along with a shared and distributed information source like the Internet, Western civilization just may avoid the hard fall that so many before had experienced, and instead might ride out the current dip. But with challengers to the throne all around, from the new economic powerhouse of communist China, to the growing powerhouses of India and Brazil, along with a resurgent and belligerent Soviet Union Version 2.0 if the West were to survive, it would need to defeat not only these external forces economically and perhaps militarily, but also the enemies from within who would destroy what previous generations had sacrificed so much to build. Whether they were immigrant and Muslim groups trying to change the way of life that created the wonderful countries they wanted to now live in, or those who would have us feel shame for actually being great countries amongst comparative cesspools, or even those who were perfectly content to sit back and live off the avails of the great Western nations while contributing nothing, all would need to be defeated.

A daunting task.

He could never understand why someone would risk everything to flee their country to come and live in one of the Western democracies, then immediately try to change their new home to be more like their old home. Acton had lost count of the number of discussions he had had with his students on the topic. They made for lively debates, and he was open to all views on the matter, as long as the arguments were civil and productive. Unfortunately he found too many times with today's youth they had too difficult a time putting together a cogent argument, and instead resorted to insults, cursing, or complaining to some civil liberties group about the professor who challenged politically correct thinking, when in fact all he was doing was forcing them to participate in the greatest freedom of all.

Freedom of speech.

He thought of the movie Raiders of the Lost Ark and how in the end the government had taken the ark and hidden it in a warehouse, the wonders of the find forever lost to history except for a cameo in a fantastic sequel with a riveting story line almost thirty years later.

But not this time.

This time the treasure they had unearthed was public.

A little too public for his liking.

And it was loaded in the hold of this very plane, a priceless trove worth almost a full billion dollars if simply melted down. But they weren't conquistadors, Spaniards melting down priceless Incan and Aztec treasures merely for the metal and gemstones. They were archeologists, trying to preserve the past.

And in this case it meant secrecy and heavy security, the former of which had failed miserably, thanks most likely to the completely inept and corrupt United Nations that had handled the negotiations. If there was one organization on the planet that needed a major overhaul, it was the UN. Any organization so warped as to name countries like Iran to head up women's rights had to be shutdown. What was needed in his opinion was a United Democratic Nations, rather than a collection of dictators constantly looking for ways to make Israel look bad instead of actually furthering human rights and bettering mankind.

And the permanent Security Council? Again, why should non-democracies like China and Russia have veto power? And for that matter, why should the United States? If the UN was supposed to be a democratic institution, even if its member states were not, why should there be veto power?

Because you couldn't trust the vast majority of the membership to not pass resolution after resolution impacting the democracies of the world. Though that wasn't the original intent of the veto power—it was more to create a balance between the West and the communists after World War II—it had now become a balance between the West and the Muslim and African nations of the world, few of which were democracies and few of which gave equal rights to all of their citizens, especially women.

Though half a dozen had died yesterday, he and Laura had made it out alive with a massive trove of gold the bureaucrats were concerned about though not the preserved archeological find they had hoped for. He had breathed a tremendous sigh of relief when the massive transport had taken off and left Eritrea behind. He had been a little leery however, the enormous Antonov An-124 Ruslan being insisted upon by the Eritreans, including a "non-Western" crew.

Acton would prefer to be sitting in the back of a good old American C17 Globemaster with a dozen armed Delta operators surrounding him, rather than their current situation of a private Russian aircraft with private contractors at the controls and those who had survived yesterday's attack of an unarmed group of security "observers", two from each of the permanent members of the United Nations Security Council, along with two from Italy, the ultimate destination of the treasure they had found.

But he did have to admit he felt a lot better when the two American observers had been introduced to him. Dawson and one of his Delta Force cohorts, a Korean-American, Sergeant Carl "Niner" Sung, were well known to Acton. He trusted them with his life despite an inauspicious beginning to their relationship years ago.

He looked back out the window, wondering if his mind was playing tricks on him, he too now certain they were descending. "There *is* a reason, isn't there? Some air traffic issue?"

There was no reply.

Acton looked away from the window and was surprised to find the two seats beside him empty, Dawson and Niner walking toward the front of the aircraft. It had been configured with several dozen seats at the front for the passengers, and behind a temporary wall was the hoard of gold bars they had retrieved. Another transport with his fiancée on board had lifted off only moments before them, carrying the remains of the ship that had contained the gold and its hallowed crew, the origin of which was astonishing.

In fact, he had found it almost impossible to believe when he had put the pieces together.

Raised voices from the front had him focus on what was going on. Dawson was jabbing a finger toward one of the private security that the Eritreans had insisted upon, someone Dawson had identified as ex-Russian Spetsnaz.

Suddenly the man stepped back and pulled a weapon, squeezing two shots off into Dawson' chest. His body sailed backward half a dozen feet, his chest shoved back, his arms and legs stretched out in front of him like a marionette that had been suddenly yanked by its master.

Acton gasped, jumping to his feet as Niner stepped forward, using a combination of moves so fast Acton's mind couldn't even process them, a mere split second later resulting in Niner with the man's weapon and a round pumped into the previous owner's head, Niner dropping to a knee and spinning to his right, firing two shots into another guard before he could react.

But his weapon did, the man's finger clenching on the trigger, firing a single round through the fuselage. Wind howled through the cabin as alarms began to blare. The plane suddenly plunged into a rapid dive, tossing all those aboard around, Acton bear hugging the seat in front of him as the oxygen masks dropped.

He pushed himself back into his seat, grabbing the lap belt and fastening it, yanking it tight as he reached up for a mask. Fitting it over his mouth, he leaned into the aisle and his heart sank.

The body of Command Sergeant Major Burt Dawson had tumbled forward against the front of the cabin.

Lifeless.

And as the plane continued its rapid descent, his thoughts turned to the one person he wished he was with this very moment, but thankful he wasn't.

The love of his life, Laura.

He reached into his pocket and pulled out the satellite phone. With one hand pressed against the seatback in front of him, he dialed with the other. It rang several times then went to voicemail, her voice, so beautiful, the last one he would hear in this lifetime.

He took a steadying breath then removed the mask from his face.

"Hi babe, it's me!" he shouted over the whine of the engines, pausing to take another breath through the mask. "I don't have much time. There's been some sort of hijacking attempt on the plane and we're going down. Dawson was killed by the private security and a stray bullet caused us to depressurize." He sucked in another breath. "We're in a steep dive, so hopefully we'll be okay."

Another breath, and one final thought.

"But if we don't make it, know that I love you, and that I treasured every moment we've spent together. These last few years have been the greatest of my life, and if I die today, you've made my life worth living. Give my love to Mom and Dad, and to Greg and his family. I love you, hon, and I'm sorry I—"

The plane jerked to the left, the pilot apparently losing control, tossing him violently, causing the phone to fly from his hand and bounce along the left wall of the fuselage toward the front of the plane. He battled to straighten himself, finally succeeding, their angle now giving him a clear view of the ground below, and the impossibly close road that had only minutes before seemed so far away.

He closed his eyes, gripping the arms of his seat hard, his mind filled with only one regret.

A regret that at this moment seemed terribly selfish.

And as the engines whined, the cries of some of the passengers competing with the turbines, he thought of all the heartache that was about to be caused.

As Pompeii claimed its last victims.

"Pliny the Elder" Residence, Misenum, Roman Empire
August 24th, 79 AD

"Uncle, what do you make of it?"

Plinius, standing on the veranda he hadn't left since the Emperor departed for Rome, turned to see his young nephew, Gaius, emerge from the house, scroll and stylus ever present. Plinius extended his hand and the young man took it, standing beside his uncle. They both stared across the bay at the sight before them. The ground continued to shake, the frequency making the pauses between tremors almost unnoticeable, and the sky across the bay continued to darken, far too early for this time of day.

Across the water the mighty Vesuvius continued to spew its innards skyward, a straight plume firing high into the sky then outward, like a tall palm tree, whatever it was ejecting eventually falling back down to earth in all directions.

Plinius looked at his nephew, a mere seventeen years old, and already about to begin what he was certain would be a successful legal career. His gaze returned to the plume that now dominated the horizon.

"I don't know what to make of it. I've never witnessed such a thing before. I've heard of it, of course, but never seen a volcano erupt with my own eyes."

"It's beautiful," murmured Gaius. "Terrifying, but beautiful."

Plinius nodded, uncertain he shared his young nephew's opinion. "It *is* terrifying." He motioned toward the scrolls. "Your studies?"

Gaius nodded. "Yes, Uncle."

Plinius pursed his lips. "Perhaps today it would be better to record what you see here. I fear history is being made, and we are to become pawns to the gods' wrath."

"I shall record everything diligently, Uncle."

Plinius put his arm around his young protégé, he himself a dull yet successful lawyer for many years while the dreaded Nero held the throne, during which it was best to keep a low profile lest the head that stood above the crowd be lopped off in one of his tantrums. When Vespasian had finally won the throne during the civil war, or as it had become known, the Year of the Four Emperors, Plinius had reemerged, eagerly sought after by the emperor as a man he could trust that was also capable.

It had eventually resulted in him being named Prefect of the Fleet, and his station here in Misenum. As he gazed out at the harbor housing the dozens of vessels at his command, he quickly came to a decision.

He snapped his fingers.

A servant rushed forward.

"Have my cutter prepared. I wish to observe what is happening across the bay."

The servant bowed then ran off as Plinius turned to his nephew. "Do you wish to accompany me? It could be of historical and scientific interest."

Gaius shook his head. "No, I think I'll remain here with Mother, you know how she is. Besides, I have a feeling observing from a distance will give me a better perspective on what is truly happening."

Plinius smiled, knowing his nephew was right. Charging into the midst of this curious phenomenon was probably foolhardy, but curiosity was always one of his weaknesses. He knew Gaius was incredibly curious as well, but he also knew his mother would never allow him to head toward the danger regardless of whether or not his uncle was foolish enough to do so.

"I think that is wise," said Plinius, who then motioned toward the scrolls. "And make no mention of our guests today. No matter what happens, history must never record that our Emperor was present."

"Understood, Uncle," said Gaius with a slight bow.

And as if to emphasize the point, the ground jerked suddenly, knocking them both off their feet.

Outside Omhajer, Eritrea
Present Day, Six weeks before the crash

Birhan absentmindedly swatted at the flies competing for access to his rotting teeth. They didn't bother him, and if any got in and were eaten, so be it, his stomach welcoming any nourishment, no matter the form. He tapped his cane on the ground at one of his herd that was straying from the road, the goat's bleat of protest preceding a leap back into the group.

Birhan chewed on his khat, it's mildly stimulating effect keeping him alert, the near constant habit making him numb to the reality of his existence if he went without. For that's all it was, though he knew little better. Existence. His wife was dead years ago from famine along with five of his six children, his only remaining child a daughter he couldn't marry off, a dowry so far out of reach it wasn't even a dream.

He had arranged to sell her two years ago, the burden of providing for her simply too much, but she had begged him not to, and once he had met the beast of a Saudi that was looking to purchase some of the village's girls, he had backed out of the deal, realizing he'd be unable to live with himself knowing such a man would be bedding down his daughter against her will.

Feeding two mouths was difficult, especially off the small percentage of the seasonal profits he was paid by the land owner whose heard he tended, but it was nice to have someone at home at the end of the day to prepare the miserly meals and keep the humble single room home they lived in clean and tidy. Abrihet was a good girl, though not terribly attractive, the poor girl cursed with his looks rather than her mother's.

Which meant she would be doomed to a lonely existence unless he could find some way to come up with a dowry so one of the men of the village would find it worth their while to take her on as a wife.

And it would have to be soon, she getting older by the minute.

A bleat behind him had him spinning, the khat having him on the razor's edge of giddiness. A goat had somehow been left behind. He cursed and shuffled after it, the creature disappearing over the nearby embankment. As he climbed the rise he paused a moment upon reaching the top, taking in several deep breaths and enjoying the sight of the Tekezé River below. On the other side of the river marked Ethiopian territory.

Birhan spat on the ground at the mere thought of their enemy.

He had lost many friends and relatives in the war, but fortunately for him he was too old to fight. Sighing at the thought of why anyone would fight over desert, he spotted the runaway about twenty paces away. Clicking at the creature, he rounded it from the opposite side of where he wanted it to go, then gave the cane a flick, the snap as it smacked the ground had the creature rushing back toward the herd, and Birhan following.

His foot stubbed something in the sand, causing him to pause and wince in pain.

What's this?

He knelt on one knee and moved some sand aside. An old, dry piece of wood was revealed. He was about to dismiss it when rivulets of sand began to slowly cascade down the hill toward the river below, revealing more of the piece of wood he had just stumbled upon.

A boat?

The piece of wood was curved, like the hull of a boat might be. A jolt of excitement raced through his worn body at the thought of his daughter's dowry possibly being buried right here, underneath the sand he walked by on a daily basis. He quickly swept away more of the sand, revealing more of the buried wood, and within minutes there was no doubt that this was a buried boat, and if it were seaworthy, it was a boat he could sell in town and provide the money necessary to marry off his daughter so she could begin her life.

And leave him alone.

The thought caused him to pause, but he realized that he must continue, his selfish moment never to be mentioned, her happiness all he was concerned about. As he cleared more and more of the sand away, he began to realize how massive the boat was, and glanced over his shoulder at the river, easily several hundred paces away.

How did they ever drag it here?

The thought it had been brought here during a flood only to be scuttled on the shore had his chest tightening as his heart began to sink, the next curved board broken only several feet into its sweep along the prow. After several more minutes of digging, it was clear that this boat hadn't been seaworthy in a long time, nor would it ever be again.

He dropped down on his haunches, exhausted from the effort, and disappointed that he wouldn't be able to see his daughter with child any time soon. He tossed a small stone into the gaping hole in the side of the boat and froze as it pinged off of something inside. He crawled over and stuck his head in the hole in search of possible salvage.

Perhaps a dowry is still possible!

He would have expected anyone who had abandoned the vessel to have emptied it of anything valuable, but perhaps what was worthless to them may not be to him.

Something glinted and he reached forward, grabbing a hard metal object. Pulling it from the hole and out into the sun, he suddenly felt lightheaded with excitement. Gripping the small metal rectangle in his hands, he held it up to the sun then kissed it.

POMPEII'S GHOSTS

And thanked the goat responsible for changing his life forever.

Lucius Valerius Corvus Residence, Pompeii, Roman Empire
August 24th, 79 AD

Valerius picked himself up off the floor, dusting himself of the ash that seemed to cover everything. Silks and blankets had been hung over all the windows and doorways in an attempt to keep the ash out, but the wind that seemed to howl down from the mountain kept a steady stream of servants busy as they tried to find ways of sealing the openings. Screams and wails from outside weren't stopped by mere silks, however, and Valerius found himself from time to time peering out into the darkness, it now barely mid-afternoon, to glimpse the hell outside his walls.

And on each peek, it seemed another arm's length of ash and pumice had fallen, a steady rain of small stones, still glowing from the cauldron that was now Vesuvius, continuing to rain down on the city, setting light to anything not made of stone.

The streets were filled with those trying to escape, and if it weren't for his charge buried on his property, he would leave himself, taking his precious family to safety.

But he couldn't. He couldn't abandon his duty.

And his duty would surely mean the death of his family.

He turned to his most trusted slave, Costa, who hadn't left his side since the horror had begun.

"Yes, sire?"

"I need you to get word to Plinius of what is happening here. Tell him we require rescue."

"Immediately, sire."

Costa was about to leave when Valerius grabbed his arm. "And tell your own family to leave immediately. I fear there is no place left in the city that is safe."

Costa bowed slightly. "Thank you, sire."

The ground shook again and a column nearby cracked, a large sliver of marble breaking away and shattering on the floor. Both looked at the ceiling with unease, then Valerius turned back to Costa.

"Now make all haste, for there isn't much time!"

"Yes, sire!"

Costa quickly disappeared and Valerius heard the sound of a horse galloping away minutes later. He turned to his head servant, Labeo. "Gather the staff."

Labeo bowed then left to execute his orders. Valerius returned to the window, pushing the curtain aside and looking at the mighty Vesuvius in the distance as it continued to belch ash and stone into the air, the entire sky now blackened as sheets of lightning raced across the rippling canvas of grays and evil. He turned and peered toward the sea, it barely visible despite being only several hundred paces away.

He coughed.

Stepping back from the window, he repositioned the curtain and took a drink from the goblet clutched in his hand since the air had become thick and difficult to breathe. He turned to see the staff assembled, patiently waiting for him to acknowledge them, but fear written across every face. They were men, women, children. Freemen and slaves. Husbands and wives, mothers and fathers. They were average everyday people with their own troubles and joys and responsibilities.

And not one had abandoned their post.

Valerius pointed outside without looking. "I have no words of comfort to offer, except this. I free you all of your obligations to me. Your obligation now is to your families, and to yourselves. Gather your loved ones and leave this cursed place. Make haste to the south and don't stop until you see the light of day and the ash no longer falls. And don't return until the mountain is quiet. And should we survive to see this through, you will all be welcome back." He looked at the dozens of faces in front of him. Women with tears flowing freely, children with trembling lips, men with expressions too serious to not betray their own fear. He hoped his own face didn't reveal the nausea he felt, his own stomach hollowed of any courage it might have once had. He clapped his hands together, the sound echoing through the room, startling many. "Now go, and may the gods be with you."

He turned back to the window, moving the curtain aside slightly as he listened to the foot falls slowly dwindle behind him, then nothing. He turned and started, his eyebrows shooting up as he saw almost a dozen of his staff still standing, now side by side in a row, four women and eight men, including Labeo.

"You have been dismissed," said Valerius. "Go and save yourselves."

Labeo stepped forward. "We have none to save but your family. We stand with you, sire."

The others all stepped forward, as synchronized as any combat troops he had ever commanded, and his heart surged with pride in the honor and courage being displayed before him, and albeit selfishly, in himself, knowing he could command such loyalty and devotion in the face of overwhelming odds.

He bowed slightly. "You honor me, and it will not be forgotten." He looked to Labeo. "Prepare two carts to carry my family to safety. Bring the horses inside the house so they can breathe. Load water and food for a journey of two days plus blankets and cloths to protect everyone from the ash. Remember to take extra water in case you need to put out a fire and to quench heavy thirst from whatever this is," he said, wiping some of the ash off a nearby vase with his finger.

"Immediately, sire," said Labeo, bowing, then rushing out of the room with the others in tow.

Valerius strode through his large home, it feeling empty now, his footsteps echoing off the marble, and found his wife, Avita, in their bedchambers spinning in a dress he hadn't seen before.

"Isn't it just divine?" she asked, holding her arms out and spinning on one sandaled foot. "It only arrived this morning." She rushed toward him. "Here, my darling, feel the material! It's so soft, it almost feels like I'm wearing nothing but my jewels!"

His eyes darted to her neck, a large ornate necklace, a gift from Plinius upon their marriage, adorned her powdered white skin along with bracelets, rings and earrings of ridiculous proportions.

"What in the name of the gods are you doing?" he yelled, grabbing her by the arms to halt her latest spin. "Don't you know what's going on outside?"

She glared at him for a moment, then her smile returned. "Oh, that? Why it's nothing, just a little tempest. It will pass."

He gripped her tighter as she tried to pull away. "What are you talking about? People are dying out there! We are abandoning the city!"

"Let go of me."

Her voice was low, almost a growl. He removed his hands from her arms, more out of curiosity as to what she would do next than any sense of obligation. She stepped over to a table filled with the accoutrements of female beauty and picked up a polished copper mirror, examining herself.

"Am I beautiful, darling?"

Valerius sighed then walked over to her. "Of course you are, my dear. As beautiful as the day I met you."

"Even after three children?"

"Even more so."

The mirror clattered to the floor and tears erupted as she collapsed into his arms, her shoulders trembling, the shaking of the room going unnoticed. "I'm sorry, darling, I-I don't know what came over me." She looked up at him, her tears having burned tiny rivulets through her chalk powder revealing faint trails of her lightly bronzed skin underneath. Never afraid of a hard day's work, she was darker than high society would like, but she rarely paid it any mind, her natural beauty more than enough to make those who would criticize behind her back dismissed as jealous.

"Forget about it," whispered Valerius, his arms now wrapped around his wife. "But now you must go, and quickly. The servants are preparing the wagons. You and the children will go with them at once."

Avita shook her head. "Not without you."

Valerius smiled, wiping away the tears under her eyes with his thumbs. "You know I can't. My duty to Plinius and the Emperor is clear."

"Forget them!" she cried. "Your duty is to your family!"

"Of course it is, which is why you are leaving now. If I leave with you, I will lose my honor, and my family will be forfeit, the Emperor free to do with as he pleases. And you know the Emperor, he doesn't tolerate failure. If I do not save the treasure kept here, he will kill us all for sure."

Avita placed her cheek against her husband's chest and moaned. "Oh, I know, I know. He's a horrible man!"

Valerius patted her head then gently pushed her away. "Far less so than Nero was, I assure you."

She smiled slightly. "This is true. What he did to the Thirteenth was inexcusable! Sending them to Britannia with a crystal skull! Voices telling him to do so! The man was insane."

Valerius' thoughts drifted to memories of his best friend, Flavus. They had grown up together, gone through training together, and his father had managed to get him a commission in the Thirteenth legion just before they had been ordered to Britannia. He remembered Flavus' pride at his Legion being chosen for such a sacred and important mission.

"According to the Emperor, we are under orders from Jupiter himself!"

Flavus was one who was easily swayed by anything to do with the gods, as were many Romans. Valerius had a more tempered approach, praying as was expected, but also not accepting without question what those of less acumen might blindly attribute to a sign from one of the myriad of gods Rome now worshipped.

Then there's that damned Jewish god and these infernal Christians.

The order had been out for some time that any Christians were to be arrested, but he personally hadn't paid it any mind. They were too well hidden for him to encounter, though Plinius had coordinated several raids under orders of the Emperor. In a discussion on the matter, Plinius had expressed his discomfort with how these people were being treated, but he was loyal to his Emperor and therefore forced to obey his laws.

Valerius would just as willingly let them go, but they insisted on trying to convert others to their cause, diverting the population away from their true gods.

It was blasphemous.

And dangerous in today's Rome.

With the economy barely in recovery, anything different that could be a distraction was viciously targeted, and Christians, trying to spread their new faith, were attractive fodder for a population needing someone to blame their travails on.

He looked down at his wife, trying to remember what she had last said. As if she could read his thoughts, she smiled and said, "The Thirteenth?"

He chuckled, letting her go. "There still has been no word on whether or not they ever made it. I'm certain if Flavus had I would have heard word, but with him being in the first line, if they encountered trouble, I doubt he would have survived."

He sat on the bed, his shoulders sagging under the weight of memories of his friend, worries and sorrow he hadn't thought of in years returning. Avita placed a hand on his shoulder, squeezing gently. "If he died, I'm certain he died with honor."

Valerius looked up at her, his eyes glistening slightly. "If only he had more experience, just a few years of fighting he would have made the second line, perhaps even the third line."

"How many years did it take for you to make the Triarii?"

Valerius stood, thinking back on his early days under Plinius. "Three, though I had the advantage of being in Plinius' favor."

Avita stepped back, dropping her dress to the floor revealing her spectacular body. She bent over, riffling through her clothes and Valerius felt a stirring he shouldn't under the circumstances.

"And just where is our Lord in this, our hour of need?"

Valerius rose and was about to throw his robes aside and take his wife right there and then when she suddenly stood straight, holding out some clothes triumphantly. She looked at him, recognizing the look in his eyes. She glanced down and cocked an eyebrow. "Put the spear away, darling, now is *not* the time."

She quickly dressed as he turned away in sexual frustration, turning instead to the nearby window. A quick glance outside had any amorous thoughts quickly tamped out, the only fires now burning those beyond the window.

"I'm ready. I'll get the kids," said Avita as she left the room leaving Valerius alone with his thoughts.

Plinius, where are you?

Outside Omhajer, Eritrea
Present Day, Six weeks before the crash

Birhan couldn't keep his heart from slamming into his ribcage, the excitement too great. What he had found was staggering, unfathomable in its magnitude. In fact, it was so life altering, it was terrifying. He was a simple herder, with no concept of true wealth. In fact, his subsistence living meant that he barely saw money beyond a few coins, his life one of barter and trade.

But he wasn't too much the fool to not know that what he had found was worth killing for.

After he had confirmed what he retrieved was but one of many—so many in fact it was more than he could possibly count or carry in a hundred trips—he had decided to rebury his find, then bring the herd back in without mentioning it to anyone. The slab of metal in his pocket, a metal he was positive was gold, weighed heavily on him, threatening to pull down his pants with each step.

"Birhan!"

He nearly soiled himself as his good friend Hamid yelled a greeting. Birhan waved, forcing a smile on his terrified face as Hamid crested a nearby hill with his share of the herd. Their boss, Yemane, was wealthy—the wealthiest man Birhan knew—his herd large, needing six men to tend to it on a daily basis. The pay was fair, but Yemane was ruthless should something go wrong. Lose an animal? It came out of your share, even if it wasn't your fault. As far as Yemane was concerned, any animal that cleared the gates was no longer his. And his foreman, Sheshy, was the most vicious man Birhan had ever encountered, he rumored to have killed an American soldier. Birhan had always wondered how the story could be true since he had never known Sheshy to have left the village his entire life.

Maybe we can go to America with the money I get from the gold?

The thought excited him and he almost forgot to keep his herd separate from that of Hamid's. A couple of flicks of the wrist had his herd on the right side of the road, Hamid's on the left as they covered the final distance to the farm.

"Good day?" asked Hamid.

Birhan hesitated, desperate to tell his friend of several decades what he had found. After all, why shouldn't his friends share in his find? There was far too much gold in the hold of the boat he had discovered for him to ever use.

"Yes," he finally replied, and immediately upon hearing his voice he knew it sounded uncertain.

And Hamid called him on it.

"You don't sound sure. Did something happen?" His jaw dropped, his hand instinctively tapping his cane, causing a slightly larger gap between their two herds. "Did you lose a goat?"

Birhan shook his head. "No, but thanks for trusting me that I wouldn't try to merge our herds and claim it was yours that had fallen," he said, nodding toward Hamid's cane.

Hamid looked confused then looked at the cane, realizing what Birhan was referring to. He roared in laughter, causing the two herds to rush ahead slightly, startled. "Sorry, my friend, I'm used to working with Woldu. You know how that bastard is."

Birhan smiled, nodding. If there was one man who couldn't be trusted, it was Woldu. He'd sell out his own father if he thought it would save him facing the consequences of any of his own actions.

He was a truly despicable human being.

Not like Hamid, who was just like Birhan. He too was saddled with progeny, three daughters. *Three!* The mere thought was enough to make up his mind.

"I found something," he said, lowering his voice so it wouldn't carry.

"What? You found something, did you say?"

"Yes. But don't say anything to anyone. I'll show you later."

Hamid shrugged. "Why, is it valuable?"

Birhan nodded. "Which is why you must say nothing. You'll understand once I show you."

Hamid seemed to be getting excited. He glanced all around them, joining Birhan in his nervous surveillance of their surroundings. They appeared to be alone, but Birhan couldn't risk it. But Hamid seemed unable to control himself. "What is it? Tell me now!"

"Quiet!" hissed Birhan, immediately regretting telling his friend.

It's this damned khat, it makes the tongue loose!

Hamid frowned, looking angry. "Why, you don't trust me?"

"Piss off, you know that's not it," he hissed, now certain he had made a mistake. But if he couldn't share with his best friend, who could he? He motioned for Hamid to come closer, stopping. He reached into his pocket and, looking around to make certain once again they were alone, pulled the bar halfway out in the rapidly fading light.

Hamid gasped, his already wide eyes bulging in shock, his jaw dropping revealing a mouth that had been devoid of teeth for as long as Birhan had known him.

"Where did you find it?"

Birhan slipped the bar back in his pocket and continued after his herd, tapping the cane to keep them apart as Hamid scrambled to keep up. When he was once again by Birhan's side, he replied. "By the river, a couple of miles back. There's a buried ship."

"A ship? Buried?" Hamid's eyes narrowed as if he didn't believe what he had just heard.

"You doubt me?" exclaimed Birhan, immediately regretting his loud outburst. If there was one thing he couldn't stand it was being called a liar. His life was so simple and pathetic, what could he possibly have to lie about? His temper was something he always ended up regretting, the beatings he had put his poor wife through on numerous occasions shames he still lived with to this day.

He took a deep breath and lowered his voice.

"It looked old. Very old. Probably shipwrecked centuries ago."

"Oh. That makes more sense."

"What do you mean?"

"Well, I thought you meant somebody buried a *ship* in the sand. That would be ridiculous. Ships are huge! A boat maybe, but a ship?" Hamid poked the cane at his friend playfully. "I thought you were playing a joke on me," he grinned, his gums on full display.

Birhan shook his head, unable to stay mad at his companion of so many years. "I'll take you there as soon as we're finished tending to the herd. But you must swear not to say anything to anyone."

Hamid grinned again. "I promise." He looked away. "How many of them are there?"

"Huh?"

"Gold bars. How many?"

"Hundreds. Thousands. I don't know, I can barely count my herd!"

Hamid laughed. "Then there's more than enough for both of us!"

Birhan nodded in agreement, suddenly realizing his friend was assuming his intention was to split his find between the two of them. He felt his blood boil at the arrogance. The thought had never occurred to him to share the find. Certainly he would give him some—there was more than enough to take care of the entire village if he wanted to. But he didn't. The more he thought about it the more he realized he just wanted to marry off his daughter to a good husband, then move to America where he could live in a big city like New York. He had seen a picture of it once and couldn't believe his eyes.

It must be wondrous.

There were so many people, so many buildings, he had to admit he had asked what it was when he first saw it. To think that humans could live in such a place was almost unfathomable.

Where do your goats graze?

The question he had felt was perfectly reasonable but had elicited laughter from all who had gathered to see the picture. He had stormed off, irate, after decking Semere, a particularly annoying asshole who Birhan knew damned well was wondering the same thing.

Follower!

As he stewed in the indignation of the recalled memory they arrived at the farm, the handover uneventful, Sheshy the enforcer his usual camel shit self, then after a few casual pleasantries with the other herders, he and Hamid left, the sun low on the horizon. As he looked at the sky he debated if he should put this off until tomorrow. He and Hamid could simply take their herds to the same area then look at the boat in the light of day.

But what if someone else finds it?

The thought had his heart racing a little faster and his pace quickening as he decided they must return now, and carry as much of the gold back to their houses as they could, just in case.

"Is it far?" asked Hamid as they plodded forward, their weathered bare feet gently slapping the dirt path, undeterred by the long shadows hiding countless places to turn an ankle.

"No," replied Birhan, shaking his head as he pointed up and to the right. "It's just over that rise." They covered the distance quickly, almost at a jog, then scrambled over the rise and back down the bank, the gentle flow of the river the only sound. Birhan dropped to his knees and began digging at the sand, quickly finding his buried discovery.

Hamid gasped, dropping and helping his friend.

"See, I told you I wasn't lying!" muttered Birhan.

"I should never have doubted you, my friend," replied Hamid as he scooped at the sand with a furry Birhan couldn't match. Soon the hole in the hull was revealed and Birhan reached in, grabbing one of the gold bars inside. He pulled it out and held it up triumphantly, the shiny metal glinting in the sunlight.

Hamid gasped, reaching out tentatively, looking to Birhan for permission to touch it. Birhan nodded his permission, magnanimously handing it to Hamid, as if bestowing some great privilege.

It made him feel powerful.

It was a feeling he had never experienced before, and it was wonderful. In fact, it was better than wonderful—it was intoxicating. He sucked in a deep breath, filling his lungs, his shoulders slowly drawing back as he felt himself swell with pride and ego, his friend's eyes bulging as he examined the bar of gold worth more than they could earn in a hundred life times.

"We're going to be rich," whispered Hamid, reaching out and hugging his friend, thumping his arms on Birhan's back. "We'll be able to buy the whole herd!"

"What do you mean, 'we'?"

The hug stopped, Hamid leaning back, his eyes narrowing. "What do you mean?"

Birhan couldn't believe the gall of his friend. "I never said I was going to share it with you. I said I was going to *show* it to you. There's a big difference."

Hamid's chin dropped, as did his jaw as his mouth opened wide. "But you said there's thousands of these," he said, shaking the bar in his hand. "How could you possibly not share it?"

The bewilderment in Hamid's voice only leant further credence to what Birhan had suspected for years. Hamid was a complete and absolute idiot. How this naïve moron could possibly be asking such questions was beyond him.

Birhan motioned toward the gold bar Hamid was holding. "You can keep that, of course," he said, "And you'll get more, I promise. But I'm not splitting this with you. I have plans."

"*You* have—" Hamid sputtered, suddenly stopping the tirade that was about to burst forth, sucking in a deep breath, then more calmly than he apparently originally intended said, 'You have plans.' What about me? What about my plans? I thought we were friends? How can you be so selfish? There's so much here! We could help the entire village! Imagine how good our lives could be with this!"

Birhan's chest tightened as he realized the monumental mistake he had made. *He's going to tell everyone!* And if everyone knew, he might lose it all.

And that was unacceptable.

Seeing red, the blood pounding in his ears, his heart racing as if he had sprinted all the way to the village, he grabbed his dagger from his belt and raised it high, his friend of over three decades gasping as he did so, then plunged it down hard, burying the blade deep into Hamid's chest. Hamid cried out, clutching at Birhan's arm as he tried to stop the assault, but Birhan had already withdrawn the blade and buried it deep again, and as his friend's cries turned into whimpers, he continued his frenzied attack until finally there was silence.

And prying the gold bar from Hamid's death grip, he shoved it in his pocket then rolled the body into the hold of the ship that was the key to *his* future, and no one else's.

"Pliny the Elder" Residence, Misenum, Roman Empire
August 24th, 79 AD

Plinius stood with his arms outstretched as his servants dressed him in his uniform. His man Dento tugged on the ties for his abdominal plate and Plinius grunted, the fit a little too tight for his aging—and expanding—frame.

"Not so tight, Dento, I did just feast with the Emperor."

"I apologize, sire," replied Dento, the apology subdued but Plinius was certain delivered with a slight smile. He felt the ties loosen slightly.

"Better." They were tied off and he inspected himself, bending all of his key joints, making certain his mobility wouldn't be impaired. He nodded with approval. "Is my ship ready?"

Another servant nodded. "Yes, sire, it is manned and ready, and we have a favorable wind."

Footfalls from the hallway caused Plinius to turn toward the door as a man, exhausted, skid to a halt. Plinius immediately recognized him as Valerius' trusted man, Costa. He waved him in, concern growing as he realized it could only be bad news.

Costa stepped into the room, gasping for breath, bowing deeply. Valerius flicked his hand, indicating the man should rise. "Dispense with the formalities. What is it?"

"Sire, forgive me for this message is almost two hours old. I used the Cursus Publicus to get here as quickly as possible, but—"

"Yes, yes, what is it?"

"Sire, my Lord asks for rescue. The situation is dire. The air can barely be breathed, a dust has fallen like snow and is already to the waist in some areas. Rivers of thick, glowing liquid flow down the mountain and toward the sea, cutting off escape to the north. If help isn't sent soon, all might be lost."

Plinius motioned for Costa to follow him as he strode from his chambers and toward the front of the house where his carriage awaited to take him to his cutter. "And your lord's family?"

"Still at the residence last I heard, sire."

Plinius shook his head, sending a silent thought to his friend. *Save your family, Valerius!* Plinius turned to his man Dento. "Call up the fleet. Have them sail at once to begin rescue operations at Pompeii." He turned to Costa. "What of Herculaneum?"

Costa shook his head. "I fear the worst there as well, sire."

Plinius frowned, his lips pursed, as he climbed into the carriage, motioning for Costa to join him. He looked down at Dento. "Have the Second and Third sail for Herculaneum, the Fourth, Fifth and Sixth to Pompeii. They are to assist in evacuating the civilians. Have the First rendezvous with my cutter for a special mission. And have Tacitus take command and join me at Valerius' residence with as many men as he can. Take a swift horse, deliver the orders personally."

Dento bowed and without hesitating ran to the stables, moments later emerging on one of the estate's best steeds, riding it hard toward the port. Plinius looked down at his nephew who had emerged from the house.

"Gaius, should what is occurring across the bay reach here, I want you to order the evacuation of the household. Do not hesitate."

Gaius nodded, the look of concern and worry on his face obvious. Plinius held out his hand and the young man took it. He squeezed. "You have always made me proud, and your father I know would have been as well. I would be honored to call you son." He squeezed Gaius' hand harder. "Now heed my words. Should things turn here, save yourself and your mother." He let go of his nephew's hand, a smile forced on his face. "We shall see each other again, soon."

The reins were flicked and the carriage began to move, and as Plinius sat back for the short trip to the harbor, he had an overwhelming sense he would never see his nephew again.

Omhajer, Eritrea
Present Day, Six weeks before the crash

"Father! What happened!?"

Abrihet leapt to her feet, tossing the laundry she was folding aside as her father stumbled through the doorway, kicking it closed with his foot. Lumbering toward the wood table that occupied the center of their one room home, he leaned against the top and dropped something with a thud, it hidden under his shirt, several clinks causing her eyebrows to pop in curiosity.

She turned up the lantern that sat near the pile of folded laundry she had been working on and frowned as she saw her father's clothes covered in dark brown stains, his entire body covered in dirt.

"What in God's name have you been doing?" she cried as she saw the mess he was in. "Are you okay?"

He pulled his shirt out from under the load, revealing a sight that had her pause in mid stride, her brain simply not comprehending what she was seeing.

Then she gasped.

"Is that gold?" she cried, the glare her father gave causing her to slap both hands over her mouth as her eyes opened wide.

"Funny!" he laughed loudly for she assumed the benefit of the neighbors, then lowering his voice, hissed "Keep quiet!" He pointed at a chair.

She nodded and sat in one of the three surrounding the table as her father dropped into his usual chair, it the only one with arms. He looked exhausted, even more so than usual.

And terrified.

"What's wrong?" she whispered, reaching out and grabbing his arm, then motioning toward the pile of gold bars with her chin. "Where did you get these?"

"I found them," he said as he shoved some khat toward his mouth.

She swatted his hand away. "That's the last thing you need right now," she scolded. He glared at her for a moment and she feared a beating but he nodded, shoving the deleterious weed back in his pocket. "Where did you find them?" she asked.

"Near the river, buried in an old boat. Actually, the boat was buried, these were in it."

"A boat?"

"Yeah, a big one. Very old."

She frowned. "How do you know it doesn't belong to someone? They might come looking for it."

He shook his head. "Like I said, *very* old."

"What's that all over your shirt?"

He looked away, staring at the floor. She leaned in, the light from the lantern bright enough for her to see it was a rusty color, not the mud stain she had thought.

"Oh my God!" she exclaimed, then lowering her voice, she stood, backing away slightly. "Is that blood?"

He turned toward her and nodded, tears pouring from his eyes. "I didn't mean to. I just wanted to show him it, but he wanted half."

Abrihet's eyes widened in horror with each word. "You mean…" She couldn't bring herself to finish the sentence. The blood wasn't his, it was someone else's. And it was a lot. She sucked in a deep breath and squared her shoulders, anger taking over as she realized that once again her idiot of a father had let his temper get the better of him, and it would be up to her to try and straighten things out. The last time he had mouthed off to the foreman and lost his job. It was her begging and offering to do laundry for a year that had got him his job back.

What is it going to take this time?

She feared what the answer might be.

Her eyebrows narrowed as she tried to look as intimidating as she could.

"What did you do, Father?"

"I killed him!" he sobbed, his head dropping on the table, his shoulders heaving with each cry.

Melting her heart.

The last time he had cried was when her mother died. Since then she hadn't seen a tear roll down his cheek until tonight.

But he killed someone!

She walked over and put her arms around him from behind, squeezing him tight, trying to comfort the man she knew loved her, but rarely showed it.

"Killed who?" she finally managed to ask, terrified at just asking the question.

"Hamid!" Another gasped breath and a sob. "Oh God, I'm so sorry!"

Abrihet let go of her father, stepping backward toward the door, disbelief at what she had just heard written all over her gaping face. *It can't be!* Her father's best friend since before she was born, his only companion, the only one who had never turned his back on him over his temper.

Uncle!

Her father had killed her mother's brother, the man who had introduced them, who had as a boy helped accumulate the dowry that had been of such little value that her father was the only one low enough in the village to accept it.

Love had grown, but now, as she looked at him from behind, his shoulders still heaving in grief, all she saw was a twisted monster. Her eyes shifted to the pile of gold on the table, and she realized it was greed that had driven him to kill, and what this curse of a treasure would bring next, she could only imagine.

All she knew was that a sin had been committed, and she couldn't remain. She opened the door quietly, fearing what wrath might befall her should he decide to stop her, then stepped out into the night.

And fled to the only person she could think of that might be able to help her.

Father Solomon.

POMPEII'S GHOSTS

Lucius Valerius Corvus Residence, Pompeii, Roman Empire
August 24th, 79 AD

Valerius surveyed his charge and felt all hope drain from him. Everywhere he looked were neatly stacked piles of gold bars representing hundreds of thousands of gold coins melted down for transport and to guarantee their purity. His basement had been expanded quietly before the deliveries, which then took place over months, discretely.

And now it all had to be moved in less than a day.

Impossible!

Even if Plinius were to arrive with the fleet as he hoped, there was no way they could evacuate the gold in time. The treasure had been delivered in carts along the roads in perfect conditions. Now it would have to be hand carried to the shores, into the water, and onto the waiting boats.

Surely an impossible task.

Which meant there was only one conclusion that Valerius could come to.

Today would be the day he died.

And he was prepared for that.

His heart ached with the pain his wife and children would feel, but the family honor would remain intact, and for dying trying to save the Emperor's treasure, he was certain his family would be taken care of.

Even if they couldn't evacuate the treasure in time, if he remained behind to protect it from looters, his emperor would still have his gold.

But if what he saw outside the last time he looked was any indication, the chances of looters or himself surviving were slim to none. The ash was now approaching chest height in places and the roof was starting to show signs of weakness, the columns cracking. His guard, two dozen of Rome's finest, had been initially deployed to try and keep a path clear to the beachfront, but he had redeployed half of them to the roof to shovel off the rapidly accumulating ash. Their shifts were short and arduous, the air thick, and they were fighting a losing battle. Only moments before he had ordered them to concentrate only on the structure immediately above where he now stood, prepared to sacrifice the rest of the house so the treasure could be evacuated should help arrive.

He shook his head then ran up the stairs, locking the door behind him, the key around his neck having never left his side since the door was first installed. Only Plinius and the Emperor himself had copies. As he entered the grand hall he found half a dozen of his guard lying on the floor, being tended to by one of his female slaves. They struggled to rise but he waved them off.

"Rest," he said. "I fear we will all need whatever energy we can muster before day's end."

The head of his guard, Silus, walked in from the patio, pushing aside the coverings. His face was blackened with the falling ash, his arms and legs covered in a mix of the dark matter and sweat, his hair, normally a brilliant blonde now a dusty gray. He took a goblet of water from one of the slaves, swished it in his mouth then spat in a proffered bowl. He then poured the rest of the water over his head, passing the goblet back and wiping his face with the palm of his hand. Silus looked around the room then his eyebrows raised in recognition as he spotted his liege.

"My Lord, I have good news!"

Valerius' heart leapt, praying silently it was the only news he could think of that might be good. "You have word of the Prefect?"

Silus nodded. "Perhaps. A scout has spotted the Prefect's cutter making for the shore and the fleet has left port. Other civilian craft are also coming to rescue who they can. The shores are filled with boats taking away the civilians."

Valerius felt a surge of pride in his fellow Romans, and with Plinius near, there was renewed hope. "This is indeed good news. Keep the path to the shore clear, and keep men on the roof. We can't risk having this hall collapse." He lowered his voice. "Now that we know the fleet will be here soon, pull the guards off the gates and have them begin to move the treasure below to the main level. We won't get much moved, but we will at least get some. The bottleneck is the stairs."

Silus snapped to attention. "Yes, sire!" He strode away to execute his orders as Avita and the children entered the room, followed by several servants.

"The carts are ready, darling. Are you sure you won't come with us?"

Valerius shook his head. "You know my place is here." He turned to his servant Labeo. "I place my family in your hands. Get them as far south as you can. Stop at nothing, stop for no one. Show no quarter to those who would interfere. When you find safety, send word to the Emperor, his people will find me or Plinius." He pulled a purse filled with gold and silver coins from his belt, handing it to Labeo. "This should smooth your way."

Labeo bowed, taking the purse. "You honor me, sire."

Valerius turned to his children and held his arms out. The three youngsters immediately leapt forward, hugging their father tightly. He ruffled the hair on each of their heads, returning the hugs, paying particular attention to his seven year old daughter, the youngest of the trio. "Now you listen to your mother and Labeo, and do me and your Emperor proud, understood?"

"Yes, Father," came the reply in unison. He felt his chest tighten as he wondered if he'd ever hear their tiny voices again. He looked at his wife, his eyes glistening, hers ready to erupt with further tears as he could tell she knew what he was feeling.

"My wife," he whispered, taking her in his arms and hugging her tightly. They said nothing, neither trusting what might happen in front of the children and their staff should they dare speak. After what Valerius knew wasn't enough time to say goodbye, he let go and forced a smile on his face, his eyes never leaving those of his cherished companion. "Go now, swiftly, and I will see you after we have evacuated with the fleet."

His wife nodded and followed Labeo out the front door and to the carriages. The horses were already covered in ash, and Valerius noted that each had a hat tied around its head with silk veils to try and reduce the amount of ash they might be exposed to.

Clever.

He waved as the carts departed, one with his family, the other with the supplies they would need. As they disappeared into the ash he returned inside and unlocked the cellar door for the waiting soldiers. Within minutes a small pile of gold began to form in the center of the hall and as he turned to join his men in the human chain they had formed, he heard a tremendous roar and the entire house shook. Dust exploded from the hallway that led to the bedrooms and he knew the south wing of their home had just collapsed under the weight of the ash.

You better get here soon, Plinius!

Omhajer, Eritrea

Present Day, Six weeks before the crash

Father Solomon jerked up in his humble bed positioned near the only window in the room, allowing for a usually slight but sometimes welcome stiff breeze to naturally cool him, air conditioning a luxury almost unheard of in rural Eritrea. He wiped his eyes free of sleep and listened for what had awoken him.

Pounding on the door and the desperate cries of a woman had him leaping from his bed, his middle-aged bones protesting, but still spry enough to effect a fast arrival at the door to the small church at the edge of Omhajer. When he had been assigned the outpost by the Vatican he had of course been thankful on the outside, but inside he had been terrified, horrified, disgusted—you name the negative emotion, he had experienced it, and it had shamed him. He knew it was his duty to go where God needed him, and nowhere did God need him more than in Africa, of that he had no doubt. But he had spent his life escaping Africa, and to be sent back after so many years was what he had least expected.

He hadn't wanted to go—he had been hoping for a North American or European posting. But to be thrust back into the middle of Africa, only a few days journey from where he had been born, was like going backward, losing decades of his life. It felt like a punishment that he didn't deserve, but as he toiled with the emotions, he realized his selfishness was the very proof that he did deserve this assignment, and the only way out, was to embrace God's penance, and excel in his work.

And he felt he had. In time he realized the Vatican's wisdom in putting a local in charge of the small church. It meant he wouldn't attract as much attention from the Muslims, and to their credit, they had left him alone so far. His small church was thriving, the decrepit state it had been in nothing like the renewed condition it now stood. Volunteers from the congregation had undertook repairs when word had come of a new priest arriving after so many years of there being none. The poor faithful had been forced to conduct their own services, and without an actual priest, baptisms, marriages and confessions had either been ignored, or were undertaken with great inconvenience through travel to another town.

Father Solomon had been embraced by a weary community, and it didn't take long for him to fall in love with his flock, and realize the infinite wisdom that was God. Returning him home had been the wisest decision not only for him, but for the parish he now ran, and helping these people allowed him to finally begin the process of healing himself.

But as the pounding and cries continued to urge him toward the doors, he wondered what calamity might be befalling the small community tonight? He removed the bar holding the doors shut, then pushed them open to find Abrihet, one of his most faithful, crying hysterically.

"Oh Father, you must help me!" she cried, falling into his arms as her strength gave out. He helped her inside, placing her on one of the pews, then closed the doors, noting many of the nearby houses already taking notice of the commotion, their front doors occupied with curious onlookers.

Placing the bar back across the door, he returned to Abrihet who stared at him wide-eyed, flushed, her eyes red from tears. He sat beside her and took both her hands in his.

"What is it, my child?"

"M-my father," she stammered, her chin dropping into her chest as her shoulders heaved. "My father, he—"

She stopped, stuck on the words, her gasping breaths coming faster now.

"Shhh," he soothed, knowing already what might be wrong, the mere mention of her father enough. He had heard the stories of his wicked temper, a temper he had apparently taken out on his wife on numerous occasions, and his fellow villagers from time to time. "What has your father done this time?" He asked the question as gently as he could, knowing Abrihet loved her father deeply and was known to fly to his defense whenever someone spoke poorly of him behind his back.

Her own temper will be her undoing.

"He killed Uncle Hamid!"

It was Father Solomon's turn to be shocked, his mouth falling open. "Are you sure?"

She nodded emphatically. "He was covered in blood, and he told me he did it."

"But why?" Father Solomon pulled at his thinning hair. "They were best friends. Since they were children!"

"He found gold!"

Father Solomon's eyebrows climbed his forehead as the words sank in. "Gold?"

Abrihet nodded, her tears starting to subside as she finally was able to articulate her feelings to someone. "Bars, about this big," she said, illustrating with her hands what she had apparently seen. "Lots of them."

"Where did he find them?"

"In some old boat."

Knocking at the door interrupted them. It was gentle but insistent, and Father Solomon approached the door cautiously, knowing full-well that Hamid was Muslim, and Birhan was Christian. The marriage between Birhan and Hamid's sister had been controversial at the time, but allowed merely because the dowry in question was so low, the Muslims satisfied that none of their men would have taken it, and among the Christians, they could care less, many simply happy that Birhan had found a mate.

But now? With a Christian murdering a Muslim?

We could have a bloodbath on our hands!

"Who is it?"

"It's me, Father, David!"

Father Solomon breathed a sigh of relief as he recognized the voice of his altar boy, David. He removed the bar and opened the door slightly, letting the young man inside, then before closing it up again, taking a look.

A small crowd had gathered.

"What has happened?" asked David, his voice a whisper. "There is talk in the village that Birhan killed someone?"

Father Solomon barred the door once more, nodding. "It appears he killed Hamid."

David's hands clasped at the cross around his neck. "It can't be!"

"I'm afraid so. Apparently it was over some gold that Birhan found."

"Gold?" David's eyes widened with a look Father Solomon recognized too well.

"A lot of it apparently." He motioned to Abrihet. "Watch her for a minute, I need to go to my office."

David nodded and sat beside the still sniffling young woman, a woman who was almost ten years older than the boy now expected to provide comfort, but there was no choice. He rushed to his rectory and sat at the desk, grabbing a pen and pad of paper, quickly writing out the situation and requesting instructions from the Vatican. If there was a significant stash of gold nearby, it could cause the entire village to disrupt into violence that could spread across the entire area. He needed the local authorities—which meant all the way from the capital as there were none that could be trusted here—to be dispatched with the full understanding that the Vatican knew what was happening. If the Eritrean authorities were to arrive with no external oversight, all of their lives might be forfeit.

A scream from the church had him leaping to his feet, tearing off his letter and folding it as he ran. Pounding on the doors had his heart leap into his throat, shouts of "Let us in!" and "Send her out!" growing in intensity.

And Abrihet looked terrified.

As did David.

Father Solomon handed the letter to David. "Take this to the Bishop. Tell him it is urgent we get help otherwise I fear the worst."

David nodded, his hands shaking as he took the folded piece of paper.

"Go out through the back. If there are people there, tell them where we are, then when they are busy coming in here, you can slip away."

"But Father, you'll be killed!"

Father Solomon shook his head, a gentle smile on his face as he took the boy's face in his hands. "Have faith that God will protect us." He said a silent prayer, only his lips moving, then let go of the boy. "Now go!"

David sprinted for the rear of the church then into the rectory. Father Solomon heard the door open then slam close, no altercation taking place, those gathered mostly Muslim therefore unfamiliar with the layout of the church. If David were able to escape unseen, he just might be able to get them help.

By tomorrow.

More pounding on the door and more shouting had Abrihet springing from the pew and into his arms, her entire body trembling.

"We have your father!" shouted a voice, everything suddenly becoming quiet. "If you want him to live, you'll come out now!"

Why do they want her?

It made no sense. Birhan he could understand. He was the murderer. But why would they want the daughter? She had done nothing. She was innocent in all this. Why would they want her?

Then it occurred to him, and it made him physically sick, his stomach churning and his mouth filling with bile as he fought the urge to vomit. He looked down at the poor girl and realized she had no idea the danger that now faced her.

She looked up at him, her eyes filled with innocence. "I must go," she whispered, her bottom lip quivering. "They'll kill him."

Father Solomon shook his head. "No, they will kill him anyway. We must get you out of here before it's too late."

A man screamed in agony and Abrihet made a run for the door, almost slipping from Father Solomon's hands. Another scream of agony and he wrapped his arms around her, holding her tight, trying to cover her ears with his chest and forearm, but he knew it was no use. The distinctive thud preceding each scream was something he had heard before, when he was a child, and it threatened to tear him from this place and thrust him back to a childhood he had blacked out, a day he should never forget, but had forced himself to.

The day his own father had been hacked to death by Muslim extremists, in the center of the village, for the egregious sin of converting to Christianity.

And right now, on the other side of the doors of this hallowed place, he knew the same thing was happening. A man, a guilty man, a man who had committed the ultimate sin, was being murdered in revenge, rather than justice, and he knew what the next phase of the revenge would be.

The same as it had been for his mother and sister.

And he made a decision that he would die before he would let what happened to them happen to this poor girl now trembling in his arms as she listened to her father being hacked to pieces mere feet away.

"You must remain quiet," he whispered in her ear as he led her to the rear of the church. He placed his ear to the rear door that led from his rectory and heard nothing. Opening it a crack he gasped as a hand reached in and grabbed him by his robes, pulling him outside as a group of men surged into the church, Abrihet screaming as they grabbed her. He struggled against those holding him, but they pushed him inside, holding his head, forcing him to watch as the poor girl was stripped naked then bent over the very desk he had just written the letter requesting help on.

And as the first man took her, she screamed in pain, in agony and in fear, her innocence torn apart by a tradition too vile to acknowledge, too unfathomable by civilized standards to understand, and too common to deny.

He tried to tear himself lose, to throw himself at those assaulting the poor girl, to stop the vicious attack as it began, but the grips on his arms were viselike, and as the first man finished, a look on his face not of self-satisfaction that he had just delivered justice to a guilty party, but one of sexual gratification and lust, Father Solomon prayed for the strength to help this poor innocent.

He glared at the first man, his name Abdal Jabbar, a man he had thought of as decent until this very moment, a man who had shown his true colors by the unforgiveable act he had just committed. And there would be no forgiveness for this sin, no room for him to forget. He felt hatred fill his heart, swelling his chest with a rage he had never felt, as the second man took the tiny Abrihet, another on the opposite side of the desk, pulling her arms, urging the man on.

And with a strength he didn't know he possessed, as if Samson himself were now sharing his body, Father Solomon broke away and charged toward the table, and just as his eyes met those of Abrihet, her face having gone slack, her body entering shock, her once bright eyes now dim, he felt something hit him across the back of the head and he collapsed to the floor, blacking out to the sounds of the desk creaking with each thrust, and innocent Abrihet whimpering with each violation of her broken body, now no more than a piece of meat for the carnal pleasures of the gathered men, their excuse of punishment for the entire family a pathetic justification for their sexual urges.

And as a third man stepped over him to take his turn, Father Solomon pictured his own mother, so many years ago, forced to endure her repeated punishment dozens and dozens of times, while her son watched, too young to understand what was truly happening, too young to understand why his mother's eyes slowly died in front of him, the will to live drained with each penetration, as the same evil was unleashed upon her daughter, whose hand she held the entire time, next to her.

Oh God, please help her!

Approaching Pompeii, Bay of Naples, Roman Empire
August 24th, 79 AD

Costa gripped the rail of the cutter, the smaller vessel far swifter than the mighty vessels of the fleet that he could see lining the horizon behind them, strangely lit by the late afternoon sun as he struggled to see in the dark of the thick gray cloud overhead, any sign of the sun blotted out. A curious light powder, dark gray in color, fell all around them, reminding him of the ash left over from a hearty fire.

As they neared the shore the powder thickened, making it harder to breathe. He glanced over at the Prefect and he seemed to be labored in his breathing. Costa had overheard once of Plinius' problem breathing after heavy exertion, and grew concerned. Plinius glanced at him and pointed at a barrel of water. Costa nodded and quickly filled a cup, bringing it to the man. He downed the fluid then shoved Costa to the deck as he himself ducked.

Rocks the size of fists began to rain down on them, but as they hit they exploded into smaller stones and dust, the embers left behind smoldering then extinguishing themselves in wisps of smoke.

"Watch for fires!" ordered Plinius as he continued to ride the prow of the boat, his eyes peering at the shore.

"My Lord! It's too dangerous to land here!" yelled the Legate captaining the boat.

"We have no choice!" replied Plinius, turning his head back toward his underling. "Fortune favors the brave!" he yelled. "Make for the shore, there!" He pointed slightly to starboard and Costa felt his heart leap as he recognized the shore mere paces from his master's home, the once brilliantly white abode now shrouded in a blanket of darkness. As he peered into the storm of what tasted like ash he thought he saw movement on the roof, and after a few moments he was able to make out the forms of soldiers desperately trying to sweep away the accumulating debris. Costa looked at the deck of the boat and noticed it too had already amassed enough that their footprints were now obvious.

As the boat neared the shore he gripped the rail, watching the house for any sign of his master, praying he had had the sense to abandon it long ago, but knowing in his heart that he never would. He spotted several soldiers with brooms and a path that had been kept clear from the house to the shore when he heard Plinius gasp audibly. Costa's eyes darted back to the house and his jaw dropped as the entire south wing collapsed.

The cutter sliced into the sandy beach and came to a halt, the sails dropped almost immediately, Plinius jumping over the side, Costa far more clumsily following. The chaos seen from the bay poorly foreshadowed the reality on the ground. The ash was deep, small porous rocks covered the landscape, many giving an unearthly glow as if Hades itself were trying to push through to this realm. The air reeked of rotten eggs, the ground was piled almost waist high in ash, some areas appearing even deeper. The water was a thick sludge that clung to his bare legs. Though the sun was completely hidden above them, the temperature was higher than normal, almost uncomfortable to bear and he quickly found his body dripping in sweat as he followed Plinius to the main hall of the home, the Prefect using the path kept clear by the soldiers, all of whom looked exhausted.

This is hell on Earth!

He stumbled through layers of silk and cloth hanging across a doorway and into the large dining area of the home that opened out onto the veranda overlooking the bay. Dozens of torches had been lit to provide light, none coming from outside, and all of the windows and doors had been covered to prevent ash from entering. Despite their efforts, a thin layer still covered the floor, at the center of which was more gold than Costa had ever seen before.

His jaw dropped and he immediately began to picture what just one of those bars could do for his family.

Or two.

It would change their lives. They could buy their freedom, perhaps open a shop in Rome itself. The dreams were almost overwhelming and he found he had tunnel vision, his eyes seeing nothing but the gold, his ears closed to the sounds around him. It took a tug of his tunic to snap him from the fantasy, a slave offering him water. He drank gratefully, several cupsful, then looked to his master, Valerius, who was embracing Plinius.

"Thank the gods you have arrived!" cried Valerius. "I had feared you wouldn't come."

Plinius smiled, still holding the younger Valerius by the arms. "Never doubt that I would be foolish enough to do that which brave men would fear," he replied with a wink. He turned to the growing pile of gold. "I see you have begun."

"As soon as your ships were spotted, I gave the order. It may only save minutes, but minutes may be all we have."

Plinius nodded. "I noticed men on the roof?"

"To keep the ash off. If it gets too heavy this entire room will collapse and we along with the Emperor's gold will be trapped here."

"A wise precaution. And your family?"

"I've sent them ahead. Hopefully they will find refuge south of the city."

Plinius squeezed his second's shoulder. "I've given my nephew and sister similar orders should the need arise. I'm certain the gods will watch over both our families." He stepped back and looked at the exhausted guard as they handed bars of gold to each other, the human chain slowly transferring the treasure from the chambers below. "This will take some time," observed Plinius. "As more ships arrive we will begin the transfer in earnest. For now, I suggest we relax. Have some food and drink, some good conversation. It will calm the nerves. I have ten good men with me." Plinius turned to one of his men. "Have your men relieve those on the roof and the path. Switch every fifteen minutes. Let me know as soon as the first ship arrives."

The man slapped his fist against his chest and disappeared outside, past the cloths trying to preserve some semblance of calm inside. Valerius turned to Costa. "Have food and drink brought, enough for everyone including the servants, then wash yourself up. Also, prepare an area for our soldiers to sleep. They can barely walk and need their rest."

Costa bowed and rushed toward the kitchen, thankfully in the still standing north wing of the house, his eyes having to tear themselves away from the pile of gold in the center of the room. He couldn't believe how obsessed he was with it, and it wasn't until he had left the room that he realized the grip it held on him even now. Having never seen that much wealth in one place before, he felt almost overwhelmed with how much just a tiny portion of what his master possessed could change his life for the better, and began to feel a tightness in his chest as a rage of jealousy overtook him.

He gripped a nearby doorway as the entire house shook, a woman's scream from the kitchen area beyond snapping him from his shameful thoughts. Shaking his head and voicing a silent apology to his master for his unforgiveable lapse, he rushed to the kitchen to see if anyone was hurt. All he found was a young female slave whimpering in a corner. He ushered her from her hiding place and passed on his master's orders.

"Food and drink for everyone, including yourself. Just keep bringing it out to the main dining area. Get whoever remains to help you."

The woman nodded, grateful it seemed to have something to occupy her mind. A creaking sound overhead had their eyes darting to the ceiling, Costa's heart picking up several beats as he saw the extensive cracking. He rushed from the room, spotting two slaves and redirecting them to the kitchen as he left to prepare the room for the guards to rest.

And to do so, he had to pass through the main chamber once more, and again he found himself mesmerized by the sight of more wealth than any one man could spend in a lifetime.

There for the taking.

Edge of the Nubian Desert, Egypt
Present Day, Two days before the crash

"James!"

Professor James Acton leaned out the window of the supply truck, waving as it made the final turn into the Egyptian dig site his fiancée was running—and funding for the most part. It hadn't changed much since the terrorist attack of last year, and the loss of the tomb they had discovered was heartbreaking, but the original dig, of an ancient Egyptian village along what was once a tributary to the mighty Nile, was back on track, albeit with more security.

An Egyptian military checkpoint on the only road leading to the dig was constantly manned with half a dozen men only five minutes away, with a radio at the camp that could be used to call for help. And of course due to the fact the love of his life, Professor Laura Palmer of University College London, was filthy rich thanks to a massive inheritance from her late brother, they had a significant contingent of private security, mostly ex-Special Forces, many of them former Special Air Services, England's most elite soldiers.

After some had paid the ultimate price saving the lives of the two professors and their students, the contingent had been doubled from four to eight, and the self-defense training—voluntary of course—had continued. Though Acton had experience from a stint in the National Guard years ago, what he had learned over the past couple of years from these men had proved invaluable, saving his life and countless others many times. He felt he was in the best shape of his life and had more confidence than he could remember.

Though he'd trade much of that in for a somewhat more peaceful life.

Far too often they were in the thick of things, and he prayed the two weeks he was about to spend here with Laura would be uneventful in every way except for scientific discovery and a little nudge-nudge-wink-wink.

As the truck ground to a halt in the dirt he jumped out the passenger side and into the arms of Laura, her long auburn hair tied back in a ponytail, her customary—when on the dig site—tan shorts and shirt, rolled up at the sleeves, dusty from a day's hard work, her cheeks glowing he hoped in the excitement of seeing him for the first time in weeks.

Their attempted marriage had been aborted by the Pope just before he stepped down, and they had yet to set a new date, but neither were in a rush. They loved each other—of that there was no doubt—and that was all that mattered. Formalizing it wasn't important, but was on the agenda.

Not to mention his parents had nearly flipped when they had found out. His mother was thrilled with the idea of course, but wanted to be there to see "her baby" get married.

His dad had grunted his agreement.

As he breathed in her scent, feeling her body pressed hard against his, he lost himself in the moment of true love that still burned with the passion he had only before felt when the relationship was new. Perhaps it was the distance, he in the US, her in England, his dig in Peru, hers in Egypt. Whatever it was, it meant reunions were fantastic.

He eyed the tent, then the midday sun.

Patience, Jimmy Jr!

The embrace broke and she wiped the tears from her face as the students gathered around to greet him, many of them having returned after the events of last year, determined to not let those who had died to have done so in vain, and those who would spread terror win. As hands were shook, hugs and kisses exchanged, he was gently led to the main tent by

Laura, the whirlwind of excitement ending as he stepped through the secondary entrance, the cool, crisp air from the camp's only air conditioner greeting him.

"Oh God that feels nice!" he exclaimed as he took a wide stance and held out his arms. "I've been stuck to that vinyl seat for over eight hours." Laura grabbed a bottle of water from the fridge and tossed it to him. He caught it easily and sat down at a table with a map of the dig rolled out on it. Laura came up behind him and began to massage his shoulders. He moaned, leaning his head back against her stomach. "Mmmm, that feels nice."

"How was the flight?"

"Usual pleasantries at the border, but other than that, uneventful," he replied, his eyes closing as he gave himself over to her tender ministrations. "Everything fine here?"

"Perfect. Dig is going great. We just found the edge of something big this morning. It looks like it may go down quite a bit."

Acton's eyes popped open for a moment. "Where?"

"At one of the exploratory digs to the east. It looks like the top of something, perhaps buried in a sandstorm thousands of years ago."

"Cool!" Acton could feel the excitement of a new discovery begin to fuel his system. "Who do you have on it?"

"Well, it was Terrence's exploratory dig, so I've left it in his hands for now. I think he deserves a shot after everything he did last year."

Terrence Mitchell was Laura's star grad student who had risked his life to help warn them of the impending attack, nearly dying in the ensuing battle. He was a brilliant but awkward lad who had found love during those difficult hours, eventually marrying Jenny just two months ago.

Yet we *move at a snail's pace!*

"Glad to hear our newlywed is doing well," said Acton as Laura patted him on the shoulders, ending her massage. Acton rose and stretched. "Thanks, I needed that." He sniffed his armpit and winced. "And now I need a shower and a change of clothes."

Laura waved her hand in front of her nose. "Please!"

Acton's hand darted out as he leapt forward and smacked her butt, she squealing as she tried to dodge the hit, unsuccessfully. He feigned another blow which he let her escape as she laughed, putting the table between the two of them. His shoulders slumped. "I'm dead. I think I'll take a nap after the shower."

"Rest today, there will be plenty to do tomorrow," replied Laura as she rounded the table and gave him a peck on the cheek. "And for the love of God, shower!" She raced for the exit before he could react.

Acton chuckled as he grabbed a towel and snapped it at her. She winked at him then ducked back outside while he retrieved his toiletries and headed for the showers, the water provided by an underground well that had been dug for the camp when it was first set up. One of the advantages of a Professor Laura Palmer dig was her money, which she would use to provide the little extras for her students when possible. She was even known to extend her generosity anonymously and pay the way for some students who couldn't afford it. And that philanthropic spirit had been extended to his students as well, many benefiting.

As he washed in the cool but not cold water, he began to unwind, his muscles relaxing from his long trip. Washing his shoulder, his fingers ran over the scar from where he had been shot only two months before, and he instinctively winced. The wound was healed, but the strength hadn't completely returned. He did daily exercises to help stretch and strengthen the area, but he found it still tired easily, and after a particularly hard day, it would ache enough to tempt him to take some pain killers which he was usually able to resist. If Laura was with him she was always able to distract him in some way, but if he was alone with his thoughts, he found them quite often returning to that day and his near death experience.

He had learned later that his heart had most likely stopped and that he may actually have been dead. The Delta Force operator, Niner, and an Israeli medic, had saved his life in the field, and when it was all over, their discovery handed over to the Triarii, an ancient organization descendent from the Roman Thirteenth Legion sworn to protect the world from the supposed destructive powers of the crystal skulls, they had heard nothing since.

Not a peep.

Even their good friend and member of the organization, Detective Inspector Martin Chaney of Scotland Yard had gone incommunicado. Chaney's former partner and now INTERPOL Special Agent, Hugh Reading, also a close friend of Acton's, had grown concerned and discovered Chaney had taken an indefinite leave of absence before he had left England to claim their find, the excuse given that he needed more time to recover from being shot at this very dig site. It was reasonable considering he had only come out of his coma a few days before filing his request.

Yet despite that they were all concerned.

And there was nothing they could do about it except hope Chaney was okay, and that he was merely on Triarii business.

Acton knew his good friend Reading was climbing the walls over this, he very close to the younger Chaney, almost thinking of him as a son. Acton didn't know him as well, but a bond under fire had been formed that could never be broken, and it left him thinking of Chaney frequently, wondering just what had happened to the man.

A thumping sound in the distance had him freeze in the shower, cocking his head to see if what he thought he had heard was real. The hair standing up on the back of his neck and the goose bumps spreading across his body was all the indication he needed. He quickly rinsed himself off then shut off the water as the thumping got louder. He pushed aside the wood door to the shower and stepped out into the open as he wrapped a towel around him, nobody noticing his momentary nakedness as all eyes were on the horizon.

"There it is!" yelled one of the students, pointing to the east.

Acton looked and his heart leapt into his throat as a large chopper cleared the rise, heading straight for them. The security team, led by former SAS Lieutenant Colonel Cameron Leather, raced into position, an alarm sounding that sent the students scrambling, weapons being broken out as everyone, well-drilled, took up defensive positions.

Acton raced toward the main tent, plunging through the double canvas entrance, pulling on a pair of shorts, shoving his feet into his boots, then running back outside with the satellite phone and the Egyptian walkie-talkie. As he burst from the tent he nearly ran headlong into Laura who was now packing a Glock 22 on her hip, a second in her hand along with several magazines.

"Expecting anyone?" he asked, already knowing the answer.

"No," she said, shaking her head. "Here." She handed him the spare weapon and mags, he handing her the satellite phone and radio. "Let's go!"

The two of them sprinted toward where the helicopter was landing, and as they rounded the tents, finally giving them a full view of the massive vehicle up close, Acton's eyebrows shot up at the white paint job with blue lettering.

United Nations?

Sand was being whipped around, causing them to stop and shield their eyes as the vehicle bounced to a landing. The engines immediately began to power down as the side door was slid open, two crew members jumping to the ground, followed by a man in a business suit then a woman in a skirt and heels.

Both looked and were completely out of place.

As the wind died down, Acton and Laura stepped forward as the man waved to them. The woman made several false starts then finally bent over, removed her heels and tossed them into the open helicopter. The man extended his hand to Laura as he approached, the helicopter now quiet, its blades still spinning, but slow enough to now watch the hypnotic rhythm.

"Professor Palmer?" asked the dark-skinned man, his accent British.

"Yes," replied Laura, exchanging a quick, quizzical glance with Acton as she accepted the man's hand.

"And you must be Professor Acton," said the woman, pure southern drawl giving away her country of origin. "A pleasure," she said, reaching out for Acton's hand. "I'm Tiffany Reese, United Nations. This is Reginald Wangari from the International Monetary Fund."

Introductions finished, Acton asked the obvious question. "Why are you here?"

"Is there someplace more private we can speak?" asked Reese, motioning toward the gathering throng of armed students.

Laura nodded. "Follow me," she said, then turning to the students and her ex-SAS head of security Leather, said, "False alarm, everybody go back to whatever it was you were doing."

They walked to the main tent in silence then stepped inside, the cool air reminding Acton that he was going commando. Laura pointed to the table. "Please have a seat," she said. "Can I get anyone something to drink?"

"Water, please," said Reese quickly, her thin white blouse already sticking to her body.

"I'll second that," said Wangari as he pulled at his shirt. "This is nice. Air conditioning in the desert! If my grandparents had this, they may have never left Kenya!" He laughed as he took the bottle from Laura, twisting off the cap and downing half it.

"Excuse me for a minute," said Acton. "You caught me in the shower."

"Oh, don't put on more clothes on my account!" laughed Reese, batting her hand at Acton. "I'd die to have a pair of shorts and a t-shirt right now. Instead they grabbed both of us out of a meeting in Dubai and had us on a plane in minutes. Can you believe they made us leave our luggage behind?"

Acton stepped behind a privacy screen with his suitcase and quickly dressed as the conversation continued on the other side.

"What could be so urgent?" asked Laura.

"There's been a discovery. Archeological in fact, which is why we're here," replied Reese.

"A discovery of monumental importance," added Wangari. "Something that could destabilize the entire region if word were to get out."

Acton's eyes narrowed as he slipped on a pair of underwear. *An archeological find that could destabilize a region?* "What did you find?" he asked from behind the partition.

"I'll wait until you're decent," said Reese. "You have to see it to believe it."

"Where was it found?" asked Laura.

"In Eritrea, along the Tekezé River," answered Reese. "By a goat herder, no less."

Acton finished dressing, opting to forgo his boots for expediency's sake. He stepped out from behind the partition and took an empty seat beside Laura.

"Now, how about we see what you found?" he suggested.

Reese nodded and Wangari placed his briefcase on the table, snapping open the catches with a loud double-click. He opened the top and reached inside, removing a small bundle, carefully wrapped in cloth. He placed it on the table with a gentle thud.

Acton looked at Laura, curiosity etched on both their faces. "What is it?" she asked.

Reese motioned toward it. "Open it."

"Let me get my tools," said Acton, beginning to rise.

Reese waved her hand. "There's no need. It's not fragile and it's been in dozens of hands by now."

Acton frowned, and noticed Laura doing the same.

How are we supposed to examine a find that has been handled so poorly?

He sat back down and reached for the bundle, pulling it gently toward them. Flipping it over he found the edge of the cloth, and carefully unwrapped the item, which felt to be about a pound in heft, and when he caught the first glint of the surface, he heard Laura gasp before he had the chance.

"It's gold!" she said as he revealed the full bar in all its glory. About the size of a small candy bar, the dense metal made it deceivingly heavy for its size. Flipping it over again revealed markings that had both of them leaning forward.

"This was minted during Vespasian's rule," said Acton, pointing at the writing. He looked at their guests. "You found this in Eritrea?"

"Yes."

Acton shrugged, leaning back in his chair. "It's a curiosity, obviously, but I fail to see how this could impact the balance of power in the region, or why it merited a visit from the UN and the IMF."

Wangari smiled then jabbed his finger at the bar of gold now sitting untouched on the table. "What if I told you there was more where that came from?"

"I'd say it belongs in a museum, and ask the same questions."

Wangari grinned. "I knew I'd like you," he laughed. "Your file doesn't do you justice. Look," he said, leaning in and lowering his voice, "enough dancing. Full disclosure. What if I told you they found an ancient ship buried in the sand, and it contained tens of thousands of these bars worth over one billion dollars?"

Acton's chest tightened and his eyebrows raced up his forehead. "I'd say you better get it some place safe before every criminal in the world tries to get their hands on it."

"If the find is authenticated, we intend to do exactly that," replied Reese.

"So why are you here?" asked Laura. "I fail to see how this involves us."

"We are here, Professors, because you are the closest experts to where the hoard was found, and about the only two in the region that the permanent members of the UN Security Council could agree on to send."

"Send?" asked Acton, red flags suddenly springing to attention.

"Yes, *send*," said Reese. "We need the two of you to come with us to Eritrea and confirm the find, and if it proves genuine, extract it, prepare it for delivery, then see it safely out of the country."

Acton looked at Laura, his eyes wide in shock, then at the two suits. "Are you kidding?"

Reese suddenly became serious, any trace of her Southern hospitality erased. "I never kid when it comes to lives, Professor Acton."

Acton shook his head slowly. "Can we at least think about it?"

Wangari smiled, spreading his hands out as he stood up. "Of course! Please, talk about it among yourselves. We'll wait outside. But"—he tapped his watch—"we leave in ten minutes."

"*If* we agree," added Acton.

Wangari smiled again with a nod. "Of course, Professor Acton, of course. You are of course free to choose, but I am confident you will come to the correct decision."

"And should you not," said Reese, holding the flap of the tent open, "we will be…" Her voice drifted off, then she smiled, again all pleasant. "Well, never mind that. I'm certain you'll come to the right decision."

And Acton was certain he heard in her tone two important, unspoken words.

Or else.

Market Road, Pompeii, Roman Empire
August 24th, 79 AD

Avita huddled under a blanket, her three young children surrounding her, the boys on either side, her daughter in her lap. All had their heads under the blanket to keep the ash out, which made their slow, arduous journey all the more terrifying, her imagination filling in the blanks of the horrors she heard on the other side of the thin canvas of the wagon.

The wagon suddenly came to a stop, Labeo cursing from the front, the incredibly brave and loyal servant refusing to be relieved, instead remaining at the reins the entire time. Avita lowered the blanket to see what was happening and almost immediately regretted it, her imagination not doing the devastation justice.

The entire area before them had a dull orange glow that seemed to pulse with an energy all its own. Sunlight was nowhere to be seen and she wasn't even certain what time it was. Leaning forward the night sky was a rippling mass of black clouds, strange flashes that looked almost like lightning streaking across, yet no rain fell. Houses all around them burned, at least those that had the misfortune of being thatched or topped with wood. Others had collapsed inward, the weight of the falling ash proving too much, and her mind flashed back to her own home and the collapse of the south wing just as they were leaving.

It had leant a feeling of permanence in their flight, a warning to never come back, to leave Pompeii be, to allow its victims to rest in the peace their final moments denied them.

"Let us in!" cried a man's voice. "Please, my wife can barely walk, she's pregnant!"

"Off with you!" yelled Labeo. "Out of the way or I'll run you down!"

"No, please! Have mercy on us!"

Avita crawled forward and looked down at the source of anguish so close and saw a man she didn't recognize, his tear streaked face blackened from the ash, his hair now an unnatural gray, his wife, on the street, clinging to his leg, her head on her chest in exhaustion.

Upon seeing Avita, the man immediately turned his attention to her. "My lady, please, have mercy! At least take my wife!"

"No!" cried his wife, "I won't leave you!"

Avita looked at Labeo who shook his head slightly, and she knew he was right. If they took them, then when would it stop? Their tiny caravan was already barely moving along the coastal road, it clogged with broken carts abandoned by their owners and people, many dead or dying, ash almost as high as the top of the wheels.

But part of being Roman was to be compassionate to other citizens when in need—or at least that was the way she was raised. And if this wasn't a time of need, she didn't know what was.

"Let them come up, then make haste," she said, Labeo frowning for a brief moment then nodding. The elation in the desperate man's eyes was evident and it momentarily warmed Avita's heart as he helped push his wife up into the carriage. The man followed and Labeo immediately flicked the reins, their procession moving forward once again as the two new passengers situated themselves in the now cramped quarters.

Avita handed them a flask of water as the children eyed the new arrivals with curiosity, especially the swollen stomach of the wife. The woman looked at her and forced a smile on her weak face.

"Thank you," she whispered, her eyes fluttering then shutting as her head collapsed on her husband's chest. He kissed the top of her head then drank some more water, pouring some on his hands then wiping his face free of the ash. He had a hacking cough that slowly subsided as he drank more water, then suddenly he grabbed his stomach and spun around, sticking his head out the canvas and vomiting, his shoulders heaving with each wretch, the horrible sounds almost like strangled screams, loud enough to wake his wife who turned to tend to him.

Avita held her children tight, the sounds terrifying them all, it so close and within sight that it brought a dose of reality to their until now sheltered exposure to the disaster. After several minutes the man turned back, wiping a black grime off his chin as if he had vomited the very ash that surrounded them.

"Back under the blankets," she ordered, covering her children's heads and putting her own mouth and nose under the covering. The man took several more drinks then seemed to relax, his cough gone and his breathing returning to normal. "I'm Avita," she said, finally realizing introductions had never been made.

"I'm Flora," replied the young woman who motioned toward her husband. "This is Seneca."

The man nodded, handing the water to his wife. "Thank you again for taking us. You wouldn't believe how bad it is out there," he said, his voice raspy but gaining strength.

"It's unlike anything I could have ever imagined," agreed Avita. "It is as if the gods have abandoned us."

Flora shivered in fright, snuggling closer to her husband. "I fear how far this hell has spread." She lowered her voice, leaning forward. "People are desperate out there. I fear if we don't get out soon, we never will."

Avita glanced ahead but could see nothing, the canvas cover supplemented with blankets that hung over the normally open front.

"Labeo, how goes it?" she called.

A head poked between the blankets, covered in black, streaks around the eyes and mouth where he had tried to wipe them clean. "Not well, my lady. This ash continued to deepen and the horses are having a hard time of it. I have lost sight of the second carriage—I fear they may have broken an axle."

"We must stop for them!" cried Avita, her head emerging from under her blanket.

"No, my lady. There is no time nor can we take the increased load, it is too hard on the horses. Even with the extra two they are struggling. If we do not escape the city soon, we never will. The others can follow on foot."

"But—"

Labeo cut her off, rather impudently she thought if the situation weren't so dire. "My lady, please, think of the children. My lord was very clear in his orders. I am to stop at nothing to save you."

Avita nodded, resigned to the fact that no matter how distasteful the decision had been, it had been the right one. The priority had to be the children. The others in the supply wagon could walk, and if lucky, catch up, for they seemed to be barely moving. A brisk walk wouldn't even describe how slowly they appeared to be progressing, and if it weren't for the air outside, she would suggest it was indeed better to walk.

A tortured whinny from behind had them all turn.

"What is it?" asked Avita.

Labeo's head disappeared for a moment then the cart came to a halt. His head poked back in for a moment. "It's the second carriage, they've just caught up but have just lost one of their horses." He turned to Seneca. "Are you well enough to help?" The man nodded, climbing to his knees then out the front. Labeo looked at his mistress. "I'll get water and some food. I'll be back shortly."

Labeo disappeared behind the blankets and Avita felt the carriage rock as the two men stepped down. The horror on the other side of the canvas continued, strangled screams, wails of sorrow, cries of children, and the near constant shaking of the ground terrified her even more now that they weren't moving and their only protection, Labeo, had gone, despite him only paces away.

Suddenly she heard a shout behind them and the distinct sound of two swords clashing. She spun around, the children spilling to the sides as she pushed a blanket out of the way and peered into the darkness behind them. She gasped at what she saw. The servants in the supply wagon were nowhere to be seen. Seneca was leaning against the body of one of the horses, his stomach opened by a blade, his life force pouring onto the ash that was up to his waist. Labeo was fighting their attackers, but was outnumbered three to one. Avita knew he was a skilled swordsman, but he was already wounded on his right arm, near the shoulder, and he was now forced to fight with his left in his weakened state.

He thrust forward, plunging his blade into the nearest man, his screams of pain added to those coming from every home and every street within earshot. As Labeo withdrew, he was set upon by the other two and before he could parry the next attack, he was struck in the leg. He fell to one knee, turning his head toward Avita's carriage, their eyes meeting.

"Go!" he yelled as a blade was thrust through his back, his eyes bulging, his chest bursting forward as his shoulder blades pulled back. Blood burst from his mouth as he gasped then before he collapsed into the ash, his lips moved once more, mouthing his final word again.

"Go!"

Avita pulled back inside as his body disappeared into the blanket of ash. She dove for the front of the carriage, throwing the blanket aside and climbing into the seat once manned by Labeo. Grabbing the reins, she flicked them, yelling at the horses to proceed. They jerked forward, straining against the weight they carried, and after several false starts, they began to move, Avita letting out a sigh of relief.

As a strong hand gripped her arm, yanking her onto the street below.

She cried out, covering her face as she hit the ground, but surprised at the lack of pain, the ash acting like a massive cushion protecting her from the hard stone underneath.

"You're a pretty one, aren't you?"

The lechery in his voice was obvious even to her, her upbringing affording her little opportunity to ever hear such a tone, it simply not tolerated in polite company. Her heart skipped a beat as she felt her breast pawed by the animal and she spun around, her fist clenched, opening it as it emerged from the ash, filling the man's face with the powder. Cursing, he stumbled back and began to cough, visibly sucking in the thick ash with each gasp. Realizing what was happening, he covered his mouth with his robe and fell to his knees, his sword falling from his hand.

A cry from the cart had her heart in her throat as she realized the horses were continuing forward without her at the reins, her children still in the rear. She scrambled through the ash, trying to grab hold of the cart as it began to pick up speed but stumbled and fell, losing sight as she collapsed into the powder. With the presence of mind to hold her breath and close her eyes, she began to push herself to her knees when somebody gripped her by the hair, painfully hauling her to her feet. She cried out in agony, her children responding with their own cries as they heard their mother in pain. She looked up and saw the blade of her assailant's sword swing toward her neck. She twisted her head to the side, her hair ripping from her scalp, and sunk her teeth deep into the man's arm. Crying out in pain he loosened his grip, his swing slowing as he tried to wrench his arm loose.

Avita yanked herself free and jumped to her feet, rushing after the cart. Grabbing the side, she tried to pull herself up and cried out as she began to slip. Suddenly a hand reached out from behind the blankets hanging over the front and grabbed her arm. As she was pulled inside she saw Flora emerge, her tear streaked face grimacing with the effort.

Avita pulled herself the rest of the way and grabbed the reins, flicking them hard, screaming at the struggling beasts who immediately responded. The cart began to pick up speed but Avita had little confidence they would be able to escape their attackers. She looked about for something, anything that she might be able to use as a weapon but saw nothing. Turning back, she was about to ask Flora to search for something when the pregnant woman pushed through the blankets, holding a hammer. Without a word she handed it to Avita then plunged back into the rear and out of sight, Avita switching the hammer to her left hand.

A roar of rage from her side had her instinctively swing the hammer back, the satisfying sound of bone crunching as it made impact allowing a slight smile to emerge as her attacker's growl turned to a cry of agony, the distinct sound of him falling giving her a surge of hope.

As she peered into the darkness she couldn't see beyond the snouts of their saviors as they struggled valiantly against impossible odds. With each rotation of the wheels they put more and more distance between them and their attackers and the poor, valiant Labeo and Flora's husband, whose name escaped her.

Suddenly the horses stopped, and no amount of urging would send them forward. A gust of wind cleared the ash enough for her to see a cart blocking their path, one of its rear wheels askew, and no room in the narrow streets to go around it. Her shoulders sank as she realized there was no way they would be able to proceed. Twisting around, she pushed her head through the blankets.

"Let's go! We'll have to walk from here!"

The children scrambled forward and she pulled them through, helping each to the ground. Flora handed the water and food forward, along with several blankets, then crawled out herself. Avita was the last to jump down and she was about to unhook the poor horses so they might have a chance to survive, when an enraged man's voice overwhelmed the din around them.

"Forget them!" cried Flora, tugging at Avita's arm, urging her forward. Avita reluctantly allowed herself to be pulled along as she said a silent goodbye to the terrified animals that had done their best to save their masters.

As they pushed forward, the ash so high the children were barely visible, she suddenly realized they were only moments from being separated. "Everybody join hands!" she ordered as she grabbed her two youngest by the hands, pulling them in her wake as she followed Flora who held the oldest.

Suddenly the entire ground shook harder than it had since this calamity had begun, knocking them all off their feet.

"By the gods!" cried Flora as she pointed to the horizon. A massive plume of red hot flame was spewing from the top of the mountain, thousands of feet into the air.

We're going to die if we stay out here!

Over Eritrean Airspace
Present Day, One day before the crash

Night was fast approaching as their helicopter raced across the arid landscape. It had been a whirlwind of activity once they had agreed to go with Reese and Wangari, and despite the fact the impression was left they had little choice, they would have gone regardless. It was one of the many things they had in common.

A drive to discover.

And if there were thousands of bars of ancient Roman gold in Eritrea, the mystery begged to be solved.

It was supposed to be a quick in and out operation. Simply verify the find as genuine, tell those on the ground what they needed to do to preserve the find according to international antiquities laws, then leave.

"Look!" exclaimed Laura, pointing out the window. Acton leaned over his fiancée and peered through the small round window of the large transport chopper, it brimming with personnel and equipment. There had been no time for introductions, and Acton had the distinct impression that the vast majority were military, yet there wasn't a gun in sight.

Below he could see the winding Tekezé River, then in the distance a massive area bathed in bright lights, illuminating the entire scene as if it were under the midday sun.

"That must be it," he observed as he leaned back in his seat. He pulled out his phone and activated the Maps app, showing their location to Laura. "The border to Ethiopia is just across the river."

"Isn't this disputed land?" she asked.

"It has been," said one of the men sitting across from them. Pleasantly plump, he smiled, revealing deep dimples as he extended his hand. "Charles Tucker, UN," he said, shaking both their hands, the professors introducing themselves. Tucker motioned out the window. "Eritrea and Ethiopia fought a two year war over this area about fifteen years ago. Before that they fought a civil war over the area, Eritrea gaining its independence. That one lasted the better part of thirty years. And before that? Well, let's just say British colonialism isn't the only colonialism to have screwed up this country."

"Ottoman, Italian then British, wasn't it?" asked Acton, who knew the answer full well, but was enjoying having someone informed to talk to.

"Indeed. You know your history well, Professor." His eyes narrowed. "You're not an historian, are you?"

"In a manner of speaking," replied Acton. He nodded toward Laura. "We're both archeologists."

"Then I've been showing off to experts!" laughed Tucker, his cheeks flushing. "I apologize if I came off as arrogant!"

Acton laughed, shaking his head. "Not at all, not at all. Once you get to know me, you'll realize I'm always sharing my infinite wisdom, whether people want to hear it or not!"

"Tell me about it!" said Laura with a wink and a smile.

Acton elbowed her gently in the ribs.

Tucker motioned to the engagement ring on Laura's hand. "You two wouldn't happen to be…" He let the question trail off, his eyebrows climbing inquisitively.

Laura held up the ring, beaming. "We're engaged."

Tucker smiled, holding up his left hand, revealing a gold wedding band. "Fifteen years next week." He frowned. "I'm afraid I might miss it if what they have here is the real deal."

"What have they told you?" asked Acton.

Tucker shrugged. "Not much beyond a hoard of Ancient Roman gold bars found on a buried shipwreck. The Eritreans threatened to melt it down and sell it on the open market if we didn't negotiate. If the estimates are correct, there's enough gold there to be equivalent to over a quarter, possibly half their GDP. It could completely destabilize their domestic economy, and depending on what they decided to do with the money, which we suspect is purchase weapons, could trigger another war with Ethiopia. There's also a lot of tension with the Sudanese, what with the ongoing Muslim on Christian violence. Anything that tips the balance in this region is never a good thing."

This was more information than Acton had been expecting. "What did they agree to?"

"Essentially we agreed to pay them double what the raw find would be worth, but over a ten year period."

"They agreed to that?" asked Laura, her surprise clear.

"Once we told them we'd delist any exchange that agreed to buy the gold, they really had no choice."

Acton's head bobbed. "Ruthless."

"You should see me negotiate with my teenage daughter."

Acton's smile spread up his left cheek. "You lose every time, don't you?"

Tucker tossed his head back, roaring in laughter. "You're absolutely right! I can negotiate favorable deals with foreign nations, but my daughter's bedtime keeps creeping up!"

The helicopter suddenly began to bank, the large lit area now viewable to everyone through the windows.

"Looks like you were right," whispered Laura in Acton's ear.

Acton nodded, his stomach tightening slightly as he surveyed the site, it clear there were at least hundreds of armed soldiers everywhere.

"There's trouble," said Tucker.

"What?"

"On the other side of the river."

Acton leaned forward and noticed a large number of lights were aimed at the opposite bank of the river.

Revealing what appeared to be hundreds of troops accompanied by dozens of armored vehicles.

"I think our jobs just got much more urgent," he muttered.

"Indeed," agreed Tucker. "This will continue to escalate. If the Eritreans can't maintain the balance, the Ethiopians will cross that river and snatch the gold before we have a chance to get it out."

Acton exchanged a concerned glance with Laura, taking her hand and squeezing it.

Perhaps agreeing so readily wasn't such a good idea after all.

Lucius Valerius Corvus Residence, Pompeii, Roman Empire
August 24th, 79 AD

Costa sat in a corner, eating some chicken with grapes, a goblet of wine sitting on the floor next to him. The room was quiet save the constant stories Plinius regaled them with. He knew it was in an attempt to calm everyone, and to his surprise, it was working. The man had led an extraordinary life, and Costa found himself riveted by almost every word, occasionally even able to tear his eyes away from the massive pile of gold in the center of the room.

A steady stream of soldiers was now at work, the fleet having arrived almost an hour ago. Word had arrived that the wind was not cooperating, and there was no way to set sail away from the coast, but they were hopeful in the morning the winds would turn. Plinius seemed unconcerned, indicating that until the gold was loaded aboard, the winds could do as they will.

Soldiers continued to hand bars of gold from the basement, up the stairs and into the chamber in which they all sat, but now instead of adding to the pile, a double line of troops continued handing the newly arriving gold, and the already stacked gold, out of the house and down to the shore. Costa was impressed with how efficiently it was working, the amount of gold being moved remarkable. Those outside would switch to the resting room after fifteen minutes, with those inside moving outside, and those resting, resuming work on the inside. Those battling the ash on the roof and on the path were also switching off, the initial troops who had done battle still resting in another chamber, many quite sick from what they had inhaled.

Plinius suddenly stood, his story over. "Now I shall sleep. Wake me in the morning."

"My lord!" exclaimed Valerius as he jumped to his feet, quickly rushing to Plinius' side. "The fires! They grow closer and larger! Should we not at least stay on the boats until the treasure is loaded?"

Plinius batted his hand at the air. "Never mind the fires, they're merely from the untended hearths of panicked farmers." He gripped Valerius by the shoulder. "Don't worry, my friend, all will be fine." He walked briskly out of the room and toward a guest room that had survived the collapse, ending the conversation. Costa was relieved to find he wasn't the only one shocked at this pronouncement, the dropped jaws and wide eyes of the few that remained revealing what he was thinking.

How could you possibly sleep at a time like this?

As if to punctuate the idiocy, the ground rumbled once again, more plaster dust shaking from overhead as the entire structure of the house continued to weaken, the marble floor cracking and heaving before finally settling. Valerius' head was shaking in his own disbelief before he finally caught himself and turned to those who remained.

"We'll remain in this room, it is safest. Costa, have pillows and blankets brought and have the staff get some rest. We will need our energy in the morning."

Costa nodded, motioning to one of the slaves to fulfill the order then another to pass on the message that all should rest in the main hall. Within minutes bedding was provided to everyone, all but a few torches were put out, and the only sounds were that of the chaos outside and the grunting of the soldiers as they continued to move the treasure.

A treasure that Costa lay facing, his eyes wide as they caught every glint of the precious metal.

Outside Omhajer, Eritrea
Present Day, One day before the crash

Professor James Acton was on his stomach, lying in the dirt as he wiggled his way as deep as he could into the hold of the ancient vessel. The level of preservation was remarkable, most likely aided by the dry, arid conditions, and the protection from the elements provided by a healthy covering of sand deposited over millennia.

He felt Laura's hand on his leg and a harness around his waist should there be a collapse. He knew she was disappointed at not being the first in, and was hiding it well from the others. But he knew her. Better than he had ever known a woman. They were alike in many ways, different in all the right ways. But in the pursuit of their chosen professions, they were identical, and both wanted to plunge head first into the mysterious tunnel, to jump down the rope into the unknown cavern. They lived for the thrill of discovery, no matter what the pace, whether it was crawling into the hold of a ship that could collapse at any second if some idiot drove a truck over the berm it was resting against, or whether it was simply brushing the dust off a piece of earthenware jar at a staked out dig site, the adrenaline rush was always there.

Who had used that jar? And for what? Had they made it themselves? Or traded at a market for it? What had they traded? Why had they left it behind? This was what so many people outside of his profession didn't think of. When we move, we pack up our belongings in a truck and move to our new residence, unpacking all of our old stuff. Sometimes we leave things behind, but someone either takes over using them, sells them, or throws them in the garbage.

The same was true thousands of years ago. In today's throwaway society, it's so easy to simply toss out things and repurchase them at the new destination, but before the twentieth century, belongings were far fewer and far more precious. Things were only abandoned or left behind for a reason, and those reasons were rarely good.

War, famine, pestilence, natural disaster. People forced to abandon their villages due to war, it burned to the ground by the marauders, the villagers never returning. That was a common reason found in their digs. Some natural phenomenon such as landslides, earthquakes or volcanos, forcing a rapid escape, or worse, the calamity creating a tomb not only for their possessions, but themselves.

Pompeii popped into his mind as he reached the first of the gold bars, the brand of Emperor Vespasian, who died only weeks before the eruption of Vesuvius, clearly marked on the bar by the assayer two millennia ago. The eruption had been violent, catastrophic, and when the end finally came, so devastatingly swift, the city was essentially abandoned, it impossible to salvage anything after the destruction wrought by the sleeping giant that was Vesuvius.

Over the ensuing centuries Pompeii, and the neighboring town of Herculaneum, were forgotten to history, life moving on as an empire collapsed. It wasn't until 1738 that the lost city was rediscovered, and even then it took decades before any real excavations began. Now thousands of tourists roam the streets of the nearly perfectly preserved ancient city, flash-heated in time.

Acton peered deeper into the hold then held up his cellphone, snapping a rapid series of pictures in panorama mode. As the flash snapped, he spotted a partial skeleton at the far end, and said a silent prayer for their soul. It was a common misconception that the bodies famously preserved in Pompeii were the actual hardened or petrified remains of people. Instead, they were actually plaster casts of the voids created by the bodies of the victims. When the final disaster struck, super-heated air rolled down the mountain and through the city, instantly "cooking" everything. The heat was so intense it caused many of the victims' muscles to contract, which resulted in many dying in the fetal position, as opposed to actually having already been in the position when the final blow came. These bodies were then buried in tons of ash that solidified over the centuries, and as the bodies decomposed to nothing, voids were created in the ash.

When archeologists began to excavate, they came upon these voids, and curious, one decided to fill one of them with a plaster of Paris mixture. After it solidified, they carefully removed the ash from around the now solid void, and were shocked at their discovery. Over one hundred bodies to date have managed to be preserved, their death throes now on display for all to see, from man, woman, child and beast.

But not here, not today. He had no doubt they might find more skeletons, but nothing preserved like the human voids in the ashes of Pompeii. Examining the skeletons, however, might give some indication as to how they died, and at least some of their uniforms might have survived, which could answer another important question. Was this vessel from the time of Vespasian, or was it from much later, merely transporting gold minted in Vespasian's time?

"Coming out!" he yelled as he began to shuffle backward. He felt a gentle tug on his harness as the slack was pulled out along with him, and within moments he was back outside, lying on his back, gasping in the fresh air. He held up his phone to the crowd circling him, all looking down with expectant expressions on their face. "I took a panorama of the inside."

Laura grinned, grabbing the phone as Tucker pulled Acton to his feet. They all rushed to what had been identified earlier as the Command Tent, it containing computers hooked into a diesel generator available for the gathered to use. Laura hooked the phone into her computer, sending the image to a large display for all to see.

Gasps filled the tent.

For as far as the eye could see into the hold, which was at least several dozen feet deep, sat stacks of gold bars. The estimate of thousands definitely correct, tens of thousands most likely so. As Laura zoomed in on the gold, the assayer's brands of the Vespasian seal were obvious.

"It appears that all of the gold is from Emperor Vespasian's rule," she said for those who weren't familiar with the history. "He ruled from about 69 AD until 79 AD."

Acton looked at the picture, standing only a couple of feet from the television, off to the side. A quick glance at the gathered throng suggested they weren't very impressed by the historical significance of Vespasian. "Fun fact," he said to the room. "Vespasian built the Coliseum in Rome." A round of "Ahhhs!" had him satisfied they were sufficiently engaged. He turned to Laura. "I saw a partial skeleton, farther down the left side. "Can you zoom in on it?"

She nodded and manipulated the image. Soon they were looking at the enlarged skeleton, the bones mostly collapsed into a pile. "What's that?" asked somebody in the crowd, stepping forward and pointing at a round disk sitting to the right. Laura zoomed in some more, and Acton's heart raced.

It was an Imperial crest, worn by senior officers to identify their family, along with their unit and the emperor at the time. Acton looked back at Laura, a grin on his face as the implications of what they had discovered sank in. "It identifies this man as a member of the Roman Navy, stationed at Misenum under the Admiralty of Pliny the Elder!" The excitement was evident in his voice, and as he looked about the tent, only Laura was as excited as he was.

"Don't you see?" he asked the room, his hands and arms opened wide, begging for someone to get it. "Misenum was a city on the Bay of Naples where the navy for that area was stationed. Pompeii was on the other side of that bay. Pliny the Elder was the Prefect who sailed the Roman Navy to Pompeii to try and rescue the citizens. His nephew, Pliny the Younger, provided the written accounts of the eruption."

Silence, then finally Tucker spoke up. "Meaning?"

"Meaning if this man's uniform says he was under Pliny's command, then this ship could very well be from Pompeii!"

"Pliny the Elder" Residence, Misenum, Roman Empire
August 25th, 79 AD

Gaius grabbed his mother, Plinia, holding her tight as the ground quaked beneath their feet. It was approaching morning and none had slept, the terror across the bay now spreading quickly. The stars overhead had been blotted out throughout the night, the hint of the morning sun normally expected at this time lost in the orange glow pulsing against the bottom of the dark cloud from Vesuvius now covering the entire sky. A steady accumulation of ash, drifting down like a heavy snowfall, had begun hours before and was now several inches high already, with no sign of abating.

And then there was Herculaneum.

Hundreds of evacuees had already reached Misenum, telling of the horrors they were seeing, fewer still with word of Pompeii farther to the south. But if Herculaneum was as bad as described, Pompeii must be an absolute nightmare. Most of the household that remained after their master Plinius' departure sat or stood on the veranda overlooking the bay, watching the calamity on the other side as if some great Greek tragedy were playing in a theatre, the characters an angry, erupting mountain, its true nature long forgotten, several towns built ignorantly in its shadow the victims, and Gaius and the others the audience, the orchestra provided by nature herself, rumbles and booms the percussion, the trumpets creatures fleeing in terror, perhaps wiser than their human counterparts who instead watched in horrific fascination.

"Are you two mad!" exploded a voice from behind that had Gaius and his mother spinning. Gaius smiled as Barbatus stormed in, his usual tempestuous self, a comical foil to his uncle's usually calm demeanor. How the two had become friends he would never understand, but in the field of battle strange bedfellows indeed were made.

"Barbatus, so good of you to come. To what do we owe this honor?" asked Gaius, letting go of his mother and motioning for their guest to sit. Barbatus shook his head, waving off the seat, but taking a glass of water brought by one of the servants, which was when Gaius noticed the family friend was covered head to toe in Vesuvius' dust. He motioned to one of the servants. "Bring water and towels so our guest can properly clean himself."

The servant bowed and disappeared into the bowels of the house, returning moments later with the requested items, and as Barbatus washed his exposed skin, his mouth continued to run.

"Do you not see what is happening out there?" he demanded of them, not waiting for an answer. "Your Uncle, *your* brother"—he took a moment to stab the air between him and Gaius' mother—"would want you safe, not sitting here, watching the happenings as if it were a play and you were immune to its effects."

"I will not leave while my brother's fate is unknown," said Gaius' mother, sitting resolutely with her arms crossed, her eyes on the horizon.

"Nor I," replied Gaius as he returned to his seat, picking up his volume of Livy with the intent of defying the gods by reading in the face of their wrath. As he tried to read the next paragraph, he could feel Barbatus' eyes upon him, but he was determined to ignore him. Perhaps it was the impetuousness of a seventeen year old boy, desperate to be a man, demonstrating to a real man how ill prepared he was for that role, but he found the glare continued to eat at him, forcing him to distraction as he read the same few sentences over and over, absorbing nothing.

He snapped the volume shut, returning it to the table then turned to Barbatus.

"Must you stare at me like that?"

"You're fortunate I don't put you over my knee!"

"You wouldn't dare!"

"Don't tempt me." Barbatus turned his focus to Gaius' mother. "And you, how dare you put your only son at risk like this!"

Plinia blanched slightly, turning away from the criticism, her mouth opening to reply when Gaius jumped in, saving her the embarrassment of on excuse.

"I stay by choice!" he yelled, leaping to his feet, his chest shoved forward, shoulders back, chin jutting outward, as fierce a look as he could conjure plastered on his face like a mask used by an actor in the theatre, the terror he felt on the inside hidden behind the façade he desperately tried to project.

Barbatus swelled by merely taking a deep breath, his muscles rippling as he clenched his fists, the man a veteran of innumerable battles with real men, not words on a page that had been Gaius' foes, his uncle pushing him mentally rather than physically.

He felt his bladder muscles relax and if he hadn't just relieved himself minutes before, he might have stained his robes right there. Instead he spun around and stormed toward his uncle's study just as his mother screamed. He rushed to her side, as did they all, she pointing across the bay.

And what he saw would have terrified even the bravest of warriors.

"Uncle," he murmured, unable to find the air to give the word volume.

He felt a hand on his shoulder, gentle, comforting, and he looked over to see Barbatus by his side, his own jaw dropped, his eyes glistening with the knowledge of what was happening across the bay.

There will be no survivors.

Tekezé River, Eritrea
Present Day, One day before the crash

"That's quite the leap, isn't it, Doc?"

Acton recognized the voice immediately, but couldn't find the owner. The crowd parted as someone stepped forward and when the face was revealed, Acton's eyebrows jumped with surprise.

Command Sergeant Major Burt "Big Dog" Dawson, leader of the Delta Force's elite Bravo Team, stood before him, along with Sergeant Carl "Niner" Sung. Acton stepped toward them, hand extended, smile on his face as he suddenly felt a whole lot more secure. "Sergeant Major, great to see you!" They shook hands, as did he and Niner as Laura gave them both pecks on the cheek. "I wasn't expecting to see you."

"I'll explain later," replied Dawson for the benefit of the room. Acton nodded, realizing their reunion could wait. "You were saying," prompted Dawson, motioning toward the screen.

"I was saying that this vessel could potentially be from the eruption of Mount Vesuvius."

"And *I* thought that was a leap."

"In his *expert* opinion," added Niner. "He's renowned worldwide for his expertise in archeological matters."

Acton had come to know many of the Delta Team Bravo members over the years, but had to admit Niner seemed to deliver more jokes than serious lines by an alarming proportion. He was sure some psychologist somewhere would accuse him of overcompensating for some missing aspect of his childhood, but Acton never paid too much attention to that sort of thing. Niner was an expert in his field, and had saved Acton's life the last time he had seen him. If it wasn't for Carl "Niner" Sung, Acton might very well be dead.

"There's no way to be certain, we'll need to do a proper excavation of the site," replied Acton. "But the time period definitely fits, and might explain how a boat became lost."

"Lost?" asked Tucker. "I'm not sure what you mean, Doctor."

"Well, the likelihood of a Roman vessel of the time sailing to this point and beaching, then abandoning a cargo like this is next to nothing," explained Acton. "Most likely the crew either died, or the boat slipped its moorings, unmanned. If the latter were the case, ships would be sent to immediately retrieve it, unless there was some disaster occurring that either prevented a retrieval, or prevented those in the area from knowing the boat had left."

"Seems unlikely that a boat with this much gold on it would ever have been left unmanned," said Dawson.

Acton nodded. "Agreed, which is why I think this vessel *was* manned, at least initially."

"You mean they might have abandoned ship?"

Acton shook his head. "No. Remember, at the time Ancient Egypt was a part of the Roman Empire and a major power. There is no way a vessel of this size would have been able to enter the Nile and sail down it this far unchallenged. If the vessel were abandoned, it would have been boarded, searched, and with this cargo, claimed in the name of the Empire."

Niner raised his hand as if in school. "If it didn't leave port unmanned, and it wasn't abandoned by its crew, then what are you suggesting."

"I'm suggesting it's a ghost ship."

Tucker raised his hand, Niner having set the precedent. "A what?"

"I'm suggesting that this vessel was manned, that all of the crew were killed somehow, and that it sailed itself south and into one of the many entrances to the Nile, was challenged by Roman vessels of the time, and allowed to continue on its way, unmolested."

"What makes it a ghost ship?" asked Niner.

"If they had just been killed in battle, they would have been boarded. Something spooked those who challenged it. What, I'm not sure, but a thorough examination of the find might reveal the cause."

"And just how long will that take?" asked Tucker.

Acton exchanged glances with Laura. "To do it properly, months."

The room erupted in protest, and didn't calm down until Tucker raised his hands to calm them. "Professor Acton, we don't have months."

Acton nodded. "No, you don't have months with respect to the gold. Remove the gold, and nobody cares about this site again, correct?"

Tucker nodded, smiling. "You have a keen grasp of the situation."

"Good. Then I don't see why, if we use manpower rather than machine, we can't empty the hold of its cargo beginning almost immediately."

"That could take days!" exclaimed someone in the back of the tent.

"Then let it take days!" replied Tucker. "Part of our job here is to preserve the find from an archeological standpoint, not just evacuate the gold."

"Just whose decision is it?" asked the same voice. "Yours?"

Tucker shook his head. "Nope, not mine."

"It's mine," said Reese, stepping forward. "As the ranking member of UNESCO ultimate authority has been handed to me."

Acton turned to her. "Then what's your decision?"

"We begin removing the gold immediately under your and Dr. Palmer's direction, until either it is all removed, or until the situation on the ground changes to make it too dangerous to proceed slowly," she replied, stepping in front of the monitor, taking center stage. "Remember, the priority here is the recovery of the gold. The secondary priority is preserving the find."

"And what about the hundreds of Ethiopians massing on the other side of the river who believe this is their territory?" asked the same voice, the woman it belonged to stepping forward, her black jumpsuit with Chinese flag on the shoulder suggesting she was one of the two there to represent this permanent member of the UN Security Council. It made Acton wonder immediately if that was why Dawson and Niner were there.

And if Dawson and Niner, two Special Forces operators had been sent, then most likely the same type of personnel had been dispatched from all five Security Council member states. Acton had to wonder how these ten people could possibly work together. The Americans and Brits, no problem. The French? Probably. The Chinese? Most likely not. The Soviets—scratch that, Russians? He wouldn't trust them with a ten foot pole. In fact he had come to think of them as Soviet Union 2.0 over the past few years, recent events in the Ukraine only confirming his long held belief that the Russian President was a man who simply couldn't be trusted, the ex-KGB spy yearning for the "good old days" where the CCCP acronym was feared, the hammer and sickle certain to raise heart rates around the world.

Reese nodded a welcome to the Chinese woman as she reached the edge of the circle surrounding Acton and the UNESCO representative. "That's why *you* are here," Reese replied. "To monitor the security situation, advise your prospective representatives here on the ground, and myself, so an informed decision can be made as to when it is no longer safe to remain."

The Chinese woman fixed her stare on Reese. "Ma'am, it is my opinion that that time has come and gone. It is already no longer safe to remain here."

Reese didn't bat an eyelash. "I'm open to hearing your evidence."

The Chinese woman nodded and a man in a matching jumpsuit Acton hadn't noticed plugged a memory card into the TV, the television automatically switching the signal source. A series of satellite photos began to loop on the screen, showing night vision shots.

"What are we looking at?" asked Tucker.

"These are satellite images taken by my government less than fifteen minutes ago," replied the woman. She pointed out several bright clusters of dots. "These are tanks, artillery and armored personnel carriers moving into the area. They will arrive by dawn. We also have evidence showing a number of gunships moving into the area, along with at least one thousand troops only hours away. The time to remove the gold is now!"

Reese watched the photos cycle by one more time, then nodded. "You assume they are going to attack. The Eritreans have significant forces here as well, and the United States government has pledged to defend our position, several vessels just off the coast on standby should it become necessary."

The Chinese woman smiled, her eyes narrowing as she glanced over at Dawson and Niner. "Yes, I'm sure the American military is prepared to support us, just as they did in the Crimea." She sighed as the two Russian observers glared at her. "That is the problem with you Americans. You assume the other side is as peace-loving as *you* claim to be. The sad reality is that in most of the world that isn't so." Her smile broadened. "Present company excluded, of course."

Reese bowed slightly. "Let's hope you're wrong in your interpretation of intentions." Reese turned to Acton. "Begin your extraction immediately."

Acton nodded, heading out of the tent, Laura by his side, before anyone else could suggest otherwise.

For his interpretation of events was exactly that of the Chinese woman.

Tomorrow the Ethiopians would attack, and even if the American Navy responded, it might be too late for those stuck on the ground in the initial assault. He looked at Laura and he could tell by her concerned expression she had the exact same fears as he did.

He plunged inside the hull, determined to work as fast as he could, otherwise yet another piece of history might be lost to violence, and if he were right about his theory as to the origin of this ship, more lives lost to Vesuvius' wrath.

POMPEII'S GHOSTS

Lucius Valerius Corvus Residence, Pompeii, Roman Empire
August 25th, 79 AD

Plinius woke to a scream, pushing his aging bones to an upright position on his bedding. The house rocked violently and this time several more screams erupted from nearby. He scrambled to his feet, brushing himself free of the fine layer of ash that coated him from head to toe, then coughed, a twinge of fear pushing itself above that which he had felt since first arriving ashore yesterday. He had decided a brave face was necessary to keep the troops motivated, but late in the evening even he too was beginning to give in to his fears and had decided sleep was the best way to hide his true state.

He was shocked to now find he had actually been able to sleep.

He felt weak, his chest tight, his lungs gasping for air, an attack of what his physician called asthma beginning. He covered his mouth with his robe, leaning against one of the pillars and steadied his breath. Spying a carafe of water nearby, he poured himself several glasses, downing them and feeling the tension relieve slightly, the cough at least abating.

But he knew if he didn't get out of here soon, he was at great risk.

Outside was certain death for him which was why he had insisted on staying inside despite the risk of collapse. He had never shrunken in fear from anything in his life, but this situation was testing him like nothing before. He had weathered storms at sea that would send the bravest of men running for the mountains, not to mention famine, drought, fire and more.

But never before had he seen the wrath of the gods, the very earth itself spewing forth death, blanketing everything in its path as if to snuff the very life out of any beauty that may have once been. And now he felt his lungs burning in response, increasing his fear, and again increasing the stress on the essential organs.

Forcing a brave face and a smile, he marched from the room and out into the common area. The soldiers continued to move the gold, slower now than when he went to bed, but with no less sense of urgency he was certain. He surveyed the small group, finding none asleep and all standing in archways, Plinius wondering if it was someone's knowledge of architecture that led them there, or just dumb luck.

Valerius stepped forward. "My lord, I highly recommend we leave. The north wing just collapsed and we lost several of our men on the roof and two of my slaves. The house has become too unstable."

Plinius pretended to ignore the recommendation, instead motioning for washing supplies to be brought. A slave rushed over with a bowl of water, towel over his arm.

"And the gold?" he asked as he bent forward and sank his hands into the bowl of cool water, rinsing his face several times, then washing the back of his neck.

"One ship has been loaded and is now in the center of the bay with Tacitus aboard."

Plinius grunted as he toweled himself dry, pleased it was someone he could trust. "Good, good. He shall marshal the fleet until I arrive." He tossed the towel back to the slave who rushed out of sight, Plinius shoving his shoulders back, his elbows out from his sides as he stretched with a groan. Staring at the ceiling as he did so, he noted the massive cracks stretching across it like lightning bolts frozen in time.

Perhaps we should get out of here.

"A second ship is almost loaded, I suggest we get you aboard now."

Plinius nodded, the thought appealing from a self-preservation point of view, but only if one took a short-term look on life. Titus would surely have him executed should he not save the gold.

"How much is left?"

Valerius shook his head. "Easily six more boats worth. We must abandon it, My Lord, and return once this disaster has ended."

"And if it doesn't?"

"Then I fear all is lost, and the Emperor will have no use for his gold."

Plinius detected the note of frustration in Valerius' voice, and forgave the man. Valerius could have fled in the night, but he hadn't. Valerius could outright challenge him right now, but he didn't. He was a brave man, but all brave men had limits.

And he was certain Valerius was eager to travel south and seek word of his family. Plinius had to admit he worried of his nephew and sister as well. The boy was still young in many ways, but he could begin to see the makings of a man in him, and this was just the type of situation that could trigger that change.

Would he find him sitting on the terrace, watching with the wonder and naiveté of a schoolboy, or perhaps huddled in his bedchambers, gripped by fear?

Or would he find a man, who had saved the household by ordering its evacuation.

As Plinius shoved aside a curtain, he gasped, fearing he might never know, for the darkness that enveloped them all, despite the hour, had engulfed the entire bay as well.

Tekezé River, Eritrea
Present Day, One day before the crash

Command Sergeant Major Burt Dawson watched as the gold literally flew out of the hold, Professor James Acton not concerned with the gold being damaged, merely tossing it through the hole. He had been at it for at least a good thirty minutes, and a work crew of locals had been set up, two raking the gold away from the entrance as it hit the ground, others taking the gold, safely out of the path of Acton's pitches, and piling it on pallets supervised by the UN personnel, a forklift waiting nearby to lift the pallet onto the back of a waiting truck which would immediately leave for the capital under heavy escort.

And if it weren't for the Ethiopians continuing to amass only several hundred feet away, he'd have rested easy. But a billion dollars of gold was an incredible temptation, especially to a corrupt regime that would certainly melt down a significant portion of it, distributing it among their loyal followers.

And me without my gun.

"There's room for two now!" yelled Acton from inside the hold.

"Hold your fire!" called Laura as she dropped to her knees. The flurry of gold bars paused as she climbed inside, then resumed almost immediately, moments later doubling in intensity. Dawson hadn't seen inside the hold personally, but judging by the picture Acton had taken, and the small pile of gold sitting on the pallet, he was pretty certain barely a dent had been made, but it appeared the professor had made a wise decision by deliberately clearing space for a second set of hands.

If it were up to Dawson he'd simply use the two front loaders that waited nearby, but fortunately for historians everywhere, he wasn't in charge. Which was made crystal clear by the fact he had absolutely no weapons on him. He and Niner had just completed an undercover op in Odessa in which they proved the Russians were supplying much more than just weapons and money to the Russian-speaking separatists, but actually busing in hundreds of troops from Russia, in plainclothes, to attack and occupy the government buildings, and once secured, hand them over to locals to defend.

He hated seeing history repeat itself, and he feared this was the Sudetenland all over again, with the American president playing the part of Neville Chamberlain. Hitler had used the same excuse of protecting German speakers' rights, the exact same phrasing the Russian President now used. And the West did little, as Western Europe was too dependent upon Russian natural gas to heat their homes in the winter.

Fools!

How could anyone become so dependent upon a former enemy that the very welfare of their citizenry became tied to the whims of a country that had never truly achieved democracy, and for over a decade, while the dependency grew, led by a virtual despot? As far as he was concerned the Europeans deserved to freeze should the Russians choose to shut off the taps. There would be some short term pain while new sources were found, but once they were, the Russian's would lose their leverage when their major customer said "thanks, but no thanks, we'll stick with North American natural gas".

The Europeans had to act now, and act quickly, to begin the transition, but also stand up to the bully that was a resurgent Russia. They had already essentially seized a sizeable chunk of Georgia and never handed it back. Now they had the Crimea, and all eyes were on Eastern Ukraine. What of

Latvia, Estonia, Lithuania, Armenia, and Moldova, not to mention another half dozen countries, all within the Russian sphere of influence, with significant Russian populations? Were they all fair game simply because the Russian President wanted to restore the Soviet Union?

He frowned as he spotted the two Russian security observers standing nearby, one on a satellite phone. He had worked with Russians before, and there were a few he trusted. It wasn't necessarily the soldiers themselves that he didn't trust, it was their taskmasters. These soldiers were as loyal to their country as he was to his, and they followed orders just like he did.

It was their leaders he didn't trust at all.

Spotting something on the horizon, he grabbed the binoculars from around his neck and raised them, scanning for the bright dots he had seen. Two MiG-23s zoomed into view, racing toward their position. He pointed and announced to the general public.

"We've got incoming. Two MiG-23s from the south-east!"

The entire camp turned, all becoming silent except for the hum of the diesel generator nearby. Within moments the dull roar of the MiG engines could be heard over the chugging generator, the spots on the horizon growing in intensity.

The Eritrean soldiers rushed to the bank of the river, dropping to the sand and aiming their weapons at the other side, many with their guns pointing in the air. Several technicals, merely pickup trucks with 50 caliber machine guns mounted in the rear took up position as tanks roared to life.

This is going to go to shit, quick!

He motioned for Niner to follow him and he ran toward the opening in the hold of the ship, the steady flow of gold having halted. He dropped to his knees and found the two professors kneeling at the entrance, looking out.

"You two need to get out of there, now!" he ordered, holding his hand out for Professor Palmer. She took it and he pulled her out, Acton scrambling after her. Dawson pointed to the other side of the embankment the hull of the boat rested against. "Get to the other side, the sand will provide good cover. If shooting breaks out, keep low and move north until you're out of range, then turn east. There's a village only a few miles from here. I'll find you there."

Acton nodded and grabbed his fiancée by the hand, scrambling up the embankment and out of sight, a large group of the civilians doing the same as the dozen unarmed security "observers" were left with no weapons to help defend against any potential attack, and no authority to order the Eritreans to hold their fire.

"What do you think?" asked Niner. "What's our job here? To protect the gold, or protect our citizens?"

"Officially we're not here to protect anything, merely observe, and in all honesty act as human shields against any Ethiopian aggression. The thinking is that they won't dare risk killing soldiers from the Security Council nations."

"Did anyone tell the Eritreans that'll only work if they don't fire first?"

"I met the commander. Unfortunately the bulb seems dim. And from what I saw of his troops, I don't think he'll be able to control them once they get scared."

The roar of the jets' engines filled the area now as the two MiG's rushed their position in what Dawson was certain was merely a show of force to intimidate. They would break off at the last second, banking away, careful to not cross the border.

But if a single Eritrean soldier fired out of fear, all hell could break loose. Ethiopia's military was far more massive and they had arrayed an impressive amount of armor already. Their ability to cross the river would be limited, but they'd be able to pound this position without mercy.

Dawson spotted Reese talking with the Eritrean commander, his uniform impressively adorned with large amounts of gold and medals that were most likely earned by his troops and not himself. He was arguing animatedly with Reese, using grand hand motions to belittle the slight woman. Dawson had to admit the diminutive woman was an odd choice for the assignment in a nation where women weren't respected, but when her finger jabbed back, pointed up at his throat, the glare she delivered and the words unheard at this distance, caused the man to check himself, then walk away, yelling for his troops to hold their fire.

Before Dawson could say anything Reese spun toward him, pointing. "Where are the professors?"

"I've sent them over the ridge, toward town."

She nodded approvingly then surveyed the camp as it emptied out of non-combatants. "We need to get that gold—"

She was cut off by a burst of gunfire. Dawson's trained ear told him it was a single AK-47 that fired off half a mag before being joined in by a chorus of assorted weapons. He spun toward the river to see the two approaching MiG's break off exactly as he had expected they would, but as they did, the entire southern bank of the river lit up as muzzles flared with return fire.

Dawson shoved Reese to the ground as he and Niner hit the deck. Looking about for better cover than a nearby canvas tent, he spotted the two large front loaders less than fifty feet away, their massive steel scoops several feet in the air, but facing away from the incoming fire. Dawson pointed and Niner nodded. They both grabbed Reese, hauling her to her feet and positioning themselves between her and the river as they rushed toward the loaders.

A tank fired behind them, followed by another, the massive explosions on the other side of the river immediately escalating the response. They reached the first front loader and Dawson scooped Reese up with a yelp from the woman and tossed her inside. Niner swung up and over the lip, reaching out and pulling Dawson up just as the response to the escalation pounded the shore, their temporary shelter shaking as the mighty rounds began to hammer the beach.

"Jesus Christ, we've got to get out of here!" cried Reese, huddled in a corner, curled up into a ball as she cringed with each report.

No shit!

Dawson turned himself around so he could see what was happening and wasn't impressed. Two of the six Eritrean tanks were in flames, having taken direct hits, and dozens of their troops were lying dead or wounded, the number made even more significant with his limited field of vision. The last of the civilians cleared the berm he had sent the professors over, but several were dead, including the talkative and rotund Tucker from the meeting, his mangled corpse near one of the tanks.

He must have thought it would be good cover.

Dawson frowned. From small arms fire, a tank is fantastic cover. But as a primary target, it's lousy. If the enemy has armor, and their small arms fire is coming from across a large river, the tank is the last thing you want to hide behind. Where they were now was safe for the moment unless the Ethiopians decided to hit targets of opportunity, of which this loader would definitely qualify.

"They're launching boats!" yelled Niner, his head poking around the other side with a view of the river.

"Ballsy," observed Dawson who jerked back inside, another tank erupting as it took a hit to the turret, the crew attempting to bail as the fuel foolishly strapped to the back in jerry cans ignited. He looked at Niner. "They're going to run out of military targets soon."

"Which means we're probably next," agreed Niner. Another explosion ripped apart its target too close for comfort, sending a shower of sand over them, metal shrapnel clanging against their makeshift shield.

"Oh no!" exclaimed Reese, causing the two Delta operators to spin toward her. She was holding up a gold bar, her mouth wide open. She scrambled from her corner and shoved her head over the edge, the three of them now staring at the massive hole in the side of the now nearly completely exposed boat. The embankment had been blown away, the hull collapsed inward, the gold exposed for everyone to see, a few of the bars scattered across the sand.

"Status on the crossing?" asked Dawson.

Niner twisted his head around the side. "About half way across, taking heavy fire. Looks like the current is dragging them a bit, though. If they get across I think they'll be about half a mile downstream."

Reese grabbed Dawson by the shoulder. "We have to save the gold!"

"My job is to protect you," he replied, "not the gold. I'm here strictly as an observer. My Rules of Engagement are zero—do not engage, only observe, leave if necessary."

"But you'll protect *me*?"

"Because you're an American citizen, and I'm an American soldier. My sworn duty is to protect you, regardless of these temporary Rules of Engagement."

Reese seemed to think about this for a moment. "Then I choose to stay with the gold." She seemed to be satisfied with her reply. "Now what are you going to do?"

Dawson shook his head, turning away so she wouldn't see the eye roll.

I'll knock you out cold and carry you over my shoulder if I have to.

He turned to reason with her when she held up a finger, her glare matching that she had delivered to the Eritrean commander. "And don't you dare think you're going to carry me out of here!"

A quick glance at Niner and he saw him stifle a smile, shoving his head out the side to check on their situation. Dawson didn't have the luxury of hiding his face. "I wouldn't think of it."

Reese pointed at the gold. "If we don't get that out of here before the Ethiopians get here, there's going to be a war."

Dawson knew she was right. These two countries had fought a war recently, with over one hundred thousand killed and little settled. If Ethiopia were to steal a billion dollars of gold from the Eritreans, there was no way the Eritreans would let that go unanswered. All-out war would most likely ensue, this impoverished country spending over twenty percent of its GDP on the military compared to Ethiopia's barely one percent. It was the classic little guy who boned up on martial arts to protect himself from the bigger bullies, and when no one challenged him, became the bully to show off his skills.

Eritrea wouldn't hesitate to attack, regardless of their inability to win against the much larger foe.

Thousands would die, perhaps tens of thousands.

All over a pile of gold that would probably fit in the very scoop they were hiding in.

Bingo!

His eyebrows popped as he turned away from Reese and stared at the gold. Niner darted back inside as several rounds pinged off the massive vehicle.

"I recognize that look," he said. "What've you got in mind?"

Dawson remained silent for a moment. The gold wouldn't fit in this scoop, but they had two machines, and they just might be able to get most if not all of it, less some strays, into the two scoops and then head down the beach, over the embankment, and deeper into Eritrean territory.

He turned to Reese. "Any word on when we can expect a response from our naval forces?"

Reese shook her head. "I don't know if anything has been called in. I know I didn't, there wasn't any time and the comm gear is in the tent."

Shit!

He looked at Niner. "Do you know how to drive one of these things?"

Niner nodded. "Yup, same training you received. Which means like you I haven't done it since."

Dawson chuckled knowingly. They had been trained on how to operate most vehicles, but vehicles such as this weren't usually part of an op. He had no doubt it would come back to him as soon as he sat behind the seat. He turned to Niner.

"We're going to get this gold out of here," he said.

"Great idea!" replied Niner in an overly agreeable voice. "How?"

Dawson pointed down at the scoop they were in. "We're going to scoop it out and take it inland."

Niner's eyes opened wide for a brief moment then his head began to bob. "That's just crazy enough to work. Just one thing, though."

"What?"

"The professor is going to be pissed."

Dawson nodded, realizing they were about to destroy what was apparently a significant piece of history, but he could see no way around it. He was certain even Professor Acton would agree saving potentially tens of thousands of lives outweighed preserving an old boat from destruction.

"No choice."

Niner shrugged, poked his head out and looked at the second loader sitting nearby then took cover again. "Looks like she's still in one piece. It's a military loader by the looks of it, so there's some thin armor plating around the cabin. It should hold off the small arms fire, but if they open up with a fifty on us we're sardines in a can."

Dawson nodded, just thankful there was going to be some protection. "Okay, you get the other one fired up, I'll get this one going, but first I've got to call in an airstrike."

Reese grabbed him by the arm. "No, I'll take care of that. You two just get that gold out of here."

Dawson was about to open his mouth when he thought better of it, the beginning of a glare from Reese enough. He quickly removed his vest, handing it to her. "Put this on. Once you've called in the strike, try to get over the embankment then make your way to town."

Reese nodded as she pulled on the vest. Dawson adjusted it for her much smaller frame, it still too big but much better than nothing.

"Let's go!" yelled Reese, jumping over the edge and onto the beach before Dawson could say anything. He and Niner rolled out, Niner immediately heading for the second vehicle, Dawson first checking to see Reese racing toward the tent, her skirt hiked high, her feet bare.

Why the hell is she in bare feet?

He shook his head, quickly climbing into the cab of the loader.

Now to remember how the hell this things works.

Market Road, Pompeii, Roman Empire
August 25th, 79 AD

Avita held her finger to her lips, urging her children to remain quiet as she peered around the corner to see if they had finally evaded their pursuers. A shadow rushed toward her position, the sandal clad feet barely audible, the ash providing a soft underlay to dull any sound. But the accompanying grunts were unmistakable as the shadow pushed its way through the waist high ash—it was her attacker.

She stepped back inside, the door now stuck open due to the ash that had accumulated since the owners of this lovingly kept abode abandoned its walls for the safety of the street.

Avita knew staying here was foolish, the roof already creaking over their heads, made worse with each shudder of the ground. She looked about for something to defend themselves with, the hammer dropped accidentally in their flight to safety. She spotted a clay vase on a table by a nearby window and grabbed it, dumping the dried flowers it contained onto the floor.

"Cover your heads," she whispered to the children. They reluctantly buried their heads under the blanket Flora held up for them, and Avita returned her attention to the door and the approaching curses. She knew they would be found, the path they plowed through the ash with their bodies obvious. She positioned herself behind the door, smoothing out the ash with several good kicks of her foot, then held the jar high over her head.

"What the hell is the matter with you?" asked a gruff, angry voice.

"I can't breathe," came the reply, the voice weak and labored.

"Get up!"

"I-I can't," gasped the man.

"Severus!"

Avita could hear a commotion just outside the door and she exchanged a quick glance with Flora who like her seemed to be holding her breath. There was a grunt then a heavy thud.

"Severus! You have to get up or you're going to die!"

"Leave me," moaned the other. "Save yourself."

The sound Avita heard next, a strange gurgling sound, sent shivers up and down her spine as she realized the other man was dying. She was of mixed emotions, part of her thrilled with the knowledge they now only faced one attacker, the other part horrified that a human being had just died not paces away. Who was this man yesterday? Was he always bad, or had the situation driven him to evil through desperation and fear?

She felt the vase in her hand, still held high, ready to deliver what she hoped would be a death blow to her foe, and marveled at how different she was today from yesterday. Yesterday she couldn't imagine herself prepared to kill, but this disaster, this end of innocence, had become the great equalizer, leaving civil society behind, instead turning it into a battle of every man for himself where your station in society yesterday mattered not today.

She looked over at Flora who huddled with the children, her free hand now occupied with a vase of its own, and realized that the act of kindness that had brought them together meant that the devolution of society was a choice, not an inevitable outcome of disaster, and if they all continued to help each other, rather than look out only for themselves, there might still be hope.

"I'm going to kill that bitch!" roared her attacker's voice from the other side of the partially ajar door. Avita braced herself as a shadow cast itself across the doorway then pushed into the home.

His head came into view, his back to her, and she resisted the urge to roar her anger as her hand swung down hard, the vase shattering on his skull, the shards bursting in all directions as the man cried out in pain, dropping to his knees and grabbing for the back of his head. Flora leapt forward, no urge apparently blocking her own cry of rage as she shattered her vase over the man's head as well, it unfortunately blocked by his hand now gripping his skull.

He began to struggle to his feet and Avita looked at the final shard that remained in her hand, her eyes focusing on the sharp, jagged point.

And a decision was made.

She plunged down, burying the tip in the man's back. He cried out in pain as she yanked it free, raising her arm again and once more jabbing the tip into his flesh. Flora leapt forward, her own cry drowning out the fearful cries of the man as she plunged her shard into the now bloodied back. They traded blows, the man crumpling to the ground, his cries and groans weakening with each savage turn, until finally he collapsed and moved no more.

Avita fell backward, lying on the floor, her chest heaving as she tried to catch her breath, her blood soaked hand releasing its death grip on the shard of the once innocent vase, its crafter never possibly imagining that it would be used someday as a weapon to kill.

And to save.

Tekezé River, Eritrea
Present Day, One day before the crash

James Acton crouched on the other side of the embankment, Laura kneeling by his side. A steady stream of panicking civilians were pouring over the embankment and onto the dirt road, clearly uncertain as to where to go.

"This way!" yelled Acton, waving them toward him, then pointing down the road. "Follow the road then head inland! There's a village!"

The group seemed to crave leadership and immediately obeyed, rushing toward him then past where he was pointing. Within minutes almost all had gone past their position. The bombardment was steadily getting heavier, but so far they had been completely shielded from any fire. Several explosions indicated to him that some of the military hardware had been taken out and he wondered if Dawson and Niner were okay.

He felt a hand on his arm. "What are you thinking?" asked Laura.

He smiled at her, patting her hand. "You know me too well."

"You want to go back, don't you?"

He nodded, but ducked when another massive explosion vibrated through the ground, a fireball erupting into the air. "They're unarmed. How many times have they saved us?"

"That's their job, it isn't ours," she replied, squeezing his arm a little tighter. "Their job is to protect us. If we don't follow their instructions and go back, they're going to have to risk their lives to save us *again*. They've already saved our lives by sending us here. Now let them do their job. I'm sure they're going to be okay."

Acton nodded, knowing Laura was right, but still not feeling good about leaving them behind. He was about to rise when he heard a large engine roar to life, followed moments later by another one.

"What the hell is that?" he asked, knowing the tanks had already powered up as soon as the planes had made their run for the border. These were new engines, closer to the dig, most of the armor farther down the beach, away from their current shelter.

"Does it matter?" asked Laura, exasperated, pulling on his arm. "Let's go!"

He heard gears grinding then a loud roar as a vehicle began to move.

And he recognized the sound.

The front loaders!

His heart began to race as he realized what was happening, and that he had to stop it. Turning to Laura, he grabbed the arm that was holding his. "They're going to use the dozers to move the gold!"

She paused for a moment as she processed the words. "They'll destroy the boat!"

Both of them turned and ran up the embankment, the scientists in them suddenly oblivious to the danger, instead determined to protect their dig from wanton destruction. As Acton cleared the top he skidded to a halt, holding an arm out to stop Laura from falling over the other side.

It was chaos, like a scene from a war movie. It was nearly pitch dark, the massive floodlights from earlier turned off, and only a hint of the sun on the horizon to his left. In front however the light was provided by firepower and devastation. Several armored vehicles were aflame on both sides. Tracer fire crisscrossed from one bank to the other as heavy machine guns exchanged fire. Muzzle flashes from the large weapons were accompanied by the smaller flashes from other automatic weapons firing freely and it appeared mostly blindly.

From his vantage point he could see the Eritrean troops were repositioning to the west. He peered into the darkness and a particularly bright flash highlighted the reason.

"They're trying to cross the river!" He pointed for Laura's benefit then whipped back toward the dig site when he heard the second loader begin to move forward. Starting down the embankment, he was about to shout at them to stop when a terrific explosion not fifty feet away knocked him off his feet then showered him in sand. "Laura!" he cried, spinning around to look for her. He breathed a sigh of relief as he saw her only a few feet away, sitting up and brushing the sand off. "Are you okay?"

She nodded then smiled. "I think it blasted some sand up my knickers, though."

Acton grinned then turned his attention back to their Roman prize just as the first massive scoop hit the ground, rushing toward the hull.

"It's been hit!" Laura pointed at the enlarged hole. "There's debris everywhere!"

"So much for preserving the integrity of the dig," sighed Acton as he watched the first scoop dig into the boat, disappearing from sight. As the driver continued to push forward, obviously trying to get as much as he could in a single scoop, he suddenly stopped, jamming the vehicle in reverse and pulling out, the scoop, tipping up and rising as he did so, and as soon as he was cleared the second vehicle repeated the process, only to the left of where the first loader had dug. Acton could already see most of the gold that had been in sight was now gone, and as the vehicle turned toward him, he caught a glimpse of the driver.

Dawson!

He grabbed Laura by the arm and pulled her toward the embankment, pushing her up from behind then tumbled after her, down the other side. Moments later the first of the massive vehicles roared over the same hill at an incredible angle, the weight of the scoop and its cargo the only thing preventing it from tumbling ass over end. Clearing the top, it dropped like a rock, the front scoop hammering into the ground, the vehicle steadying itself after several bounces, then turning toward the village Dawson had indicated earlier. The second loader cleared the embankment, repeating the precarious balancing act of the first, then turned to follow.

Acton ran after it, waving at who he assumed was Niner. He heard the gears grind as it came to a halt, the cabin door opening, Niner's face poking out.

"Hey, Doc, aren't you supposed to be halfway to the village by now?" he asked in his ever cheery voice.

Acton climbed onto the vehicle, pulling Laura up beside him. "You know me, I always have to be in the thick of it!"

Niner laughed then returned to the cabin, the gears grinding as he pushed the beast forward again. Gunfire and artillery shells could still be heard above the din of the diesel engine, but as they turned away from the river and began to head north, deeper into Eritrean territory, the sounds of war were replaced with the still of the harsh landscape. It didn't take long for them to catch up to the main group of civilians who had fled earlier. Both vehicles stopped and took on as many as could find places to perch, then continued toward the village.

Niner came to a halt, honking his horn at the lead vehicle, it too coming to a halt, Dawson climbing out of the cabin to see Niner pointing at the horizon. Two dozen bright lights were streaking across the sky from the east, and within moments a squadron of F/A-18E Super Hornet fighters roared overhead on full afterburners. The crowd cheered, fists raised in the air as missiles streaked from their weapons pods, hammering the Ethiopian positions in the distance, the horizon flashing in protest as the unmatched weaponry of the United States Navy overwhelmed the light from the rapidly rising sun. Minutes later the planes, their payloads spent, ripped across the sky on their return to their carrier, several remaining behind, patrolling the area, unchallenged.

In the distance to the east, the thumping of helicopter blades ripped across the landscape, and within minutes a dozen Black Hawk helicopters rushed by, two of them splitting off from the main group, banking back toward the refugees and landing, a dozen Marines jumping out of each, quickly securing the area.

Acton jumped down as Dawson helped Reese out of the cramped cab of his loader. They walked over to greet the commanding officer, Reese looking weathered but alive. Handshakes rather than salutes were exchanged, Dawson and Niner's true background not being acknowledged.

"Report!" snapped Reese as she arrived. The Captain's eyebrows raised almost imperceptibly, his eyes darting to Dawson who nodded slightly.

"Ma'am, I'm Captain Hastings. The Ethiopian forces have been pacified, their attempt to cross the river halted. Ground and air superiority have been established, there is no further threat. I just received a report that the other forces moving into the area have turned around. Apparently with the gold gone, there's no point in staying."

"Excellent work, Captain," replied Reese, visibly relaxing. She turned to Dawson. "And thanks to you and your partner," she said, nodding toward Niner. "Your quick thinking would have prevented a war if the Navy hadn't arrived."

Dawson bowed slightly. "Thank you, ma'am." He turned to Acton. "Sorry for destroying your boat, Doc, but the Ethiopians were already doing a good job of it."

Acton shrugged. "You made the right decision. We'll go back and survey the site, retrieve the rest of the gold. I'm sure there're still lots of things that can be recovered, especially now that the time constraints have been eliminated."

Reese clapped her hands, waving the crowd in.

"I'm sorry people, but we still have jobs to do. We'll return to the site as soon as the military declares it safe. I want a head count though before we do anything else." She snapped her fingers at someone, diving into the crowd, leaving Acton and Laura with the Delta operators and the newly arrived Marines.

"How bad was it?" asked the Captain, then spotting the gold in Niner's scoop, he whistled, the question forgotten. "Jesus," he whispered, picking one of the gold bars up. "Heavier than you'd think."

Acton nodded, picking a couple up, tossing them to Dawson and Niner. "That's how you can pan for gold. It's so much heavier than the normal silt in a river that it sinks to the bottom, allowing you to wash away the sand."

"Amazing," said Dawson as he tossed the bar back in the scoop.

"How much do you think this is worth?" asked Niner as he continued to toss his from hand to hand, marveling at the weight.

"That's about a kilo, which is roughly thirty-five ounces and an ounce of gold is around thirteen hundred bucks so almost fifty grand."

"Holy shit!" Niner batted the bar into the scoop as if it were suddenly red hot. "No wonder people kill for this shit."

Reese walked up to them. "And today wasn't any different. It looks like we're missing twelve people. Hopefully they're fine and still at the site."

"I saw one civvy definitely buy it," said Niner. "The guy who was talking to you, a little hefty."

Acton's jaw slackened as he felt his stomach hollow out. "Tucker?"

"I don't know, you were talking to him in the tent. Friend of yours?"

Acton shook his head. "We just met him on the helicopter on the way in. Nice guy." He felt sick, flashbacks of Peru filling his thoughts. He had been around a lot of death over the past few years, but rarely was it someone he knew, and someone he liked.

Except Peru.

He felt Laura squeeze his hand and he looked at her, her own eyes glistening. He turned to Reese. "Let's get back there and check on the others."

Reese nodded, pointing to the two loaders filled with gold. "Captain, I trust I can leave these in your capable hands?"

Captain Hastings smiled. "Absolutely, ma'am. You can always trust the United States Navy."

Niner opened his mouth to deliver what Acton had no doubt would be a spectacular wise crack about how the army was superior, but Dawson grabbed him by the jaw before a word could come out.

"Let's get going before someone puts his foot in it."

Lucius Valerius Corvus Residence, Pompeii, Roman Empire
August 25th, 79 AD

The ground shook with a sudden jolt, sending Valerius to the floor, his elbow hitting the marble hard causing him to wince in pain. He heard yells and rolled over to see the front entry columns snap in the middle, the tops collapsing and shattering on the unforgiving floor, shards skidding across the tiles.

Followed moments later by the entire front of the house.

The tons of stone and wood used to construct the roof years ago collapsed with an initial hesitation followed by the roar of massive cracking and tearing. The soldiers still moving the gold tried to scramble out of the way, some hurling themselves toward the rear of the room, futilely, the entire event taking only seconds. Valerius jumped to his feet, rushing toward those brave men but felt someone grab his shoulder armor, yanking him back to safety as the dust from the collapse, mixed with the ash that had accumulated on the roof, rolled toward them like a bank of fog, enveloping them in a dark gray cloud.

Valerius covered his mouth, his heartbreaking at the muffled cries from under the rubble as those unfortunate enough not to die in the initial crush slowly had their lives drained away in agony, their fates sealed not only by the impossible immovable mass, but the horror befalling the entire city.

"Come, master!"

It was Costa who had grabbed him, and continued to hold him, apparently still not trusting that he wouldn't throw himself into the fray in a futile attempt to save his men. He patted the hand of his trusted servant then turned to see who remained. There were few. Plinius was in the doorway, urging him with a wave to follow him as he pushed the soldiers that had survived through the door. Valerius looked up and saw cracks rapidly spreading out across the ceiling like fracturing ice on a pond, and leapt into action, rushing toward the door.

"Every one out, now!" he yelled, pushing Plinius through the door and whipping Costa after him. A female slave huddled nearby, screaming as the rest of the ceiling began to crumble. "Let's go!" yelled Valerius, but she shook her head, too terrified.

He swiftly covered the half dozen paces between them, grabbing her by the arm and yanking her into the air, tossing her over his shoulder as he spun around toward the door. Her screams weakened as he pushed toward the door, then stopped as he felt her go limp, fainting at whatever it was she had seen. He stole a glance behind him as he crossed the threshold and emerged from what was once his home, the remaining structure crumpling in on itself, the archway he had just cleared remaining standing, his emergence punctuated with a blast of dust that momentarily obscured everything. As the dust cleared, only to be replaced by the sight of the thick, falling ash of their new reality, he gasped at the horror he had tried to avoid all morning.

It was the end of times, prophesized for as far back as time went.

He handed the young slave over to one of the soldiers and approached Plinius who was surveying the damage, coughing hard into his robe.

"What are your orders, my lord?"

His lord, master and friend of so many years dropped to one knee, hunched over as he continued to hack, his shoulders heaving with the effort.

"Water!" ordered Valerius, and a soldier rushed over with a skin, handing it to Valerius who then pressed it to Plinius' lips, squeezing the precious fluid out. Plinius took several gulps, his cough subsiding slightly, but as Valerius knelt beside him, he could hear the wheezing of strained breaths, and one glance at his Prefect had him convinced his mentor wasn't going to survive unless they escaped immediately.

Plinius reached up and gripped Valerius' arm, pulling him so his ear was near the man's mouth.

"Forget me. Save the gold."

Valerius shook his head, placing his own mouth at his liege's ear.

"I shall save both, my lord." He rose to his feet, pointing toward the water. "Make for the boats!"

Suddenly a strong wind swept down the hillside and toward the bay, momentarily clearing the ash from their view, replacing it with the stench of rotting eggs, and as Valerius tried to pull his master to his feet, he realized the air had spoiled, and he was weakening.

He dropped to his knees, grabbing Plinius by the face.

"My lord, Plinius, please! You must try!"

Around him soldiers began to drop with groans as they were overwhelmed by the sulfur, others who had immediately heeded his orders were running toward the boats, clearly visible now that the ash had been cleared by the deadly wind. He looked into Plinius' eyes, and his heart sank.

There was barely any life there.

His liege's breaths were mere gasps now, shallow, far apart. His mentor of almost his entire adult life looked up at him, their eyes meeting, and in one last gasp, he issued his final order.

"Leave me."

Valerius' heart demanded he pick up his liege and carry him to the boats, but his head knew it would mean his own death as well. His lungs were screaming for relief as he held his breath. He touched his head to that of his friend for a moment, then pushed himself to his feet, wading through the thick ash toward the shore.

One of the boats, its hull low in the water, weighed down by its precious cargo, had already turned, the wind gripping its sails and pulling them away from the shore. Plinius' cutter sat nearly on its side, the tide low, its hull covered in a massive amount of ash and its sails burned, leaving it useless.

Only one ship remained now, and as he hit the thick mud that was now the shore, the ash and water having created a mix as thick as that used by masons, he pushed through as he saw others being pulled aboard by the crew.

He gasped, finally letting go his breath and sucked in what might be his final lungsful should it prove deadly. Thankfully he felt the sweet relief of air filling his lungs, providing him with the energy to continue on, the stench still there, but not as strong as it was at the house.

The ground shook with a jolt so strong it was if he had been racing in a chariot and suddenly hit a wall. He flew through the air, toward the boat, but landed face first in the mud, his breath knocked out of him. He struggled to get up, but couldn't, the weight of the water and mud, combined with the suction power of the mixture held him tightly in place, and as he felt his life drain from him, his only thoughts were of his wife and children, and the comfort it provided him to know they had escaped this tragedy the night before.

His name would live on, and they would be protected, he dying a hero of the Empire.

Tekezé River, Eritrea
Present Day, One day before the crash

Acton tossed the last of the gold bars to Laura then crawled out into the glaring midday sun. Laid out on a table were dozens of artifacts he had found during the final clear-out of the gold. They had already been moved by the front loaders so there was no point in trying to catalog them in place other than to take photos with his phone before carefully removing each piece. It had delayed the gold extraction each time, but not by much. With Dawson and Niner's "on-their-feet" thinking from this morning, they were now way ahead of schedule with respect to the gold.

Which meant they were leaving very shortly, the Eritreans wanting all of the foreigners out with the gold, the excuse being they wanted to diffuse the situation with the Ethiopians. Acton knew very well that the Eritreans had no interest in preserving the archeological find so had taken the opportunity to preserve what he could while Laura had managed to negotiate an extra half day. Dawson had arranged a Black Hawk to deliver them to the Eritrean capital of Asmara at the same time the convoy of gold would arrive.

The Eritreans had reluctantly agreed.

"Look at this," said Acton as he took out a pocket knife and scratched away a bit of the surface of one of the broken pieces of wood that had been part of the hull. A layer of hard black sat in the palm of his hand. Laura pinched some of it between her fingers, rubbing them together.

"What do you make of it?" she asked. "It almost seems like soot."

"And look, below the surface is fresh wood."

POMPEII'S GHOSTS

Laura and Acton both looked at each other at the same time, smiles and eyes wide. "Like it was burned!" they cried in unison.

"What have you kids found?" asked Niner who was within earshot.

Acton held up the piece of wood. "It looks like the entire outer hull was exposed to severe heat, but just for a few seconds, perhaps tens of seconds, that scorched the surface, but didn't ignite the wood."

"Ancient Roman nuclear blast?" asked Niner with a smile as he took the piece of wood and examined it.

"Nope. Volcanic eruption? Definite maybe."

"Wouldn't that torch the whole boat though?"

"Not necessarily," replied Laura. "A study of Pompeii leads scientists to believe that a superheated blast of air engulfed the entire area then when the oxygen was consumed, rushed back. It killed anything that was alive out to more than ten kilometers, but the farther out, the lower the temperature, to the point where if you were far enough, wood wouldn't ignite."

Niner handed the piece of wood back. "Fahrenheit 451?"

Acton took it, returning it to the table. "Exactly. The boat was probably far enough out to only get scorched. The crew would have been killed, but the boat would have survived, and the scorching it received would have actually helped seal the wood, preserving it for all these years."

"So it looks like your theory is right, Doc. Congrats!"

"Thanks." Acton sighed, turning to face the wreck. "It's just too bad this won't get properly excavated. There's so much history here."

"Well, you've got twelve hours. Would an extra pair of hands help?"

"Make that two extra pairs," said Dawson as he approached. "They won't give me a gun, so I have to do something with my hands," he said with a smile as he wiggled his fingers.

Acton looked at Laura. "What do you think?"

She shrugged. "A quick and dirty excavation is better than none at all. This site will be looted the moment the troops leave."

Acton's lips pursed. "You're right. Let's do it!"

Acton was fairly certain the interior of the boat was empty, it having been raked clean to find every last gold bar, so the order of the day was to remove the sand from around the vessel so they could gain access to the deck. Rakes and shovels were commandeered and the four of them were soon attacking the mounds of sand, the others who remained beginning to gather around and watch them, then eventually joining in. Within half an hour almost two dozen of the UN personnel and others gathered were working in teams, removing the dirt under the supervision of the two experience archeologists.

It took hours of backbreaking work before a triumphant shout was heard from the female Chinese observer Acton had learned was named Lee Fang. "I think I found the deck!"

Acton and Laura both scrambled up the slope to the left of the boat and carefully approached her position. The shape of the exposed vessel indicated it was resting partially on its side, at about a forty-five degree angle, and the flat area now exposed by Lee's efforts seemed to suggest she had indeed found the deck.

"Excellent work!" cried Laura as she examined the decking. "It seems solid, but we'll have to be careful." She pointed to the embankment where the unexposed side of the boat was still buried. "I suggest we start moving the dirt from there. It will reduce the weight on the deck and hopefully reduce the risk of it collapsing. But be careful. Listen for any sounds of wood creaking or cracking. If you hear anything, stop what you're doing and yell 'Halt!' so we can listen. If you feel it shifting, get your butts out of there. The safest bet is to the left or right rather than over the top."

"Agreed," said Acton. He looked at his watch. "And though time is of the essence, remember that this is where you're probably going to start finding things, so if you feel something under your rake or shovel, call one of us over, okay?"

There were nods of agreement then Lee sunk her shovel back into the sand, the eagerness on her face reminding Acton of one of his students discovering the thrill that was archeology. In fact, the expressions on everyone's face had his stomach fluttering with a renewed faith in the human spirit as strangers toiled together in a thankless pursuit, dozens of people from around the world, friends and enemies, working toward the common goal of preserving a piece of history that until six weeks ago, the world had no idea existed.

It was a feeling he wouldn't trade for the world.

"I found something!" yelled Reese who had joined in only recently. She was jumping up and down, pointing at something and as Acton approached, he could see why she was excited.

A skeletal hand hung over the edge of the deck rail, the arm and possibly the rest of the body still buried.

Reese was still jumping up and down when Acton felt everything shift.

"Freeze!" he yelled.

A look of horror spread across Reese's face as she landed one last time on the sand she had forgotten was sitting atop an empty hold of an ancient ship built with wood cut two thousand years ago.

Everyone stopped what they were doing and Acton could hear a creaking sound coming from underneath. He looked about and saw about a dozen people in immediate danger. Four were near the edge of the embankment with the most risk of being buried under several tons of sand should everything collapse. He pointed at them. "You four, very carefully, climb down over there," he said, pointing to the left where they'd be able to escape down the side.

Another creak and this time he heard a slight snap.

He turned his attention to the other six still on the surface of the deck, one of whom was Laura. "You six, one at a time, head to the edge then down the slope. If you hear me yell, you all run as fast as you can and don't look back."

There were nervous nods as the first, the male Chinese observer, ever so gently stepped to the edge then slid down the slope, the rest slowly following, Laura taking up the rear.

Another creak and a definite snap.

Reese yelped, the confident woman Acton had seen for the past two days replaced by someone terrified at their current predicament. He found it slightly ironic that under heavy gunfire she had seemed calm and in command, but here, in the midst of the unknown, where she was out of her element, basic instinct had taken over and he could tell she was fighting the urge to flee.

He reached out to her, trying not to shift his bodyweight any more than necessary. "Take my hand," he said, calmly, trying to quiet her nerves. She reached out and he felt a sweaty palm as he closed his hand around hers. "I've got you." His voice was as reassuring as he could make it, his own heart slamming into his chest as creaks and groans from the boat began to echo all around them. "Now turn to face the rear of the boat, the left side of the embankment."

Reese nodded, slowly turning, her left hand grabbing his hand as soon as it could, for a few moments both gripping him tightly.

"James, it's collapsing!"

His head darted to look to where Laura's voice had come from and he found her pointing at the embankment. As if on a pivot his head swung and he saw the entire side beginning to ripple down toward the deck as the structure shifted below them again.

If only we had had the proper bracing available.

It had been a gamble, and it had initially paid off, but now, as he grabbed Reese by the hand and yanked her hard, dragging her toward the edge, he realized they had made a big mistake. His legs pumped against the wood and then the sand as the entire deck began to give way, the jumping up and down of one excited amateur finally triggering the end-of-life for this ancient marine vessel.

He felt the deck give way completely and he hurled Reese with all his might toward the edge, letting go of her hand as he dropped. His feet hit something hard and he allowed his knees to flex then he pushed upward, springing toward the daylight and the beach as darkness rushed toward him. His acrobatics however failed, and he found himself hitting the ground hard, a piece of wood digging into his side as sand quickly began to bury him.

Scrambling on his knees and elbows, he struggled forward then saw the faces of Dawson and Niner as they rushed in, Dawson leaping forward, grabbing Acton by both wrists, his grip viselike. As the dirt enveloped him, he saw Niner grab Dawson's legs, then nothing as he took one final gasp of oxygen before he was completely buried.

His eyes were squeezed shut, his lips pressed tightly together, his lungs screaming for air as hundreds of pounds of dirt crushed him, the pressure increasing as more of the embankment slid down to entomb what it had once hid.

But the grip on his wrists never wavered.

He realized Dawson's head would only be inches from his own and that he too must be buried, but he felt a tug and he tightened his grip even more.

Another tug and this time he felt his body stretch out.

And another, this time he swore he moved forward, albeit an inch if he were lucky.

Another inch.

A few more.

His lungs were screaming for relief now and he could see spots dancing on the back of his eyelids. He focused on the grip. It never wavered, it never relaxed, and with each tug he could feel himself inching toward rescue.

Suddenly he felt himself surge forward, his chest ripping across something hard, probably wood, and he cried out in pain, the last of his air erupting from his mouth, and just as he was about to suck in the surrounding dirt, he felt the coolness of fresh air, his eyelids suddenly bright.

He gasped, fresh oxygen flooding his system, mixed with a healthy dose of dirt causing him to cough as his rescuers continued to pull him out. His eyes were still closed and he felt someone haul him to his feet as he continued to cough. Water poured over his face and he reached out for the source, feeling a plastic bottle shoved in his hand.

"Drink," he heard Laura say, her voice wavering slightly with emotion. He said nothing, instead taking a large swig, swishing it around his mouth then spitting it out.

"Hey!" came Niner's voice from below him. Acton wiped his face with his hand then opened his eyes to find Niner lying on his back, gasping for air, a large wet spot on his black Immortal Freedom Fighter t-shirt, its single stylized word, Immortal, somehow perfectly suiting the Delta operator. To Niner's left was Dawson, on his knees, being attended to by the Chinese observers.

"Reese?" gasped Acton, the words caught in his throat as he wretched out a clump of sand, his airway finally completely cleared.

"She's okay," said Laura, her hands brushing off the dirt. "Oh my God, you're bleeding!"

Acton looked down and could see his shirt was ripped open, blood pouring down his chest. It looked worse than it felt, and for a moment he thought he might be in shock, then he realized what must be happening. He poured the rest of the water over his chest, washing away most of the blood, leaving a few minor cuts and a bad bit of "hull rash" that would leave a mark for a while.

"I think I'll live," he said, his voice still hoarse. He saw Reese quickly walking toward him, a look of relief on her face, she appearing none the worse for wear.

"Are you okay?" she asked.

He nodded. "You?"

She rolled her shoulder, wincing. "Other than almost dislocating my shoulder when you threw me over the edge, I'm fine. If it weren't for you, I'd probably be dead right now."

"Think nothing of it."

He turned toward the wreckage and sighed, his heart sinking as he realized their work had just quadrupled, and they had no time left. Suddenly his eyes opened wide and he pointed.

"Look!"

Everyone turned to see where he was pointing.

At the foot of the pile of dirt sat half a dozen partially buried skeletons, still in uniform, the embankment having given up its secrets at last, as if wanting to return its guests to their home, so far away.

Near Market Road, Pompeii, Roman Empire
August 25th, 79 AD

Avita lay on her back, gasping, as Flora used a broom she had found to sweep the ash out of the doorway, closing it triumphantly with a bang and a smile. It did help muffle the terror on the other side somewhat, and for a moment Avita allowed herself to relax, closing her eyes and concentrating on her breathing. A wind howled outside, blowing the ash about through the small cracks in the reasonably well-built house, when suddenly the stench of rotting eggs filled her nostrils, causing her to gag. An old story once told by Plinius had her jumping to her feet and grabbing the blankets. She stuffed one under the door, using the others to block the shutters that covered the one window in their refuge.

"Hold your breath for as long as you can!" she yelled, huddling with the others in the farthest corner. She took a deep breath, realizing it was horrible air she was proposing they hold, but the wind outside was strong and she hoped that whatever it was they were smelling would soon be blown past them.

After what seemed an eternity, but was barely a minute, her son gasped, sucking in lungsful of air. His nose curled up and his eyes watered, but he seemed none the worse for wear. She let the breath she was holding out then drew in her own first breath. It was still pungent, but not like before, and she tapped the others around her.

"It's okay to breathe," she said. "It still smells, but it seems safe."

Gasps and cries of relief erupted from the others as everyone took their fill. Avita tossed the blanket aside, it now stifling under its cover, and stood, looking around for what she did not know, she just felt she needed to look like she was taking action for the children's sake.

Flora stepped to the door and opened it slightly just as the ground began to vibrate, shaking everything in the small house. A clay jar danced across a wood table then shattered on the floor, keepsakes hung on the walls swayed back and forth.

"Come here children!" she ordered, gathering them in the center of the room where there was little that could fall on them. She looked to Flora who shook her head.

"It's not safe outside, the ash is even thicker."

Avita nodded, now on her knees, holding her children tight. "Join us," she said, the tone of her voice revealing to the only other adult in the room exactly the state she felt they were now in. Flora smiled, tears glassing over her eyes as she knelt beside them. The two boys made room for her to join their tiny circle of humanity, and they all put their arms around each other.

As the vibrations increased, she found it harder to keep her balance, all of them gripping each other harder and harder as whatever it was neared. The children were crying now, and the room began to glow an unholy orange. Avita held her children as tight as she could and, looking up at Flora, began to sing a lullaby she knew her daughter loved.

Flora, tears pouring down her face, looked down at her swollen belly and joined in, the first words gasps of agony as she realized her child would never be born, and would never hear its mother sing. They made eye contact, both faces burned by salty tears, their expressions ones of twisted torture as the rumbling continued to approach, the sound deafening to the point where they were now shouting the words at the top of their lungs. Her daughter screamed first, then the boys and when Avita finally registered what was happening, she saw Flora's eyes widen in agony just as Avita felt her own clothes catch fire, her skin melting in an instant, the intense heat pulling at her, causing her to fall to her side and slowly curl up into a ball beside her children and a stranger with child, to be discovered millennia later, exactly as they had died, their agony and horror preserved for all time.

Asmara International Airport, Eritrea
Present Day, Day of the crash

Acton gave Laura a final wave as she ducked into the Boeing 737 carrying her and their archeological find to Rome. He had been asked by Reese to travel with the gold, along with the other UN observers, and had readily volunteered, hoping to steal a few moments to simply be in the presence of so much wealth and history.

He also felt responsible for it somehow.

They had been able to excavate and preserve the skeletons of the crew that had been exposed in the collapse, and they were now on the plane with Laura, along with dozens of artifacts that in Acton's opinion—an opinion shared by his fiancée—confirmed this was a boat and crew that had witnessed the disaster at Pompeii in 79AD. The theory he and Laura had batted back and forth on the flight to Asmara was that Emperor Vespasian had hidden a stash of gold in Pompeii or the surrounding area, most likely as a hedge against a coup attempt, and his son's soldiers had tried to evacuate it during the eruption.

And they had almost succeeded, escaping by boat with the hoard but not before the flash of superheated gases killed them instantly, leaving their ship to sail itself along the prevailing winds of the season, and toward the mighty Nile, where if greeted as a ghost ship, would have been given a wide berth and left to its own designs, finally washing ashore in what was now Eritrea. Time and superstition would have it buried, only to be discovered two thousand years later by a goat herder, a simple widower with a history of tragedy.

And the allure of Pompeii's gold would claim another life.

During the flight Reese had time to fill them in on the whole story. The goat herder had murdered his friend in a greed infused rage over what was more than enough to change the lives of every citizen in his country, then only to be turned in to the local priest by his daughter, the priest nearly dying while trying to protect the daughter from the victim's family.

Reports indicated the father had apparently been hacked to death in the village square, his body scattered, his daughter repeatedly raped in revenge before the priest, badly beaten, was able to save her by organizing a group of the local women to come to her aid.

Laura had cried when she had heard the story.

The local priest managed to get word to the Holy See who then contacted the UN. Once the Eritreans found out what they had on their soil, they had very cleverly—or at least that was Acton's opinion—leveraged its intrinsic value, rather than its raw value. They announced that in exchange for a substantial sum of money, they were willing to hand over the find, otherwise they'd melt it down and use it to fund the state treasury. Negotiations ensued between the Eritreans and the Italians, along with many other universities and countries, all trying to come to some agreement, quietly behind the scenes.

It wasn't until economic sanctions were threatened that a deal—a very generous deal—was struck. It was amazing how quickly governments became agreeable when faced with the threat that any precious metal held by that country wouldn't be recognized on the international markets.

The massive Antonov began to power up nearby, the engines so loud any hope of conversation was impossible. As he watched the Boeing carrying most of the UN delegation including Laura back to Rome taxi onto the runway, he turned to Dawson and Niner, both watching the last of the coffins being loaded into the cargo hold of the Antonov.

Six had died.

POMPEII'S GHOSTS

The same number of skeletons found on the wreck.

He frowned as he thought of Tucker, a man he had only known for hours but who was so friendly, so jovial, he knew his impact would be felt for some time. The two Russian observers had been killed as well, along with one from the British and French teams. The sixth had been a UN bureaucrat that Acton hadn't met, apparently the first to die in the command tent.

Reese walked over, clearly not happy, her head still shaking from an animated conversation that had been taking place out of earshot with several Eritrean bigwigs. Her face was flushed.

"What's wrong?" asked Acton, but Reese couldn't hear him, the roar of the Antonov's engines now overwhelming. She shook her head, pointing at her ear, then motioned that they should follow her to the waiting plane. They boarded through the cargo door, Acton looking at the coffins for a moment, his attention diverted almost immediately to the cellophane wrapped pallets of gold bars. Even muted behind the semi-translucent wrap, it was mesmerizing, and he noted that none could take their eyes off the stacks of bullion until they entered the part of the plane set up as a passenger cabin near the front.

As soon as the door was closed behind them the roar of the engines was subdued significantly. Acton turned to Reese. "What's wrong?" he asked again.

She leaned in, as did Dawson and Niner.

"First off, this wasn't the agreed upon transportation. There was supposed to be a special UN charter but the Eritreans cancelled it, instead arranging this behemoth."

"And that's a problem, how?" asked Acton.

"That wouldn't be a problem except that they insisted on providing private security, six of them. They all work for the company this plane was chartered from."

Dawson frowned. "Let me guess, Russian?"

Reese's eyebrows narrowed. "How'd you know?"

Dawson shrugged, motioning at their surroundings with his eyes. "It's an Antonov in good condition. It's a fairly safe bet it's Russian or former Soviet Union."

"Well, you're right. It's Russian. And the agreement was there would be no more than two security personnel from each Security Council nation. Now there are six, and if the original two hadn't been killed, there'd be eight."

"Not to mention crew," added Niner.

"So at least another two!" cried Reese. "This is totally unacceptable!"

As if to punctuate her point, an announcement over the PA was made in Russian only as the plane began to taxi.

"It looks like we have little choice," said Dawson. "Let's just keep an eye on things." He eyeballed two of the security guards standing near the cockpit door. "Are they armed?"

"No!" Reese shook her head vehemently. "I insisted on no weapons and they agreed. As far as I know, there isn't a weapon on this plane."

Dawson didn't say anything, none of them did, but Acton could tell the two Delta operators were thinking the same thing he was.

No weapons? Yeah, right!

Acton took his seat, buckling in, Dawson and Niner sitting beside him, Reese in the row ahead. The plane raced down the runway and they were airborne in seconds, the powerful engines thrusting them into the back of their seats. As the vibrations worked their magic, Acton found his eyes closing, his body starting to drift into sleep as he gave in to his exhaustion.

But something gnawed at the back of his mind, his subconscious replaying the day's events, trying to figure out what was bothering him. Suddenly he bolted upright in his seat, Dawson and Niner staring at him.

"What's wrong?" asked Dawson.

Acton looked around to see if anyone else had noticed his sudden movements, but no one seemed to be paying him any mind. He turned to Dawson.

"I might be going crazy, maybe I miscounted, but…" His voice drifted off as he began to doubt his own memory. He shook his head. "No, I must be wrong." He shook it again, this time with more certainty. "No, I'm definitely wrong."

"What are you *definitely* wrong about?" asked Niner.

Acton smiled, a little embarrassed. "Well, I was pretty sure for a moment there that I remembered seeing seven coffins in the cargo hold, not six."

"Maybe we should check it out." Dawson undid his lap belt and leaned over the seat, tapping Reese on the shoulder. She jumped, apparently still wired, then undid her own belt, turning around to face the three men.

"What's wrong?"

Apparently their concern over something was obvious. "Probably nothing," replied Dawson. "But we'd like to take a look at something in the cargo hold."

Reese shook her head. "Not possible. The agreement is that once this thing is airborne, nobody is allowed in the back until we land. That way nobody can be accused of tampering with the gold." She nodded toward the two doors in the rear that led to the hold. Acton turned and saw two guards standing at each door. "Their orders are to let no one by, and they don't answer to me."

"Who do they answer to?" asked Niner as he turned back to face the top UN representative on the plane.

"I have no idea. The Eritreans, perhaps? They're the ones that hired them. This entire situation is bullshit, like I said before—it wasn't part of the plan. Right now we're just trying to get the gold to safety, then we can point all the fingers we want at who screwed up what. But for now?" She shrugged. "There's eff all I can do about it."

Acton didn't like the sounds of that, but then again this was a UN operation. It should come in ten times over budget and not accomplish its goals, other than to line pockets of people both inside and outside the organization.

Cynical much?

He knew from countless encounters with the UN that they were an inept, bloated bureaucracy that spent other people's money haphazardly with few if any checks and balances. Yes, many of their mandates and many of their people had good intentions, it was simply that they were staffed far too often by people from countries where graft was a way of life, and to suggest anyone was untrustworthy within the bureaucracy would immediately label you a racist or bigot.

And now they were all stuck on a Russian transport plane, unarmed, with a billion dollars of gold in the hold, and half a dozen Russian guards that no one had vetted.

Acton sat back in his seat, shaking his head. "If there's nothing we can do, then there's nothing we can do." He closed his eyes. "Like I said, I'm probably mistaken."

He closed his eyes as the others returned to their seats and tried to forget everything that had been said over the past five minutes.

Unfortunately, all he could picture was the cargo hold with six coffins in a single row, with a seventh tucked between the large pallets of gold.

Near Lucius Valerius Corvus Residence, Pompeii, Roman Empire
August 25th, 79 AD

Costa hit the ground, tossed through the door by his master. He rolled in the thick powder, looking up and seeing nothing but a dense, dark, roiling sky, a faint orange glow reflecting off the underside. It matched every description of Hades he had ever heard, and if he didn't know better, he would believe that the world of the damned had been unleashed on the living.

But he wasn't a superstitious man, nor a religious man. He had never believed in such things, and in his mind this was a horror of nature, not gods from Olympus. It was a horror that could be survived, that had to be survived, and if he were careful, would be survived brilliantly.

Voices surrounded him, his master yelling at Plinius, other cries in the night as people rushed for the water, somebody yelling 'Hold your breath!'. The stench was unbelievable and he took the advice, holding it for as long as he could, finally, when he could take it no longer, he gasped, sucking in semi-fresh air, then listened.

Silence.

At least in the immediate area.

For there was no silence in Pompeii this day.

A dull roar groaned from the ground, his ear pressed against it as he remained lying down. The cries of a panicked city filled the air like the background music of the damned, mixing with the gentle white noise of the ash as it continued to fall like snow, the sound real or imagined in his hypersensitive state.

He pushed himself to his knees, barely able to see over the depression his body had made in the ash.

He was alone.

He stood up and gasped, jumping back as he spotted Plinius kneeling nearby.

"My Lord! I thought you had gone to the ship!"

There was no reply. Costa stepped over to the Prefect and tapped him on the shoulder.

Again no response.

He knelt down and looked at the man's face and Costa's eyebrows shot up in surprise.

He's dead!

Costa breathed a sigh of guilty relief then stood, looking down at the shore. The boats were setting sail, and he wished them well—he truly did. But his fate was not with them. His family he was certain had escaped, they having left yesterday with the others. Their future however was not secure. It never would be.

But underneath the pile of rubble that was once the Lucius Valerius Corvus residence sat enough gold to set every slave free in the empire.

And all he needed was two bars of it to secure his family's freedom and future.

He circled to the front of the house and it was clear there was no way in, at least none that was obvious. Returning to the back, the nearly equally devastating sight did present one hope the front didn't—the still intact archway Valerius had stepped through carrying the slave girl.

He stepped through and grabbed a still burning torch from a sconce next to the door. Holding it out in front of him, he could see the collapsed columns and roofing spread out in front of him, and as he held his flame out, moving it slowly to spot any openings that might give him access to the basement, he stopped, a smile spreading across his face.

Gold!

The glint was unmistakable. He dropped to his knees, crawling forward and reaching under a slab of stone that sat askew across a piece of wood. A single gold bar lay discarded on the floor, probably abandoned by a soldier when they were ordered to leave. He gripped freedom and stuffed it in a pocket, the weight substantial and unexpected.

His heart raced as he pictured the future.

Now we are free. One more and we are secure.

He pushed aside the stone that had concealed the first bar, it smacking against the marble floor with a vibration substantial enough to cause Costa to freeze, listening for any evidence the house was about to shift on him again. Shoving aside some wood and straw, he found a narrow A-shaped opening created by two large portions of the roof having come to rest on a column at the far end. It was just large enough for a man.

Barely.

He shoved the torch ahead of him and began to crawl. The dust had him coughing, his eyes burning, his lungs desperate to suck in large breaths, but instead he forced in only shallow ones in an attempt to reduce the amount of dust and ash he inhaled.

Finally the need proved too much and he sucked in a deep breath, his chest heaving high and pressing into the stone above him.

He felt it shift.

He froze, slowly letting his breath out, which only exacerbated the problem, causing him to draw the next few in rapidly and hard as he tried to cover his mouth and prevent a coughing fit.

Finally under control, he opened his eyes and turned his head, looking up. Everything seemed stable for the moment, but with the near constant tremors, he knew he had to get out. He pushed himself back with his hands then reached for the torch and stopped.

Another bar!

It was just a few feet ahead, almost within reach. He pushed forward several times, careful not to touch anything, then reached out for the gold bar. Still out of reach.

And his right shoulder was now pressed against the stone above him.

He crawled his fingers forward, manipulating his body to lower his right side and managed to get a finger on the bar, but it wouldn't move.

Just a finger-length more!

He let out all his breath, lowering his body further, and shoved with his toes against the floor, moving forward just enough to get his thumb and forefinger around the bar.

He pulled.

And it didn't budge.

He tried jiggling it and it moved slightly, the sound of metal scraping on stone causing him to pause as he debated what to do next. It was clear that a piece of the roof was sitting atop this small bar of gold. The question in his mind was how catastrophic might removing it be to the delicate balance that had been established above him.

It's for your family!

He vigorously wiggled it back and forth and with a triumphant cry it came loose.

The debris in front of him shifted with a thud. His heart nearly stopped as he froze every part of his body. A creaking sound overhead that rapidly became louder had him pushing back with both hands, the torch abandoned. The stone in front of him collapsed just as he yanked his hands clear, and he shoved as hard and as fast as he could, the gold bar in his right hand ineffectual against the marble floor, his left hand all that was providing the grip. The trusses used to build the roof began to separate, snapping one at a time from where he had pulled out the keystone holding everything, including his family's future.

His breath was frantic now, his heart slamming against his chest, his hands, elbows and knees bleeding from the unforgiving shards of marble and stone he now slipped on as he tried to make his escape. He prayed to the gods he claimed to not believe in for forgiveness, promising he would never be so greedy in the future if they were to just let him survive this one stupidity, and as he neared the end of the narrow passage, he began to think his prayers might just have been heard.

And answered.

The entire tunnel collapsed just as his head cleared, but not before his hand. The hand that still gripped the gold bar. He cried out in pain as several hundred pounds of rock pinned his fingers, the rest of his body clear of the immediate danger.

The entire ground began to vibrate, a steady, growing rumble surrounding him. He pulled at his fingers with all his might, the agony incredible as he realized at least one of his fingers was broken. Lifting with his free hand, he managed to yank himself free, collapsing on his back, his chest heaving up and down as he caught his breath and tried to regain the focus lost to the searing pain.

The floor was shaking violently now, the roar intense and all consuming. He rolled onto his stomach then pushed himself to his knees. In the distance he could see an intense orange glow rapidly approaching. The archway behind him collapsed and he leapt out of the way, coming face to face with the second gold bar now under a man's weight in stone.

A weight he was certain he could move.

If only there was time.

The sea was a heartbeat's dash from where he now stood, and he could begin to feel the heat of whatever apocalypse was about to befall them all. His eyes fixated on the gold bar and what it could do for his family. He grabbed the stone with his left hand and pulled up with every ounce of strength that remained. He felt the stone lift slightly, and using his toe, he flicked the gold bar free, releasing the stone triumphantly. He bent over and grabbed it, then ran toward the terrace, leaping over the collapsed archway, then sprinting down the path the soldiers had maintained toward the shore. No boats remained except the abandoned cutter that Prefect Plinius had arrived on, but all he had to do was reach the water.

He felt the heat sucking at him, teasing him with delightful warmth, as if his entire body were sinking into one of Rome's famous hot baths, then, with the water not ten paces away, he was engulfed in a raw heat that both deprived him of breath and life, as his entire body was seared into a single, solid charred piece of meat.

And as he collapsed, two gold bars, once held in the pockets of a robe now turned to ash, fell to the ground, both freedom and future lost to a moment of greed.

POMPEII'S GHOSTS

Exiting Eritrean Airspace
Present Day

Major Anatoly Kaminski, Russian Federal Security Service (FSB), lay with his eyes closed, his body completely relaxed as he felt the vibrations of the Antonov's mighty engines massage every square inch of his being, better than any coin operated bed in a cheap hotel he had ever experienced. As he waited for the plane to reach cruising altitude, he hummed the Soviet national anthem, its proud lyrics heroically challenging the world, unlike the timid lyrics now sung when Russia's flag was raised. One of the many bold decisions made by Vladimir Putin was to restore at least the music of the Soviet national anthem though including the lyrics as part of that decision would have been unacceptable at the time. Kaminski was quite certain, however, that in time, those lyrics that had fired up a country to victory over the Nazi tyranny and to hold back the evils of Western imperialism for decades, would be restored.

Though he wasn't old enough to have been a member of the FSB when it was called the KGB, his father was and had instilled in him a fierce sense of national pride that had been tested in his youth after the collapse of the USSR. But now, under a strong leader determined to restore Russia to its former glory, he loved his country so much it hurt, and when he had been made a member of the FSB's Directorate "A", or Spetsgruppa "A", his father had actually cried with pride. Though his father was now dead, a victim of the harsh Russian economy where capitalism had failed miserably, enriching only those who embraced its full corruptness, he would never forget the day he arrived at home in his uniform, the Alpha Group emblem on his shoulder.

And after extensive vetting he had been invited into the inner circle—the Omega Team, assigned the most covert of operations under direct control of the Russian President himself, though always through an intermediary to allow for plausible deniability should something go wrong. When he had heard rumors of Omega Team's mandate—to restore the Soviet Union—he had ingratiated himself upon anyone he could think of who might be part of the ultra-secret group.

And it had paid off.

Many in the West wondered how a unit as highly trained as Alpha Group could seem to screw up on so many occasions, the most memorable the assault on the Dubrovka Theatre where fifty armed Chechens had taken over 850 hostages. What most didn't realize is that life was thought of differently in Russia. Sacrifice was acceptable of the few to benefit the many, and in this case the outrage that ultimately resulted in the end had allowed Russia to pacify Chechnya with overwhelming force—and overwhelming support from the citizenry of Russia.

His own first mission was as part of Omega Team's involvement in triggering the South Ossetia war in Georgia, a former Soviet State with a substantial Russian speaking minority. They had entered the country disguised as Ossetian separatists and shelled Georgian positions. The Georgians responded, and in the end lost the war, effectively losing not only South Ossetia, but the breakaway region of Abkhazia as well.

Another small chunk of the Soviet Union restored.

His last mission had been in the Crimea, that short but violent mission allowing Russia to reclaim what was rightfully its, and set the precedent of protecting Russian minorities throughout the world. Eastern Ukraine was already on the agenda with other regions such as Moldova and the Baltic Republics, and as long as Western Europe was foolishly dependent upon Russian natural gas to heat its homes in the winter, with leadership that seemed to either have not read their history, or instead read it and embraced Neville Chamberlain's 'Peace for our time' naiveté, Russia would be free to continue to pick apart the former breakaway republics piece by piece.

With the help of patriots like those of Omega Team.

Kaminski felt the plane level out and he slid aside the false bottom of the coffin he was inside then pushed the lid open. He knew the rear hold was supposed to be empty and he had heard nothing beyond the engines since takeoff, but he rose cautiously nonetheless. His position, tucked between two pallets of gold—a spare coffin should anyone have asked—was fairly well concealed. He slipped out of the coffin, his feet quietly touching the metal floor, then looked about to confirm he was alone.

He was.

Leaning back inside the coffin, he pulled the sidewall out of the way, the Velcro holding it in place separating with ease, revealing nine Beretta 92 Compacts and several dozen magazines, along with a nice supply of C4 to finish the job. He grabbed a weapon, loaded it then stuffed it in his shoulder holster, putting a few mags in his pockets.

He pulled out his phone and sent a direct message over a Wi-Fi network set up just for the job, the rest of his team now notified of his status. The Antonov had been customized for jobs like this in the past. A pass-through had been installed between the cargo hold and the adjoining bathroom in the passenger cabin, it allowing for items to be passed back and forth surreptitiously.

Over the next thirty minutes he would arm his entire team, then those aboard would be at their mercy.

Offshore near Lucius Valerius Corvus Residence, Pompeii, Roman Empire
August 25th, 79 AD

Valerius felt himself continue to sink deeper into the muck, his lungs screaming for relief as he instinctively held his breath, refusing to give up without a fight lest his acceptance into Elysium be risked by cowardice. His right side hit something and he rolled to his left. He shoved his right hand out to his side, feeling it break through the thick goo he was trapped in. Suddenly strong hands grabbed him, tugging at his arm and he slowly began to feel himself rise, his lungs ready to burst, his eyes seeing hot white spots on the backs of his eyelids. Suddenly he was free and he gasped, the air anything but fresh, but at least it was air. The strong hands continued pulling him up and moments later he found himself dumped unceremoniously on the deck of a boat as those who had saved him turned their attention to others still in the water. He took in several more full breaths, then rolled himself to his feet, stumbling to the helm, climbing the few steps and gaping at the view in front of him.

The entire city was engulfed in a thick cloud, the only light penetrating it the harsh oranges of fires left unfought, and the mountain that had once provided beautiful views and delicious grapes, now a boiling cauldron of reds and oranges, steaming rivers of fluid rushing down its sides toward the city below.

"Set sail, now!" he ordered, pointing to the captain of the boat. Orders were barked and he could feel the boat begin to turn, the sails thankfully catching the wind, it having turned during the night. "Head for sea!"

"But, my lord, the other boats, they're heading for Misenum!"

"Signal them to turn. We need to reach the sea if we have any hope of surviving!"

"Yes, my lord! But what about Prefect Plinius?"

"He is dead."

"But his body!"

"His orders were to save the gold. Hopefully in time we can retrieve him and bury him with the honor he deserves."

"Yes, sire."

Hearts were heavy at the thought of leaving their Prefect, but none more so than Valerius, who also left behind a friend, and the bravest man he had ever known. Plinius had sacrificed himself he knew to not only save the gold, but to save him, for Plinius would have known that Valerius would have stopped at nothing to try and save his mentor.

Thank you, my friend.

The ship turned further still and soon was bearing south-west, but as Valerius scanned the horizon, no other ships were following, all heading north-west to their home port.

A ripping sound, as if the ground itself had been torn open and all manner of hellish beasts released with a roar, signaled the Armageddon he had feared being unleashed. As he turned toward the sound he saw the entire top of the mountain was now missing, an intensely bright display of reds, oranges and yellows streaked the sky as rocks the size of houses were tossed in the air as if by Jupiter himself, raining hellfire on the entire area.

Massive explosions ripped apart entire neighborhoods, huge fires engulfed entire swaths as these flaming boulders hit the ground and continued to roll like juggernauts of evil.

And it wasn't only the land that was hit with the devastation.

On the horizon he could see at least two of his boats aflame, the cries of their crews carrying over the water, those safely on his ship all turned, silently watching the horror unfold as they sailed untouched toward the open sea, alone.

"Look!"

He turned toward the voice, that of the young female slave he had saved, and looked to where she was pointing. A massive burning, churning cloud of fire rushed down from the mountain in every direction, the speed incredible, easily dozens of times faster than the swiftest of steeds, enveloping everything within its path in an intense flame, a fire so hot that everything in its wake glowed from the heat, and as it continued to spread outward, toward the shore, he noticed the shoreline receding dramatically, as if it were in a race to escape the horrors befalling the entire area.

It was unlike anything he had ever seen before, and his heart hammered in his chest, fear gripping him as he watched the water continue to retreat, then get lost as the tidal wave of fury burst past it, engulfing the water in its red hot heat, the sound of the water instantly boiling, hissing like hot rocks tossed in a cauldron of water, filling the air. The humidity shot up dramatically and he could feel the heat as the boiling, roiling horror sped toward them, the ship valiantly racing toward the sea as fast as it could, but the gods proving more swift.

It hit the aft end, those standing there screaming out in pain as he rushed toward the prow, but it was too late, the intense heat licking at his back for an instant, searing every bit of his body into a mass of bubbling tissue. His cry of agony was muffled as the heat rushed into his lungs, sealing his ability to process oxygen instantly, leaving him gasping for a moment, until he collapsed over the prow, his entire being racked in quickly receding pain.

And as the last vestiges of the souls aboard the only ship that had stood any chance of escaping Pompeii made their way to the Elysian Fields, the heat wave sucked back toward it source, leaving nothing alive, nothing burning.

And a heavy deposit of ash covering every surface, including the bodies of Valerius and his compatriots, and the ship that now carried them out to sea.

Exiting Eritrean Airspace
Present Day

Niner's eyes were closed, resting, but still aware of everything going on. As he silently meditated, trying to create a black ball in the center of the white noise of his thoughts, he heard the voices of his seat mates in the background, almost a distant echo as if he were sitting on the bottom of a pool.

"We're descending."

It was Dawson's voice, a hint of concern there. It yanked him from his alternate reality as the explanation was given, and with a glance at Dawson they were both up, walking toward the front of the airplane to find out just why they were descending over what was supposed to be Sudan. They approached one of the private security guards at the cockpit door.

"I need to speak to the pilot, please," said Dawson in as pleasant a voice as Niner had ever heard him use with a Russian.

"I'm sorry, but that's not permitted," said the man, his accent thick but his command of the English language clear.

"I'm afraid I must insist," replied Dawson. "I'm here under authority of the United Nations Security Council and as a representative of the United States. I *must* speak to the pilot. It will only take a minute."

The man turned his back on them, activating his comm and speaking quietly to someone. He turned back around and shook his head. "Nyet. Return to your seats, now."

Dawson stepped slightly closer, jabbing at the air with his finger. "I can't do that until I know why we are descending."

A flash of fear appeared on the man's face, his eyes flaring for a split second, a sudden inhalation of breath. He stepped back two paces, reaching behind him. At first Niner thought he was reaching for the cockpit door but suddenly the man grabbed something from behind his back. Dawson stepped forward to halt him but it was too late, the Beretta suddenly appearing, the safety already off, the trigger squeezing. Two shots erupted from the barrel hitting Dawson squarely in the chest sending his body hurtling backward, hitting the aisle with a sickening thud.

Before the weapon was turned on him, Niner stepped forward, reaching out and wrist-locking the man before he could squeeze the trigger again, bending his joint painfully then removing the weapon. Niner placed a round in the man's forehead then dropped to his knee, spinning, firing two more into the center mass of the second guard who had already drawn his weapon.

Is anybody actually unarmed?

The guard's gun fired, his dead finger spasming on the trigger, sending a bullet through the fuselage. Alarms sounded and the plane suddenly began a steep dive sending Niner tumbling forward, coming to a painful halt against the wall lining the cockpit, his head slamming against something metal, his entire world suddenly engulfed in darkness.

Rosetta, Egypt
November 7th, 79 AD

The sails were full, the wind stiff but not overly so, leaving the sea calm enough for them to pull close. Dento grabbed a rope dangling from the side of the Roman vessel, its form quite familiar to these parts now that Egypt was part of the Empire, but rarely seen travelling alone.

And ignoring all attempts at communication.

From a distance men could be seen on deck, but none of the standard signals had been sent or responded to, and Dento was dispatched to investigate when the ship seemed to be heading into the mouth of the Nile without the customary docking required at the port in Rosetta.

Several of those in his boat grabbed lines, the Roman vessel rising far above their heads, it massive compared to their small harbor boat. They had called out many times on their approach but the unresponsive craft had continued to ply forward, their hails ignored, the only sounds the prow slicing through the water and the whipping of the cloth in the wind.

The vessel had an odd color to it, almost a dark charcoal, and Dento ran his fingers along the wood, wincing as he was pricked by a splinter. His fingers darted away and he looked curiously at the near black substance that covered them.

It's like from a fire pit!

He hauled himself up the rope, as did several others, his old bones not keeping up with the less aged of his crew.

Which meant he wasn't the first to see the evil that lay above.

Taurus, his trusted second screamed and dove into the ocean. Ralla, a young promising soldier who had never shown the brains to be afraid of anything cried out before he too let go of his rope, slamming into the hard deck of their own boat. Dento was certain he heard the snap of a bone, and the writhing pain Ralla appeared to now be in seemed to confirm it.

There only remained him and one other, who looked at his captain hesitantly.

"Wait for me," ordered Dento, much to the relief of the other who scurried back down the rope and into the boat. Dento pulled himself up the rest of the way and with one final effort, swung a leg over the edge, straddling the rail running the length of the boat. Ahead he could see a man, on one knee leaning over the prow. He had been spotted earlier, but had appeared drunk.

Or worse.

He seemed to be a dull gray, and unmoving. Dento looked about the deck and gasped. Everything was covered in some sort of grayish black substance, including the crew.

And they were all dead.

Some still at their posts, some curled into balls on the deck.

But all dead.

And as pale as ghosts.

His foot, now on the planking, jumped into midair, as if under its own control, Dento instinctively realizing he shouldn't be here. None of them should be. This was a ship of the damned. A crew, still manning their posts, all dead, all covered in something, unmoving, unwavering, as if made from stone.

And none with any signs of trauma.

Weapons didn't kill these men.

He glanced to his right and saw the body of a woman, lying on her side, her face twisted in agony, her hand stretched out in front of her toward the man who still knelt at the prow.

A witch!

Women didn't travel on Roman vessels. Not Roman military vessels such as this.

They must have been lured into rescuing her.

He shuddered and swung his leg back over the side.

And repaid their kindness with a curse.

Scrambling down the side, he jumped back into his boat just as Taurus was hauled from the water.

"Make for the harbor master, quickly!" ordered Dento. "We must warn them!"

"Warn them of what, Captain?" asked Taurus as he stood, dripping. "Is it as it appears?"

Dento nodded.

"I fear it is," he replied.

"What, what is it?" asked one of his crew who hadn't climbed the side, and now tended to Ralla's arm.

Dento moved to the prow, his back to his men to hide the terror that gripped him.

"It's a ghost ship," he replied, his lip almost trembling as he said it, having never seen one himself, and having never met anyone who could claim different. They were things of legend, cursed vessels doomed to ply the waters for eternity in hopes of someday making shore.

And they were untouchable.

"What shall we do?" asked the young Ralla, his pain ignored, his terror not.

Dento risked one final look over his shoulder at the cursed vessel as it sliced through the water toward one of the many entrances to the mighty Nile.

"We shall let it be, for those who dare interfere are doomed to join them."

Entering Sudanese Airspace
Present Day

Major Anatoly Kaminski, Omega Team Leader for this mission, strapped himself into one of the fold down seats that lined the rear cargo hold as the rapid descent continued. Something was wrong, that much was obvious. He was certain he had heard several gunshots just before the dive, and before he could open the door to the passenger cabin he had been thrown hard. Whatever was happening on the other side of that wall would have to wait.

As he yanked the lap belt tight the plane jerked to the left, sending his arms and legs forward, dangling in the air. The pallets of gold shifted slightly, the ratchet straps straining to hold their loads in place. The plane was at nearly a seventy degree angle and he was now almost looking down at the billion dollars of loot when a horrid thought occurred to him.

What if he banks the other way?

The load would shift back, and with the momentum built up from its current position, the straps just might fail, sending thousands of pounds of gold bars at the wall he now sat against.

And he had no intention of dying under a load of untraceable gold meant to clandestinely finance their destabilization programs.

He felt the plane begin to level out slightly, the angle improving almost imperceptibly at first, then with more momentum, the angle now fifty degrees, then forty. The tension on the belts holding the gold in place began to ease and he grabbed the latch to unlock his own belt should the need arise.

Just level out! Get it under control!

He knew the pilot at the controls was one of the best—he had handpicked the man himself. But the Antonov was massive, like flying an elephant by the ears. The fact the beast could get in the air was a miracle in itself. Landing it in an emergency was something else, especially on the airstrip they were aiming for.

I wonder if we can still make it.

It was driving him crazy not knowing what was happening on the other side of the wall. The plan had been simply to take everyone hostage at gunpoint and land. Once on the ground control would be easy, and within less than fifteen minutes everything would be over.

An emergency landing was not in the cards.

The plane leveled and he felt it begin to tilt toward his side. He snapped himself loose of his belt and jumped up, rushing toward the front of the plane as it began to level off again, the pilot apparently back under control, having overcompensated slightly. The air stopped whistling in the cargo hold and it didn't seem as thin, leaving him to wonder whether there were any casualties on the other side of the wall.

With the plane apparently no longer in imminent danger, it was time to take control. He pulled his Beretta out, flicking the safety off and unlocked the door. Yanking it open, he stepped inside the passenger cabin, quietly closing the door behind him as he surveyed their surroundings. A hole about the size of a basketball had been torn in the fuselage near the front, wind still blowing noisily from it. Four of his men already had their weapons out, pointing them at the passengers, some of whom had their hands up.

"Report!"

The entire cabin turned to see who had just taken command, his men it seemed out of relief, the others a mixture of fear and curiosity. He knew the eight remaining observers were highly trained Special Forces from their respective countries, so fear of being hijacked wouldn't really be high on their lists. Fear of their plane crashing was another thing, and the fear he was seeing on some of the faces was most likely from that. There were two civilians, one his intel told him was a bureaucrat from the UN, the other a meddlesome archeologist who had an impressively thick file at FSB headquarters.

I'll be keeping an eye on you, Professor Acton.

His third-in-command, Lieutenant Boris Shepkin marched toward him, concern on his face along with a little fear.

It better be from the plane nearly crashing.

"Sir," said Shepkin with a nod of his head, placing his mouth near Kaminski's ear so they wouldn't be overheard. "The two American observers caused a problem. They discovered we were descending and demanded to talk to the pilot. Victor shot him. The second observer disarmed Victor, shot him and shot Andrie as well."

"Are they dead?"

Shepkin nodded. "The second American observer was knocked out during the descent. We've secured him in a seat near the front."

Kaminski glanced ahead and saw the Asian American handcuffed to the arm rest in the front row. "What caused the depressurization?"

"Andrie's weapon discharged when he was shot."

"Any word from the cockpit?"

"He's got control again but Air Traffic Control is trying to contact him. Apparently we're below radar and they think we've crashed."

Kaminski grinned. "Wasn't the way we planned it, but I guess it sort of worked out. Time to cut all comms to confirm their suspicions."

Shepkin covered the door as Kaminski returned to the cargo hold. Opening a panel on the wall, he yanked half a dozen circuits for the various radios and transponders, the plane now running silent—only primary radar could pick them up now, and that was fairly limited in this part of the world.

And with us below radar, it won't matter.

He returned to the passenger cabin and headed for the cockpit. He knocked three times, standing in front of the peephole and a moment later the door opened. Stepping inside, he closed the door behind him.

"Status?"

Their pilot, Urakov, glanced over his shoulder as he gripped the shaking controls. "I've got her stable for the moment, but that could change at any second."

"Are we still on their radar?"

"Negative. The emergency descent then the loss of control pretty much took care of that. I've altered our course as planned so if they're looking for us on our previous flight path they'll be wasting their time."

"Good. ETA?"

"We should be at the airstrip in less than twenty minutes."

"Okay, maintain radio silence." Kaminski turned to leave then stopped. "And keep us in one piece until we hit the ground."

"Oh, that I can do," replied Urakov with a glance at his copilot Elkin. "It's how many pieces we're in once we hit that I can't guarantee."

Kaminski laughed, slapping Urakov on his shoulder. "Don't crash, then. I'd miss your sense of humor."

"You assume you'd survive?"

"No, I just don't assume we're heading to the same place in the afterlife!"

Urakov and his copilot Elkin roared with laughter. "Have you seen my apartment? Hell would be a vacation! Like Sochi in the winter!"

Kaminski shook his head, a grin spread from ear to ear. He grabbed Urakov's shoulder, squeezing. "Just get us down in one piece, and your job is done."

"Da, da," replied Urakov. "Now get out of my cockpit, you're distracting me."

Kaminski looked out the windows, the ground whipping by at incredible speed, the sparse vegetation and harsh landscape uncomfortably close. He decided not to ask their altitude.

"Good luck, my friend," he said then exited, returning to the noise of the passenger cabin. It was much quieter now, Shepkin just now fitting a seat cushion into the hole, the equalized pressure allowing it to stay in place and muffle the sound.

"Can I have your attention please?"

The entire cabin turned to look at him.

"Thank you. In about fifteen minutes we will be landing. We will all disembark at that point. We will be liberating you of some of your cargo, then leaving you behind. Once we are safely at our final destination, the authorities will be notified as to your location, and you will be rescued." Kaminski stepped forward, eyeballing those he knew were military. "*Any* resistance, *any* attempt to interfere with our plans, and I kill the civilians first, starting with her." He pointed at Reese, who glared back at him defiantly.

If only I had a few minutes to spare.

He felt a twitch, part of him yearning for the old days of Mother Russia where the pillaging was accompanied by a little reward for the victorious troops.

She looks like she'd be one hell of a suchka.

The intercom crackled and Urakov's voice came over the system. "Everybody buckle up, this landing isn't going to be pretty."

Kaminski knocked on the door and it was opened by the copilot Elkin, Urakov gripping the controls. He strapped himself in the empty navigator's chair, turning so he could see the ground whipping by.

"There!" yelled Elkin, pointing ahead. Kaminski leaned forward, straining to see as Urakov banked slightly to the right.

A runway was barely etched out of the sand, it an abandoned British airstrip built before Sudanese independence. His team had scouted it only days before to confirm the runway was still operational and found it in nearly perfect condition, the dry desert doing little damage. As the nose pulled up slightly to kill their speed he lost sight of the abandoned airstrip. The airframe began to shake, violently, as Elkin called out their airspeed. He knew they were coming in on a runway far too short for this plane to take off from, but it should be long enough for it to land, even if the final few hundred meters were beyond the "official" end. If the landing gear collapsed, they didn't care.

This plane was never taking off again.

"Oh shit!" cried Urakov. "Dump the rest of the fuel!"

Elkin reached forward, flipping several switches.

Kaminski leaned forward. "What's wrong?"

"I'm barely holding her together. Just assume your crash position and if you can—"

Urakov stopped talking as the plane jerked to the right, a horrendous sound coming from behind them.

"—kiss your ass goodbye!" finished Urakov as the plane slammed into the ground, the rear landing gear collapsing from the force. The front end immediately smacked against the ground causing all their bodies to be forced toward the floor, then the front landing gear sprung back, shoving them in the air, their restraints the only thing keeping them from splattering against the roof of the cockpit.

Not able to reach his ass to kiss it goodbye, Kaminski instead held on to his chair as tight as he could and watched in dismay as Urakov's hands flew off the controls from the impact, the plane starting to skid as the rear landing gear broke away. A tremendous creaking sound, like metal tearing from metal, filled his ears causing his heart to slam into his chest even harder than it already was.

"What the hell is that?"

Elkin glanced over his right shoulder and out the window. "We're losing the starboard wing!"

With a sudden jolt the horrendous sound stopped and the plane suddenly spun to the left, the rear end pivoting counterclockwise, and as they all watched in horror, Urakov no longer bothering to try and control the aircraft, instead busy trying to power down, they were treated to a terrifying view.

The entire runway behind them was engulfed in flames as the dumped fuel ignited, racing toward the now torn off wing.

"Stop dumping! Stop dumping!" cried Urakov as he realized the same thing Kaminski had.

The fuel was still pouring from their good wing, leaving a trail of flammable liquid leading directly to their fuel tanks.

Kaminski began to undo his restraints with the idea of somehow bailing from the aircraft before it erupted into a fireball when another jolt sent the plane pivoting in the other direction, Kaminski's head slamming into the console, his entire world soon engulfed in a billowing black fog of unconsciousness.

POMPEII'S GHOSTS

Hamashkoraib, Sudan

Samir spun as did they all, the entire market, a moment before filled with the shouts of negotiations as goods were haggled over in a seemingly never ending battle of wills between vendor and customer, and now silent, the wail of a lone baby finally heard by its mother.

On the horizon a large black cloud, roiling with fire and rage, erupted into the air, an odd streak of flame extending for what looked like several miles across the horizon quickly extinguishing itself, leaving nothing but a black trail the wind quickly dissipated.

Samir motioned to his men, jumping in the passenger seat of their old 1986 Toyota pickup, its original bright blue paintjob a distant memory, the color almost blasted clean over the decades from exposure to constant sunlight and blowing sand.

But the engine still ran like a dream, none of those ridiculous computers to breakdown. Any competent mechanic in town could fix it, and half his guys including himself knew how to do the basics. It was a matter of pride being able to maintain one's own vehicle, and the older the functioning vehicle, the more competent you appeared to those around you.

Tricking it out added to the respect shown as well.

His truck, purchased for only 125,000 Sudanese Pounds three years ago had been customized to mount a fifty-caliber machine gun in the rear, the weapon and mount hidden in a custom storage area welded underneath the vehicle. With it, he and his posse wielded significant power on the streets of the nearly lawless town of Hamashkoraib.

But that was Sudan today.

A mess.

It was quite often every man for himself, and he with the biggest gun usually won. And if there was a chance to get something for nothing, or little effort, the opportunity was taken, usually by the first to act.

And an explosion in the distance meant fuel, and fuel meant a vehicle, and perhaps people who could be rescued for a reward, or held hostage for ransom. Samir didn't care which, both here were merely semantics. His men jumped in the back, his driver, Abit, already pulling out as the market resumed its previous business, most people simply wanting to finish their negotiations and get home safely.

Cash!

If it were foreigners, especially Westerners or rich Arabs, today could be the day that changed his life forever. *Rescue* someone, or ideally a group, and the reward could be quite handsome. He knew the American and European governments always claimed they never dealt with terrorists, but he also knew that was bullshit. They just used intermediaries, and the ransom was almost always paid. The key was to ask for a ridiculous amount, then negotiate down, allowing the fools to think they had been successful.

What most Westerners didn't realize was ten million dollars here made you a target, not a king. But ten thousand dollars? That let you live like a king in a small town like Hamashkoraib. It meant women, alcohol, food and a nice roof over your head for years.

And respect.

He felt goose bumps on his skin as the thought of what could be surged through him.

Respect.

It was all he had ever wanted, and it was always so elusive. Respect in Sudan didn't come from being polite or presentable, from being friendly or pious. It came from fear. It came from envy. If people feared you, if people envied you, then you were respected.

And if they did both, you were king of the world.

All he needed was one good score. A few tens of thousands in American dollars and he'd be able to buy or build a big house, fill it with women and temptation, then keep the party going for as long as the money lasted, and with women and friends, cheap drugs and alcohol if you knew the right people—and money always bought those introductions—he could live for years like an uppity British lord his great grandfather Mohammed had told him once ruled over them decades ago.

Grandfather Mohammed's favorite story was of the hasty evacuation of British and Egyptian troops on January 1, 1956. After the Sudanese parliament had voted unanimously for independence only days before, the colonial forces left rather abruptly, probably, as his Grandfather said, with hurt feelings that their "children" had rebelled.

Mohammed had been a member of the Sudan Defence Force and was assigned to follow the column of British and Egyptian troops out of Sudanese territory and into Egypt, and then take over the manning of the border crossing. It had been a proud day for their country, and a proud day for his Grandfather Mohammed, but not so much for the British Governor, who rode in his prized Jaguar XK120, his uniform crisp yet dust covered, his expression one of stiff British dignity, none of his emotions revealed at the humiliating retreat.

That was until his prized car broke down and had to be hooked to a transport vehicle and hauled out of the country.

Every time Mohammed told the story when Samir was a child it became more and more elaborate, with the distinguished gentlemen kicking dirt at it, punching the hood with his fist, shooting it with his pistol. Samir didn't know what to believe, or even whether or not any of it was true, the story so outrageous. As a child he had listened in awe, as an adult, his beloved Grandfather long dead, he looked back on the stories with fond memories, meant to entertain those gathered, the only thing now ringing true the breakdown of a Jaguar.

That part he could believe.

His driver, Abit, pointed ahead. "It looks like it's coming from that old airfield!"

Samir grinned, a dentist's ears in Khartoum itching at the possible business in his future.

"Let's hope it's an airplane that's crashed."

"With lots of passengers!" agreed Abit.

"*Live* passengers."

"*Rich* live passengers!"

Samir grabbed his friend by the shoulder, shaking him hard with excitement. "What will you buy with your share, my friend?"

Abit answered without hesitation, as if it were a question he had been preparing to answer for years. "A house with six bedrooms!"

"Six? Why six?"

"One for each of my four wives," explained Abit, holding up three fingers, the fourth lost years ago in a knife game.

"And the other two?"

"One for when you come to visit me."

"And the sixth?"

"For my mistresses!"

Abit roared with laughter, Samir joining in. "A well thought out plan, my friend!"

They rounded a low hillside, the dirt road they were travelling on cut out of the valley over years of repeated use, and Abit skidded to a halt. In the distance was the abandoned airport, dark black smoke billowing into the sky still. Samir threw his door open and stepped out onto the running board, holding his binoculars to his eyes.

And he smiled at what he saw.

We're going to be rich, even if nobody survived.

Abandoned 250 Sudan Squadron Royal Air Force Airfield

Professor James Acton unbuckled his lap belt the moment the plane stopped spinning, rushing toward the front of the cabin. Almost the entire right side of the fuselage was ripped open, leaving it exposed to the outside and revealing the horrific explosions that continued several hundred feet away. He grabbed Niner by the body armor and sat him upright, a deep gash in his forehead oozing blood liberally. Acton slapped him on the cheek and the man moaned, his eyes fluttering open.

"What the hell happened?"

"There was a hijacking. We just crash landed."

Niner's eyes opened wide and he suddenly seemed to be much more alert. "Help me up."

Acton pulled him to his feet then looked down at Dawson's crumpled body, his chest tightening as a lump formed in his throat. Suddenly the cockpit door was thrown open, slamming against their comrade's corpse.

Before they could move a gun was pointed in their faces as the leader of this fiasco stepped out, nursing a nasty bump on his head. He yelled something in what sounded like Russian and his few remaining men yelled acknowledgements as if roll call had just been taken.

Acton heard two from the rear, and two from the cockpit.

Five.

That meant on top of the two Niner had eliminated, two more were out of commission from the crash. Acton stepped back, hands raised, to let the three occupants of the cockpit exit. As he moved, he took the opportunity to survey the cabin and was relieved to find that all of the "innocent" passengers seemed to be okay, they being strapped into their seats when the plane made its dive then crash landing.

The leader of this group of terrorists—or whatever they were, Acton was leaning more toward profiteers—peered out the gaping hole in the fuselage, shouting in Russian and waving his arm at someone to join them. Acton heard more shouting outside, and it quickly became clear that the evened up odds that he knew not only he was thinking of, but Niner was as well, had skewed out of their favor once again.

This was obviously where they were always meant to land.

About the only good news he could take from that was the fact they didn't seem to have gone that far off course, less than thirty minutes to the west of their original flight path if he were guessing right, which *should* mean they'd be easy to find if a standard search pattern were used.

Now they just needed to survive the theft of the gold.

"Everyone out the back!" ordered their captor, one of his men opening the supposedly locked door to the rear cargo space. "Hurry, before that fire reaches us!" he yelled, adding a little urgency to the cautious movements of the hostages. As Acton and Niner passed through the door, he took one last glance toward the front, but Dawson was out of sight, Acton's view blocked by the chairs. He said a silent goodbye and stepped through the door.

Daylight greeted them inside the hold, the rear ramp down as far as it would go with the landing gear no longer attached to the plane. At least half a dozen men were standing outside, all armed, all dressed in Special Forces style equipment with no identifiable markings, all with masks pulled over their faces.

Which made Acton wonder why the men they were with now hadn't bothered.

"They're going to kill us," he whispered to Niner.

"No shit," replied the Korean American. "First chance you get, you make a break for it."

"No talking!" yelled one of the guards, slamming Niner in the back with the butt of his machine gun. Niner fell to a knee, glaring at his attacker, but getting back up silently with the help of Acton.

They exited the plane and Acton gasped. Debris was scattered everywhere, one of the wings, torn from the fuselage and resting several hundred feet away was engulfed in flames with thick black smoke billowing out of it as the fuel burned. As they were led to the other side of the plane, Acton was relieved to find the other wing still intact, and as yet, free of any indication of fire.

As they all lined up along the side of what appeared to be a very old runway, Acton examined their surroundings. At the far end sat another plane, some sort of transport plane he thought might be a Hercules, its rear ramp down, a forklift racing from it and toward the crashed Antonov.

So that's how they're moving the gold.

But there was a problem. Several men were gathered around the front landing gear of the Herc and Acton smiled. The tires were flat, a smoldering piece of wreckage from the Antonov nearby apparently having sliced through the rubber.

"Can they repair that?" he asked, barely moving his lips.

"Not unless they brought some spares."

"So they're stuck here with us."

Two men exited the rear of the Herc rolling spare tires.

"Shit," muttered Niner.

"What should we do?"

"Forget the gold, our job is to survive," replied Niner. "Let the UN worry about the cargo. They're the idiots that let this mission proceed with these yahoos at the controls."

Reese—the senior "idiot" on the ground—edged closer. "What do you mean? You think they knew this would happen?"

"Absolutely," replied Niner. "Tell me, when was the gold considered delivered?"

"When we left Eritrean airspace."

"And who insisted on that little piece of the puzzle?"

"I don't know, to be honest. I was drawn in later, but they certainly seemed to take advantage of that clause in Asmara when insisting we take this plane instead of the one we had arranged. The clause allowed them to choose the method of transport out of the country."

"So they bided their time until they could find the right people, then put them into position to steal the gold once they had fulfilled their contract. You still need to pay them their money, and then they probably split the actual gold, coming out even further ahead."

"Good theory," whispered Acton, "and we can play the blame game later. Right now we need to figure out how to survive. Once that gold is on the other plane, it just might be 'kill all the witnesses' time."

"They never searched me. I still have the gun I took off the guy who shot BD. There's at most eight shots left though."

Acton sighed. "Better than nothing, I guess. How many do you think you could take before they get you?"

"Definitely three, maybe four or five, depending on the confusion. More if I can get to some cover. The key is what the others do. If some of our people can get the weapons of the guys I take out, they can join in. We just might have a chance at that point. And you two will have to hit the ground as soon as the shooting starts otherwise you'll get caught in the crossfire."

"Are you sure this is wise," asked Reese, the only sound of reason among the small group that had gathered, adrenaline already fueling Acton's thinking. "We could just get a bunch of us killed."

"I'd rather die fighting, than on my knees," replied the female Chinese observer, Lee Fang.

The sentiment was echoed quietly as the first load of gold was pulled out of the rear of the Antonov by the forklift.

"We don't have much time," said Acton, looking over at the wheel repair. "They've already got one of those spares on. One more tire and load of gold, and we're expendable."

"Why haven't they killed us yet?" asked Reese, it an obvious question that even Acton had been wondering about.

"They're not secure until they're off the ground," answered Niner. "If I were them, I'd secure my cargo, make sure the repairs were solid, load us all on the crashed plane, then blow it up, making it look like we all died in the crash."

"And the gold? They can't hide that," said Reese. "Whoever finds us will know that for sure."

"Not if they leave a few bars scattered through the wreckage. The UN might just assume the Sudanese got it, or some local militia."

"Militia?" asked Reese, her eyes darting around nervously. "What do you mean?"

Niner smiled. "This is Sudan. There's armed militia groups everywhere. They're basically no better than gangs."

"So no matter what, we're back to killing the hostage takers before they kill us," frowned Reese.

Suddenly gunfire erupted from the far end of the runway, a beat-up pickup truck racing toward them, its rear compartment filled with gun toting locals. Niner shoved Reese to the ground as Acton landed beside them.

This might be exactly what we need!

POMPEII'S GHOSTS

Abandoned 250 Sudan Squadron Royal Air Force Airfield

Command Sergeant Major Burt "Big Dog" Dawson was anything but dead. Sore as hell, yes, the two shots having slammed into the body armor he was wearing under his shirt and sending him sailing to the floor. His ribs were bruised for sure, cracked most likely, but it was every other square inch of his body that screamed for relief.

One thing you were trained to do when first awakening in a possible combat situation was to listen first, make sounds second. And that's exactly what he did. He remembered getting shot and blacking out, but nothing after, and judging from the state of his body, much more had happened while he was unconscious. The lack of engine sounds told him they had landed, but the smell of smoke, aviation fuel and chemically treated carpet told him he was still on the floor of the Antonov and something terrible had transpired.

He opened his eyes a sliver and found no one in sight. Orders were being barked outside in Russian and English, those in English being shouted at the hostages, those in Russian at each other, apparently a transfer operation underway.

Probably the gold.

He turned his head slightly, making sure he was alone, then carefully rolled himself toward the first row of chairs so he'd have more cover. As each part of his body touched the floor he winced. He looked at the bulkhead he must have slammed into and saw blood in several places along with a good dent in the door to the cockpit.

No wonder I'm sore.

He wiggled his fingers and toes, then rotated his hands and feet. His entire right side was a little tender, but he didn't seem to have any broken bones. Bending each knee carefully, drawing the leg up to his stomach then slowly back, he assessed his condition. Elbows and shoulders followed, all the while listening to their Russian captors. He was fluent in Russian—know thy enemy—but had made a point to not let anyone know on this mission. He wouldn't be surprised if the other Special Ops members from the observer team knew his dossier but there was a decent chance their captors didn't.

And if they did, that would indicate how well connected they were.

He rose to his knees, his lungs screaming in protest, then peered over the seats.

Holy shit!

A good chunk of the side of the aircraft had been ripped away, it appearing the wing was gone. The passenger cabin was empty except for a couple of bodies piled in the corner nearby, a bullet hole in the center of one man's head quite clear.

Niner?

He scrambled over to the bodies and quickly began a search, relieving them of two Beretta handguns and half a dozen magazines. He did an ammo check on both then stuffed one behind his back, the other he kept in his right hand. He rounded the side of the airplane where he had been sitting with the Professor, it still intact, at a crouch. As he passed each row, he looked for bodies or wounded, but found none. As he passed one of the rows he saw a satellite phone on the floor.

He grabbed it, turned it off so it wouldn't give away his position or waste the battery, then shoved it in the ball pouch just in case he was captured. Most men didn't give that area a thorough search, and in his experience, Russian men were so homophobic they almost avoided the area like the plague.

He found two more bodies, apparently killed by whatever had happened aboard, bringing the total dead to four, all bad guys. He could live with that. Satisfied he was alone, at least for the moment, he fished the phone out of his crotch and turned it on.

No signal.

It's a satphone! Why the hell isn't there a signal?

He flipped the phone over to check the battery compartment when he noticed the antennae casing was cracked.

Shit!

It might be repairable, but not right now. He pressed a few buttons and activated the video camera, then positioning himself near the window, carefully held it up, slowly turning it for a full sweep then lowering the phone, back out of sight. He replayed the video and breathed a sigh of relief as he saw Niner and Acton standing by the side of what appeared to be an old runway, along with several others including Reese and the Chinese observers. They were being watched by two guards, but not closely.

He checked his watch and figured he had been out for maybe half an hour.

We're probably in Sudan, maybe an abandoned airstrip from the Brits.

But this plane wasn't going anywhere, and he could hear sounds on the other side of the temporary wall that something was happening in the cargo bay. If they were after the gold, which obviously they were, then their plan must have been to transfer it to an alternate transport. Sudan was too barren for them to be going by truck, so there must be another airplane. He crawled to the other side of the plane and peered out from under the seats through the tear in the fuselage.

I hate being right all the time.

A Chinese Shaanxi Y-8, a rip-off of the Soviet Antonov An-12, sat several hundred feet away, its cargo ramp down. Several crew were replacing the front tires and appeared almost done, while what looked like the first pallet of gold was being loaded into the back by a forklift. If he was going to stop them, he didn't have much time.

Why stop them?

The gold was of no concern to him now that it was out of Eritrea. These guys were Russian, so obviously stealing it either for themselves or some foreign interest, almost definitely not African, so destabilization was no longer a concern. His primary concern now was to save the civilians and Niner.

Gunfire erupted from the opposite end of the runway, the distinctive sound of AK-47s filling the air, a weapon he had already noted none of their captors seemed to be carrying.

He ducked back down as several rounds pinged off the fuselage.

Was a third party intervening?

Abandoned 250 Sudan Squadron Royal Air Force Airfield

Acton looked at Niner who nodded. Both of them jumped to their feet, rushing forward and tackling the two guards. Acton lost sight of Niner as his target hit the ground with a grunt, Acton landing on top of him. He punched the man several times in the face as quickly as he could to stun him, then leapt forward, placing his knee on the man's neck, using his bodyweight to push down on the man's carotid artery, slowly cutting off the oxygen to his brain.

The man struggled under him, but the element of surprise had worked, and Acton had the upper hand, and with every second that elapsed, he knew his opponent's resistance would weaken, Laura's ex-SAS security team excellent instructors.

The slaps against his legs became weak and soon stopped, his man out cold. Acton grabbed the gun from his hand then retrieved several mags from his pockets. He looked up to find Niner already walking over to him, his man being secured by the two Chinese observers, the Brit and French having taken charge of Reese, moving her to better cover as the gunfire continued from the new arrivals, return fire now underway in earnest.

Niner grabbed the man by the shoulder, Acton gripping the other, and they retreated behind a stack of rusted out oil drums, any fuel they might have at one time contained long having leaked out and contaminated the soil. As they rounded the drums to join the others, Acton and Niner tossed their man to the ground, he immediately set upon by the Chinese who bound and gagged him within moments.

Acton poked his head up and saw the attacking vehicle veer to the right, beating a hasty retreat as the concentrated fire from the Russians scared them off. Niner tossed his spare weapon and two magazines to the surviving British observer.

"Thanks, mate," he replied, readying the weapon. "How many does that make?"

Acton looked at his gun, not wanting to give it up but realizing there were others more qualified than him. "I've got a Beretta and three mags," he said, holding them out. "Anybody more qualified than me?"

The Chinese observer Lee Fang held out her hand. "No disrespect, Doctor, though your file is impressive, I do believe I am more qualified."

Acton smiled with a nod, handing her the Beretta. Niner held up the weapon he had relieved Dawson's killer of. "I've got this and two mags. So that means we have three weapons and seven spare magazines. We need to make these last and hope that they'll just leave with the gold if they think we're too risky a target to take out."

Acton felt naked without the weapon and his eyes began to seek out other sources of protection when he spotted the forklift racing back toward their position, several guards hanging off it, the others protecting the plane having retreated inside the cargo hold.

Something in Russian was yelled.

"They know we're missing," said Niner.

"You speak Russian?" asked Lee.

Niner nodded. "Don't you?"

"Of course," she smiled. "Know thy enemy."

Niner grinned at her. "Which is why I also speak Chinese."

"And I English." Her smile wasn't as forthcoming, but it was there.

Now if we can all just keep getting along, we might make it out of here alive.

Two guards rounded the rear of the plane, scanning the area. One pointed to the drums they were hiding behind and raised his weapon. "Allow me," said the Brit, squeezing off two rounds, each man dropping to the ground. The Frenchman and the other Chinese observer bolted forward, grabbing the weapons from the two fallen men as the three armed members of their party covered them.

Gunfire tore up the ground to their right and they were forced to abandon their search for ammunition, instead both rolling away from the shots, putting the massive cargo plane between them and the shooters. They scrambled back to the safety of the oil drums as the others conserved their ammo.

A shout from down the runway had Acton turning his attention to the other airplane. It appeared they had successfully replaced the front landing gear tires and the pilot was now powering up the engines. The forklift with the second and final pallet of gold was rushing toward the cargo ramp, and moments later it was swallowed up by the interior, the props now at full power.

A burst of gunfire then the sound of bullets pinging loudly off the drums in front of them had everyone hugging the deck, the thieves retreating toward the waiting transport, pouring heavy fire onto their hiding place.

The two Chinese observers returned fire, emptying their magazines. Lee tossed a spare to her partner, reloading her second last mag as the Brit and Frenchman took over. Several more guards dropped, speeding along the retreat of the others, the last of them jumping onto the rear deck as the ramp rose, the plane beginning to taxi to the end of the runway.

The engines roared, the plane holding in place as the pilot applied the brakes while the power continued to build. Gunfire from the other end of the runway coincided with the plane suddenly bursting forward, rushing toward the return of the locals.

In far greater numbers.

Abandoned 250 Sudan Squadron Royal Air Force Airfield

Samir gripped the seat with one hand, tight, the other balancing his AK-47 on the side view mirror as he pumped lead toward the massive aircraft roaring toward them. Whatever was onboard must have been valuable, the two planes here the biggest he had ever seen, and the amount of fire power impressive enough to cause him to order their initial retreat.

Luckily several others had arrived to investigate the fire just as they had found cover over the crest of a hill, and after quick negotiations, the owners of the vehicles had agreed to a three-way split and resumed the attack.

But if the plane left the ground, not only was any cargo lost, but so were the valuable hostages. And as their weapons pumped away at the military transport, he realized it was of no use, the thickened skin designed to resist small arms fire.

The nose lifted off the ground, then the rear wheels with a puff of smoke, leaving them all to duck as the massive plane passed over them. The three vehicles screeched to a halt, most of the men turning to continue firing at the rapidly departing plane. The gunfire began to wane and eventually stop, everyone dropping back in their seats disappointed at an opportunity lost.

"Look."

Samir turned to look where his driver Abit was pointing. Beyond the wreckage of an even bigger transport plane lay about a dozen fuel drums, and through the rusted out holes it was quite evident that at least one person was hiding behind them.

He jumped up in his seat, poking his head through the window and pointing toward the drums, yelling, "Hostages!"

His driver hammered on the gas, their Toyota racing toward what Samir hoped would still be a generous pay day, though now split three ways. He would need to figure out a way to rid himself of the others but there was time for that later. As they rushed toward the oil drums and a possible retirement fund, he motioned for the others to break off and surround whoever might be hiding.

Abit brought them to a skidding halt as Samir and the others jumped out, their AK-47's aimed at the drums, the other trucks doing the same.

A man stood up, his arms raised.

A white man, dressed in Western clothes.

Samir smiled.

When the other ten stood, almost all white, his smile turned into an outright grin as he exchanged triumphant looks with the others.

We're rich!

Dawson retreated deeper into the plane after watching the Shaanxi Y-8 take off under fire. As his friends and the others were surrounded, he used the phone to take a quick video of what he was facing, then turned it off again as shouts in Arabic were barked by what appeared to be competing chefs, no one man seeming to be in charge.

That could prove useful.

Somebody shouted for the plane to be searched. Dawson stuffed the phone, guns and mags in one of the seatbacks then rushed to the back corner and dropped to the floor, dragging the body of one of the dead Russian hijackers over top of him. He knew it wouldn't hide him from their sight, but it might just make them ignore him if they thought he was merely another dead body.

Shouts from the cargo hold in the now quiet deserted airport neared, the door between the cargo and passenger areas thrown open only feet away.

Shouts in Arabic of "Hands up!" and "Look for valuables!" filled the air and he felt the body covering him moved as someone yelled "I've got some bodies over here!". A hand grabbed his shoulder and he forced himself to relax, slowly breathing lest the red face of a held breath give him away.

"There's nothing here!" yelled another near the front. "Let's go back outside!" His shoulder was let go and the voices and footsteps faded, leaving him once again alone with the dead.

And perhaps the only hope for his comrades now held at gunpoint.

Yelling outside had him pushing the body on top of him aside and he carefully looked out the window. The hostages were being searched then loaded into the back of the vehicles. When the last were aboard the gunmen who could fit climbed on then the three vehicles peeled away leaving six men behind, looking at each other and the ground as they kicked at rocks, none willing to acknowledge how low on the totem pole they really were to have been left behind.

"Let's search again. Maybe there's something that they missed," suggested one, his loud, probably khat fuelled voice carrying through the torn opening in the fuselage. The others nodded and Dawson realized these men had nothing left to do but a thorough search since they had no ride home. He scurried forward, retrieving his weapons and magazines along with the phone, then rushed over to the huge opening. Sitting nearby were two small bottles of water, held against the fuselage by some netting. He grabbed them both and shoved them down his shirt.

Glancing outside, he saw no one, the voices now coming from the cargo hold. Careful not to cut himself on the torn metal and exposed wiring, he jumped down to the ground, rolling to absorb the impact, his ankle twinging slightly, his ribs screaming in protest. Rushing forward while scanning his surroundings, he took up position at the front of the aircraft, the bottom ground into the runway, its gear collapsed.

He listened.

Still only the voices from inside the plane. The oil drums would provide temporary cover, but he needed better. Several hundred feet beyond was an abandoned building, half fallen in on itself. If he could reach there with no one seeing him, he'd be free to leave the entire area, using the building as cover.

But if just one of the half dozen left behind looked out a window, he'd be done for. With his ribs the way they were, a long distance chase was out of the question. Any other day? No problem. But today it would end up being a shootout, six against one, with him possibly in the open.

Not too bad odds, but still not good if he hoped to save the hostages.

Taking one final look, he dashed for the oil drums and hit the ground with a grunt, his ribs screaming in agony and a puff of dust revealing his position. He cursed himself for his stupidity, the pain overcoming his training for a moment. Peering through the holes in the drums he saw no reaction from the plane, the locals all aboard seeking whatever treasures they could.

Now or never.

He took a quick look behind him and saw some dried brush about halfway between him and the collapsed building and decided to crawl it. Flattening himself, he pushed the water bottles to the sides so they wouldn't burst, then began to push across the arid landscape as quickly as he could. Just as he was about to reach the bushes he heard someone yell in Arabic, "There's somebody out there!"

That's my cue!

He jumped to his feet and hustled it toward the broken walls, his lungs demanding he stop as his ribcage screamed in rage. Gunfire erupted, several rounds bursting the stone in front of him as they neared their mark. With only feet to go he leapt through the air, diving through one of the few remaining windows and slammed into the ground, his hip smacking a pile of brick that had once been part of an interior wall.

He winced in pain, but forced it to the background as he swung around and took up position by the window. All six men were storming his position, several with their weapons firing on full automatic.

No ammo concerns?

He hoped they were just idiots not thinking they needed bullets to shoot after the magazine they had emptied, but he couldn't risk his life on that assumption.

He rose up and squeezed off three rounds, the lead three hitting the ground, dead or dying, before the other three could react, diving behind the oil drums. Blind fire erupted from their position as they shot their weapons in his general direction, most of the bullets missing blindly. Dawson knelt down, the hard dry brick providing sufficient cover for now, content to let his enemy waste their ammunition.

The sound changed, one of the three weapons clearly shifting position as it fired. Dawson moved to the right of the window and caught sight of the hostile trying to take his left flank. The first shot caught the man in the shoulder, but he kept running and firing, the next shot brought him down in a heap. Swinging back for a quick look out the window, he saw the other two had taken advantage of the distraction and were just disappearing out of sight to the right.

The gunfire stopped and he heard rubble move on the other side of the wall. He stepped through the window, crossing the front of the building and stopping at the one-two corner. He took a quick peak and saw the second man disappear after the first around the back. Weapons fire erupted and a quick look back saw puffs of dust blow out the window as his previous position was sprayed with gunfire. He took advantage of the noise to rush the two-three corner and just as the gunfire stopped, he rounded the corner, weapon raised, and fired two shots into his would-be killers.

They never knew what hit them.

An engine revved and gears shifted in the distance. Dawson peered out from around the wall and saw an old World War II era jeep bouncing toward the wrecked Antonov, several more gun wielding fanatics aboard. He grabbed an AK-47 from one of the men, all of their ammo, of which there were only two mags, then ran in the opposite direction, using the building as cover. He crested a small hill and soon had nature to provide cover. Looking up at the sun, he determined the direction the vehicles with the hostages had gone, and set out at a brisk walk in pursuit.

As the hot African sun beat down on him, still high enough in the horizon for him to follow any trails, but not low enough for the air to cool, his mind began to plan for possible contingencies.

Assuming he could find them.

If they went too far, I never will.

Fiumicino–Leonardo da Vinci International Airport, Rome, Italy

"What do you mean they lost contact with them?"

Laura's chest was tight, her stomach doing flips as she tried to maintain control. She hadn't expected much of a welcome when she arrived, the entire mission hush-hush until the gold was secure, but what she found when she exited the gangway were dozens of reporters, glaring camera lights, and microphones shoved in her face and those of her colleagues.

"The plane with the gold, it crashed!" cried one of the reporters, the glee in her voice at having another story to capitalize on human misery evident. It made Laura sick with rage, these hounds so eager to ambush people with the news of a dead loved one, to stick cameras and microphones into the faces of the bereaved, all to score higher ratings and perhaps advance an otherwise pathetic career.

News isn't the news anymore.

Her beloved James' words echoed through her head. He was right for the most part, though she still felt there were a few respectable news organizations out there. CNN had lost all credibility for her with their coverage of the missing Malaysian flight. For an anchor to actually seriously suggest wormholes? For their prime time news hosts to actually run with stories that they had evidence of it landing on a secret runway and that the passengers were alive? It was irresponsible and an insult to journalists everywhere, not to mention an atrocity to the families.

She had changed the channel and never gone back.

I hope the BBC never gets that ridiculous.

She had no idea what was going on now, and she just pushed her way through the throng and into her waiting limo, several others from the flight joining her.

"What the hell are they talking about?" she asked, looking at the IMF's Reginald Wangari.

He shook his head. "I have no idea, give me a minute." He pulled his cellphone out as the car pulled away, the noise of the reporters fading. Laura pulled her own from her purse and turned it on. As it connected to the network her phone vibrated indicating a message. She quickly hit the button to listen, entering her code then pressing *1*.

She immediately recognized James' voice, and knew right away he was in trouble.

"Hi babe, it's me! I don't have much time. There's been some sort of hijacking attempt on the plane and we're going down." Her heart slammed against her chest as she pressed the phone against her ear, holding up a finger for everyone else to be quiet. "Dawson was killed by the private security"—she gasped, her stomach tightening—"and a stray bullet caused us to depressurize. We're in a steep dive, so hopefully we'll be okay."

Tears rolled down her cheeks as she realized that if what the reporters had said, this would be the last words she would ever hear him say. A cry erupted from her as she pictured him in his final moments, his words breaking her heart. "But if we don't make it, know that I love you, and that I treasured every moment we've spent together. These last few years have been the greatest of my life, and if I die today, you've made my life worth living. Give my love to Mom and Dad, and to Greg and his family. I love you, hon, and I'm sorry I—"

There were several bangs and screams then the message ended.

And she knew the only man she had ever truly loved was dead.

"What is it?" asked Wangari, his voice gentle as he leaned forward and touched her knee.

"A message from James," she whispered, her voice cracking. She replayed it, putting it on speaker, everyone listening in silence. When it was done, she hung up and curled into the corner of the seat, her eyes watching the streets pass by blindly as she sobbed gently to herself. Wangari was on his phone, and after a few minutes of getting connected to the right person, put it on speaker.

"Go ahead, Adam, you're on speaker. Tell us what you know."

"Hello everyone, Adam Lee here, UN. All we know is this. The plane went into a slow descent near the Eritrean-Sudanese border and ignored all hails from Air Traffic Control. At about twenty thousand feet, it went into a steep dive and disappeared from radar. We received no SOS, however the transponders were still sending telemetry indicating the plane was leveling off, then we lost all contact, including transponders."

"What does that mean? They crashed?" asked someone, Laura still not focusing.

"We believe they had some sort of malfunction, then either a depressurization that required an emergency dive, or an engine failure resulting in the same. Then once they regained control, the plane either exploded or broke apart."

"Can you be sure of that?" asked Laura, turning toward the phone, her mind still a haze of grief and confusion.

"Not yet," replied Lee. "We're trying to get search crews in there now, but the Sudanese aren't cooperating. We think they're going to make an attempt at the gold."

"How did the word get out?" asked Wangari.

"The Eritrean president made an announcement in front of the press about it as soon as the plane left their airspace, which technically meant they had fulfilled their part of the bargain."

"So everybody in the world knows there's a billion dollars of gold possibly scattered across the desert of Sudan," muttered Wangari.

Laura winced, then replayed the voice message, searching for some comfort, some hope, in James' last words. *We're in a steep dive, so hopefully we'll be okay.* That meant the depressurization was about to be dealt with. There was no way there was a bomb on board—why blow up the gold? Hijack the plane absolutely, but don't blow it up—the retrieval effort would be insane.

And wasn't this some huge *military* transport? How could a *military* plane be taken out by a single gunshot? It didn't make sense. She put the phone back in her purse, returning to the conversation.

"I don't think they crashed," she said, interrupting whatever was being said.

Nobody spoke for a moment, then Wangari smiled sympathetically. "We all hope that, but the evidence—"

"Tells us that they were slowly descending, that there was a gunshot, they depressurized, there was an emergency dive to deal with that, and then all communication was lost."

"What gunshot?" asked Lee over Wangari's phone still on speaker.

"I have a voicemail from my fiancée, Professor James Acton. He said there was an attempted hijacking, some shooting that caused the plane to depressurize and then they went into a dive. This plane was hijacked. They were obviously descending to land somewhere they weren't supposed to when they were discovered. A gunfight ensued, they depressurized, the pilot took action, then they shut off all communications."

"That's quite the assumption," said Lee.

"Only the last part, and frankly, no more so than your assumption they broke apart in the air. Isn't this a military transport? Are you telling me a single bullet can break it apart?"

There was silence on the other end of the line, everyone in the back of the limo staring at the tiny Blackberry held in the palm of Wangari's hand.

Lee finally spoke. "Even if we assume they landed, there's not much we can do. The Sudanese aren't cooperating, and we have no idea where the plane is to even start looking."

"Wouldn't they land somewhere along their flight path?" asked Wangari.

"If we assume a hijacking, highly unlikely. My guess is they were going to descend smoothly until they were below radar, cut communications, then change course. They could fly for hours in any direction, which I'm certain is what they did if they didn't crash."

Laura clenched her fists in frustration. "But where can they land a plane that big without anyone noticing?"

"It's North Africa. There are hundreds of abandoned airstrips left over from the war that they could land at."

Laura held her breath for a moment, her mind reeling in a desperate attempt to prove James was still alive. "*Then* where would they go?" she finally said in triumph.

"What?"

"They would have to land somewhere where they could offload the gold, then transport it to another location. That means they would need to have been able to get transportation to the abandoned airfield, including equipment to offload those pallets of gold. They can't be too far from civilization."

Wangari's head was bobbing, Laura pretty certain she had convinced those in the vehicle with her that there was still hope for their colleagues. But the silence on the other end was what needed to be swayed.

"I agree there's a chance the plane landed," replied Lee at last, "but I have to point out one thing. If it did land as planned, there would be no reason to keep the hostages alive. They would have landed probably hours ago, offloaded the gold, killed the hostages, then left." There was a pause. "I'm sorry Professor Palmer, but at this point in time, we must treat this as a recovery operation, and keep our eyes open for unusual gold trades. Wangari, I have to go to a briefing. I'll call you when I have more."

The call ended and Wangari returned the phone to his pocket, looking at Laura. "I'm sorry," he said.

Laura looked at him, anger filling her with a warmth she desperately needed right now.

"The UN may have given up on them, but I haven't."

Reading Residence, London, England

INTERPOL Special Agent Hugh Reading sipped his warm milk, easing under the covers of his bed, his love of which had been recently renewed by his son's thoughtful gift of new bed linens for his birthday. Microfiber sheets with an equivalent thread count of 1400. They were so incredibly soft, smooth and cool compared to the harsh burlap he had apparently been using for decades that he wondered how he had ever been able to sleep before.

And they were made all the more comfortable because they came from his son.

Spencer was twenty-three years old now—a young man setting out on his own to establish a life Reading prayed would be a happy and fulfilling one. He no longer hoped that his son would have a better, more prosperous life than his—the job market was just too tough for those types of dreams anymore. Perhaps in time, but not now. All he wanted was for his son to be able to do something he enjoyed doing, and make enough at it to pay the bills and put a little aside to one day start a family of his own.

Grandchildren!

The thought made him feel old.

Very old.

But it would make him happy, especially now that he felt he'd have a chance to see them. Spencer had been slowly letting his father back into his life, their relationship strained over the years since Reading had divorced his wife when Spencer was young, and it had been selfishly easier to simply pull back, which Spencer seemed eager to let him do, eventually wanting nothing to do with him beyond a forced five minute conversation at holidays. But something had changed inside Reading, perhaps when he realized he was getting too old to be a cop and left Scotland Yard. Time was getting short, and he realized his son was quickly approaching the age he was at when his own father had passed away, and there wasn't a day that went by where Reading didn't regret spending more time with his father.

You take for granted that your loved ones will always be there tomorrow to see them, so you put off today's plans. Then suddenly tomorrow arrives, and there's another excuse, then one day you get the call.

"Your dad has cancer."

Those four words devastated him. Especially when he was diagnosed with at most a few months to live. Reading had spent almost all of what turned out to be only five weeks with his father, and they had become closer than ever in that time, and he wouldn't have traded it for another decade of the distant relationship they once had.

It was almost thirty years since his death and he still missed him, and he didn't want his own son going through the same or worse. At least Reading and his dad had been on good speaking terms, they just didn't take advantage of it. Reading and his own son were cordial at best until recently, and he hoped things would continue to improve so his son wouldn't have the same regrets. Old age was creeping up on him, and with his choice of friends of late, the old Reaper seemed to be stalking him at times.

He flicked the light switch off, resting his head on the small memory foam pillow with built in cooling gel he had received from his son at the same time. In a confession, his son had told him he had bought it six months before for Christmas, but when it arrived from China, it stank so bad he had to wash it several times and air it out for months before it became giftable.

His phone vibrated on the nightstand, its display lighting up, casting a faint glow on the ceiling his now open eyes stared at, curses muttered under his breath.

There's just no way a man can go to bed early!

Sure it was only nine in the evening, but when did the rule of etiquette of not calling after that hour get struck from the books? He didn't get the memo, and if it weren't for his job, he would set his phone up so that after nine in the evening it would go directly to voicemail.

His eyebrows narrowed.

You did do that.

He frowned, rolling over and grabbing the phone, the call display showing "Palmer, Laura". As he hit the Accept button on the display, he realized he had programmed in a series of contacts that would be put through at any time.

Speaking of friends who have brought the Grim Reaper into my life.

"Hello?"

"Hi Hugh, it's me, Laura. I hope I didn't wake you."

Reading sat up in bed, flicking on the lamp on the nightstand. "Don't be silly, it's only nine o'clock. Where are you?"

"Rome."

"Not another job for 'you know who'?"

"No, I don't expect any more now that he's retired."

There was no hint of her usual jovial self, and Reading could tell this conversation was about to go south. He grabbed his pad and pen from the nightstand, readying it should it become necessary.

"What's wrong?"

"James…" Her voice drifted off and he heard a squelched cry as she snapped off a sob.

His voice lowered, more tender than his usual brusque self. "What is it, love? What's happened?"

"We were in Eritrea, retrieving a large hoard of gold from Ancient Rome under the auspices of the UN and IMF."

"I never heard anything about that."

"It was hush-hush. There was an attack, some people died, but we got away. I took a flight out with the artifacts from the dig site and James went on another flight with the gold, along with some unarmed UN observers, including two friends of ours."

"I see." Reading knew exactly what type of friends those were, though he didn't bother asking which two. "And what happened?"

"When we arrived we were told the other plane had crashed. I checked my voicemail and there was a message from James. He said the plane had been hijacked, that one of our friends had been shot, and they had depressurized. They were in a steep dive when he got cut off."

"And what's the UN doing about it?"

"Nothing!" she cried. "Nothing! They say the Sudanese government isn't cooperating. They think they're going after the gold themselves."

"How much gold?"

"Over a billion dollars on the open market."

Jesus Christ! That'll attract every nutter on the planet!

"Do they think the plane crashed?"

"Yes, but they came to that conclusion before they knew about James' message! I think they landed safely. They were on one of those monster Russian planes—"

"An Antonov?"

"Yeah, I think that's it. That's a military transport, isn't it?"

"Yes, and not likely to be taken out by a shot or two," said Reading. "What can I do to help?"

"I don't know. I'm at a loss."

Reading sucked in a deep, slow breath through his nose, replaying the conversation in his head, looking for some angle they could use.

He smiled.

"You said two of our friends were on that plane?"

"Yes, as UN observers."

"I suggest you contact them. Something tells me those guys won't rest until they know what actually happened to their mates."

Reading could almost hear the smile through the phone. "That's a great idea! I'll make a call right now!"

"And I'm going to catch a plane to Rome at once. What hotel are you staying at?"

"The Westin Excelsior."

"Sounds expensive. Can I sleep on your sofa?"

Laura laughed, the first hint of her usual self he had heard so far. "I'll get you a room, don't worry about it."

"It's good to be the Queen," he replied with a smile, shaking his head. *If I had her money, I'd burn mine.* "I'll contact you as soon as I have my itinerary. Let me know how you make out with our friends."

"Okay, Hugh, we'll see you soon," she replied. "And Hugh?"

"Yes?"

"Thanks."

Reading felt his chest tighten slightly. "No need to thank me. You'd do the same. Now make that call and get the ball rolling."

"Yes, sir!"

He ended the call, launching the Expedia app on his phone, a ticket booked within minutes for a flight leaving in a couple of hours. It was expensive, but he never worried about it. Somehow, miraculously, small deposits always ended up in his account within a few days that covered these surprise excursions to help Laura and Jim. He had told her the first several times it wasn't necessary, but she had denied doing it with a slightly sly grin.

He gave up complaining, instead finally accepting that this was what it was like to have a ridiculously rich friend.

And if the unexpected trips weren't always accompanied by gunfire and kidnappings, he'd be even more grateful.

Yet here he was heading off to Rome then most likely Sudan, one of the most violent countries in the world.

I must be bloody daft!

1st Special Forces Operational Detachment-Delta HQ, Fort Bragg, North Carolina
A.k.a. "The Unit"

Sergeant Major Mike "Red" Belme nodded to Maggie, Colonel Thomas Clancy's secretary. She looked tired—worried. *Has she been crying?* His eyes narrowed as he was about to ask her what was wrong when he heard the Colonel's bark beckoning him.

"If that's Sergeant Major Belme then get in here!"

"Yes, sir!" replied Red as he continued through the outer office and into Colonel Clancy's sanctuary. He closed the door behind him and took a seat, the Colonel never one for ceremony. The Colonel was a soldier's soldier, his rank more of a burden than an achievement, he always having preferred to be on the front lines whenever possible. Though he had never been Delta—that reserved for Sergeants—he had seen combat during his career, the walls covered in various forms of recognition evidence of that.

Burt "Big Dog" Dawson, Red's best friend and pseudo-commander—command structure loose within Delta—respected Clancy, trusted him even, and that was enough for Red to feel the same way. The Colonel had never let them down, had never abandoned them, and had stuck his neck out for them on more than one occasion.

Red knew that Colonel Clancy would do whatever he could to save his men, even if Washington told him to do nothing.

But today Clancy looked tired. He stared at his screen for a moment longer then leaned back in his chair, running a cigar under his nose. Red's eyebrows shot up at the sight. The Colonel had been trying to kick his cigar habit for the past couple of years on the urging of his wife, and this was the closest he had seen him come to failing in that endeavor.

"Don't worry, Sergeant Major, I'm not lighting it," he said, as if reading Red's mind. "I couldn't if I wanted to. I don't have a match or lighter in the damned room." His eyes drifted to the top-right drawer of his desk. "Now, I could shoot the tip off, that might light it, but then there'd be paperwork." He sighed then opened the very drawer holding his sidearm.

And tossed the unlit cigar inside, slamming the drawer shut.

"It's days like today where a man needs his vices," he muttered.

"What's happened, Colonel?"

"BD and Niner are missing, presumed dead."

"What?" Red couldn't control his outburst, this information coming from as far left field as he could imagine. He knew they had been on a mission in the Ukraine, but that had been completed and they were on some babysitting mission for the UN. "What the hell happened?"

Clancy shook his head, his entire face seeming to have aged ten years since yesterday. "It appears the plane they were on went down. There's been no communication for several hours but ATC had them on a rapid descent before they went off radar."

Red dropped his head between his knees, his hands gripping his shaved head as flashes of better times played across the back of his eyelids. He suddenly sat up. "Has anyone notified his family yet?"

Clancy shook his head. "We're waiting for confirmation."

"So there's still hope?"

Clancy again shook his head. "Not from what we've been told."

The phone on Clancy's desk chirped, demanding attention. Clancy frowned, hitting the button. "I said no interruptions."

"Yes, sir, I'm sorry, sir, but there's a call I think you'll want to take," came Maggie's voice over the intercom.

"Who is it?"

"Professor Laura Palmer."

Clancy and Red both exchanged surprised looks. *Palmer?*

"Get her number." He jabbed the button, cutting off the conversation. "Professor Acton was on that plane."

"Huh?" This meeting was full of shockers for Red, enough to actually leave him at a loss for words.

"I'm going to read you in because as soon as you talk to Professor Palmer, you'll know everything anyway. BD and Niner were our representatives for a covert mission to transport over one billion dollars' worth of gold from Eritrea to Italy. It was found at an archeological site, which is why the two professors were involved. It was top secret because of the amount of money involved. Palmer was on a flight with the dig site relics, BD and Niner were on a privately contracted Antonov with a group of unarmed UN observers, originally two from each of the permanent members of the UN Security Council countries, and two from Italy."

"Originally?"

"The Ethiopians attacked the dig site, killing several of the observers." He leaned forward, pointing his finger at the phone. "If she's calling, either she knows something, or she *thinks* she knows something. My hands are tied since this was a UN op, and you know how useless they are." He leaned back in his chair. "I suggest you give the woman a call, and should you feel it necessary, visit her personally to offer your condolences on her loss. Perhaps take a few of the boys with you."

Red knew exactly what was supposed to be read between those lines. He nodded, rising. "I'll be sure to pass on your own as well, Colonel."

"You do that." He flicked his wrist toward the door. "Enjoy your vacation, Sergeant Major."

"Thank you, sir." Red exited the office, closing the door behind him so the Colonel would be able to honestly say he hadn't heard any conversation between his secretary and a soldier under his command. Red rounded

Maggie's desk and leaned over, putting a hand on her shoulder. "How're you holding up?"

Maggie's eyes erupted with tears and she buried her face in Red's stomach. He patted her head gently, not saying anything, as the woman who had only recently expressed her interest in Dawson demonstrated how much she had given of her heart. After about a minute she pulled away, dabbing herself dry with a tissue.

"I'm sorry," she said, her voice rough but still with a hint of the strength that Red thought Dawson found appealing. She had almost insinuated herself into Dawson's life, and he had reluctantly accepted it, which delighted his friends and team. Dawson had always been a loner. In fact, Red couldn't remember a relationship lasting more than enough dates to get a few romps, then his friend would close himself off, ending the relationship. Red knew why, they all did. Red himself was married initially due to a wonderful accident, his son Bryson—and Dawson's Godson—and it had terrified him at first, getting married and having a family with a job so dangerous.

But hundreds of thousands—millions—of servicemen the world over had married and had children, during peacetime and war. It was the human imperative, to bond and procreate, and he didn't regret a single day of his relationship with his now wife and their amazing kid.

But Dawson was so married to the job Red knew he was worried getting attached would cause him to ease up, to avoid taking the risks he always did, which Red was certain Dawson felt would put his men at risk.

And Red had called bullshit on it a few weeks ago when talking with Dawson over a beer in his basement while watching the Rangers game. "You're too good a soldier for that," he had said to his friend. That had elicited a grunt, which in some cases for Dawson was a font of information. The more he saw them together, the more comfortable they seemed, and when he came to the range humming one morning, something his friend only did when he was *particularly* happy, fist bumps had been exchanged secretly by the team, everyone knowing the "boss had got some".

He didn't let up on them that day, though.

Maggie quickly wrote down a number on a pad and tore off the sheet, handing it to him. "This is Professor Palmer's number."

"Did she say anything?"

"Only that it was urgent she talk to someone."

Red nodded, holding up the sheet. "Thanks." He rounded her desk and before opening the outer office door, looked back at her. "Don't lose hope yet. If there was any way to survive this, BD would find a way."

She smiled weakly, he himself not buying the words coming out of his mouth. *If there was any way...* Who was he kidding? A plane in a rapid descent from tens of thousands of feet slammed into the ground nothing like a piano on a Disney cartoon character. You didn't just push up from under the wreckage and walk away.

You died.

But why would Palmer be calling him?

Correction. She was calling the Colonel, not him. And it was too soon to be passing on condolences to your secret friends in Special Ops.

Which meant she knew something she felt they needed to know. He closed the door of one of their secure communications rooms behind him and sat down, dialing the number.

"Hello?"

"Professor Palmer?"

"Yes."

"This is a friend of Mr. White's."

"Oh, hi, I recognize your voice. What should I call you?"

"Call me Mr. Black."

"You heard about the plane crash?"

"Yes."

"I have something you need to hear."

"Go ahead."

A voicemail message from Professor Acton began to play, and his heart sank as he heard of Dawson's death. But if this had started as a hijacking, it gave a plausible explanation as to why the plane had been lost on radar, and it meant Niner might still be alive. His mind raced as the voicemail ended.

"I can't get any action from the UN, they say their hands are tied because the Sudanese aren't cooperating."

"I heard the same thing here."

"Can *you* do anything?"

Red smiled, hoping this conversation was about to go where he knew only she could take it. He had no idea how rich she was, but he did know she was rich enough to make a difference. "With the right resources, yes."

"I'll write you a blank check."

"Where are you now?"

"Rome."

"I'll text you an account number. Put a hundred grand in there. I'll see you before morning."

"Consider it done."

The call ended and Red leaned back, closing his eyes as he remembered the first time he had met his good friend. Then when he had asked if Dawson minded taking Niner on the latest mission since Bryson had a school play he was desperate for his father to see him in.

He knew he shouldn't feel guilty, but he did.

And now if there was a chance at saving Niner, he would do everything he could to bring him home.

And if not, he'd kill everyone involved in the death of his friends.

Outside Hamashkoraib, Sudan

Dawson's body armor had been tossed long ago, the pants turned into shorts, one of the torn off legs fitted over his head like a bandana doubling as a hat, the other hanging over the back of his neck and shoulders to cut down on the sunburn. His first bottle of water was empty, the cap carefully replaced, the bottle tucked inside his shirt in the hopes condensation might form inside the bottle to give him a few drips later if desperate, and be uncontaminated by salt if he were to find a water source.

A watering hole would be nice!

He had his shades to help block the sun, his utility belt which included a multi-purpose tool, knife, mini-first aid kit, water purification tablets, matches and some plastic ties, not to mention two Beretta 92's with six extra magazines and an AK-47 with another two mags.

And no food.

You can't eat bullets.

Though Atlas had once on a dare from Niner.

He was following a dusty trail, not a road by any civilized sense, but it was a route that had been recently frequented by several vehicles, the tracks still fresh. If he were lucky, they might just lead him to where the hostages were now being held. He had taken several photos of the tire tracks with the satellite phone just in case he needed to compare later. The phone still had about half its battery power left, but was useless as a communications device so he had it shut off to conserve juice. If he had a chance later he would spend a few minutes tinkering, but was reluctant to risk frying the device as it had proven useful already. He had all of the hostages and hostage takers on video. Should he be rescued, he'd be able to hand that video over and they might be able to identify the locals involved and send in a team to retrieve his comrades.

He stopped.

The trail seemed to join up with another more travelled one, then split into two again, forming almost an elongated X, he currently on the bottom left of the X, the heavier traffic the right side. The tracks he was following were lost in the jumble, it clear traffic passed here regularly. The last discernable track that definitely belonged to what he was following showed no indication of turning hard right, so he had to assume they had continued forward.

But had they exited left on the road less travelled, or right, on what appeared to be a fairly major road for the middle of nowhere?

He knelt down and examined the tracks heading left and it didn't take him long to spot the distinctive defect in one of the vehicles' tires, a gouge at a forty-five degree angle that left a repeated gap in the sand with every rotation.

A motor revving had him spinning, looking for cover. Several large rocks nearby were all that was available. He rushed toward them, ducking behind just in time as a beat up van, a Dodge Caravan if he wasn't mistaken, faux wood paneling from the eighties still partially intact, crested a rise from the top right of the intersection. It appeared to have one occupant, a middle-aged man singing at the top of his lungs, his smile and demeanor befitting small town USA.

Dawson jumped out from behind the rocks, pointing his AK-47 directly at the man's head as he slowed to make the turn. The man's eyes bulged as he saw the gun and he slammed the brakes on, raising his hands. Dawson flicked his weapon and the man nodded, turning off the engine then climbing out.

With English one of Sudan's two official languages, Dawson took a chance. "Do you speak English?"

The man nodded.

"Good, just do what I say and you won't get hurt." He motioned in the direction the van had just come from. "How far to town?"

"About five kilometers."

"Are you healthy enough to walk it?"

The man nodded rapidly, his eyes still bulging with fear.

"Do you have any weapons?"

The man nodded. "In my glove box. Only a fool travels here without a weapon."

Dawson motioned to where he thought the hostage takers had gone. "Where does that lead?"

"To town, but the north side. It's rarely used, very rough."

"The name of the town?"

"Hamashkoraib."

"How big?"

"Not very." The man's eyebrows narrowed. "Are you American?"

"I'm asking the questions."

"Sorry."

"Are there any Western representatives there? Government, embassy, church, companies?"

The man shook his head. "No. This is a very poor town, mostly controlled by gangs. The government leaves us alone, we leave them alone."

"Phones?"

"A few of the warlords have satellite phones, but they won't help you."

"So there's no way to communicate with the outside world?"

The man shrugged. "We have an Internet café."

Dawson's head dropped slightly, his eyes rolling up. "You have no cellphone coverage, but you have Internet."

"It uses satellite I think."

Dawson opened the passenger door, retrieving a piece of paper and a pencil from the glove compartment, along with the gun, an old six-shooter Remington with four bullets. He tossed the paper and pencil on the hood. "Draw me a map on how to get to this café."

The man nodded and quickly mapped out the twists and turns that were necessary. Dawson took the map, folded it up and put it in his pocket. He flicked his gun toward the trail the man had just come from. "Start walking, don't look back."

"What about my van?" asked the man, his eyes pleading, it obvious it was as precious to him as any child.

Dawson frowned, then took out the map. "Write your name down and your address. If I can, I'll get word to you where your van is when I'm done."

The man eagerly jumped forward, taking the pencil and paper. "Do you have email?" he asked.

Dawson chuckled. "Of course."

"As do I." He quickly wrote down a Hotmail address. "Email me here when you are done."

Dawson smiled as he read the address. "Isn't that The Camel Man 76 in Arabic?"

The man's head bobbed eagerly. "I started out selling camels. Now goats, horses, you name it, I sell it." He frowned. "I have deliveries in the back. What will you do with them?"

Dawson had visions of Noah's Ark stuffed in the back of his commandeered vehicle. "What kind of deliveries?"

"eBay purchases. I buy for people and arrange delivery for a commission."

Dawson didn't bother asking how this worked in the middle of nowhere, but with families splitting up and immigrating around the world, he wouldn't be surprised if this man had a brother in New York handling one end of the operation.

"I'll leave everything in the van unless I need something."

The man nodded slowly, not exactly pleased with the "unless" rider.

"Now start walking," repeated Dawson, flicking his weapon at the man, "and don't come looking for me or I'll be forced to kill you." Reluctantly the man began to walk back to town, cresting a rise within minutes. Dawson jumped in the van, fired up the engine, then turned the vehicle around, taking the left hand road to where he hoped he might find evidence of the final destination of the local criminals who had taken his friends and colleagues.

As he followed the trail, there no indications of any vehicles having turned off it, he was careful not to travel too fast; he could miss a turnoff, or worse, run headlong into the dozen or so armed men holding the hostages, or into yet another group that as of yet had no involvement.

His eyes scanned the sky for any sign of a contrail, anything airborne, but again came up empty. By now for certain the authorities knew the plane had gone down—it had been hours. And with a carrier off the coast of Eritrea, sending in search aircraft or even drones should have been an easy matter.

But there had been nothing.

He could have missed a drone, that he could accept, but not an aircraft. They were too loud, and the billowing smoke, a hint of which had still been on the horizon to the south before the sun began to set would have been visible for hundreds of miles in the air. Even if they had gone off course, they couldn't have gone that far since he had only been out for about half an hour. That meant at most three to five hundred miles from their intended course, and a wide search pattern from altitude would have spotted the thick black smoke of aviation fuel.

There could only be one explanation.

Nobody was looking.

Now the question was why. If he had to guess, it was that the Sudanese weren't letting anyone in their airspace because they wanted the gold. The Sudanese should be arriving soon, if they hadn't already. When they did they'd discover the gold was gone, and would hopefully at that point let the search begin since they had nothing to lose and everything to gain through goodwill.

He came around a bend and saw the town of what he assumed was Hamashkoraib before him, lights just starting to dot the landscape, some electric, some natural fires and candlelight. It was a quaint, peaceful sight from his perch, but somewhere in the mix of this small town were almost a dozen Western hostages, including two of his friends. With the dusk quickly settling in he decided to leave the trail and find a place to hole up so he could renew the search tomorrow.

Parking behind a large outcropping of rock carved out millions of years ago by a forgotten river, he flicked the light on in the back of the van and started to look through the goodies left behind by its owner. A grin spread across his face when he found several boxes taped together—two Froot Loops and one Cap'n Crunch.

And a case of bottled water.

God bless The Camel Man!

He tore free one of the bottles and unscrewed the cap, downing as much as he could before coming up for air. After a few more swigs he carefully refilled his smaller bottles, those easier to carry on foot. As he made himself comfortable, he realized the van had been tricked out by its owner to double as a mobile home, most likely for when he was making distant deliveries. All the side and rear windows were tinted a dark black and a thick curtain could be pulled across the front seats blocking any light to the back seats. The driver side seats in the rear, two extra rows, were already positioned down with fresh linens, Camel Man's wife obviously caring enough to keep him comfortable, and he showing his appreciation by having a picture of her and several children in a wood frame screwed into the roof.

You'll definitely get your van back, my friend.

These personal touches humanized his "victim". Though Dawson didn't feel guilty—he had done what needed to be done for the greater good—it simply reinforced the need to make amends when it was possible.

A small gas lantern hung from a rope strung across the back. He lit it and turned the light up about halfway. A toiletry bag stood out and he took a bottle of water along with the soap, toothpaste and shaving kit, and gave himself a quick bird bath with the side door open and the lamp turned off so he wouldn't be seen. Refreshed, he climbed back inside, opened the windows enough to let a breeze flow through, locked the doors, and lay down in Camel Man's bed, the broken satellite phone and his multi-tool lying beside him.

After fiddling for half an hour, he decided it was beyond his ability to repair, and instead put things back together, praying it still had the non-communications functions intact.

It did.

As he turned down the lamp and settled in for the night, his weapons and the handgun from the glove compartment stripped and cleaned, he almost immediately fell asleep only to be woken minutes later by gunfire in the distance. He jumped up, grabbed the phone and exited the vehicle.

Down below in the valley he could see the muzzle flashes. He quickly snapped several photos then changed the phone to low light mode and took several more as what he figured was celebratory gunfire continued at the edge of the village for a few more minutes.

And what better thing to celebrate than the capture of a dozen Western hostages?

Hamashkoraib, Sudan

James Acton jolted awake, gunfire erupting from outside along with laughter and cheering. He looked around the plain room to find most of his companions were awake as well, Reese frightened the most it seemed, the soldiers all taking it in stride, quickly returning to their attempts at slumber. Reese made eye contact with him and rose, taking her blanket with her as she approached him. She knelt down in the empty space beside him.

"Do you mind if I sleep here?"

Acton shook his head, his mind immediately wondering what Laura would have to say to that. Niner rolled over and gave him a quick grin and a wink as Reese lay down her blanket then snuggled in with him. He realized—or at least hoped—she was just terrified and was looking for comfort from the one person she had known the longest—an entire 48 hours. She was flirtatious, but even the most flirtatious woman wouldn't try something in a room filled with a dozen hostages.

Would they?

He hoped not. He had never been unfaithful to any woman in his life, and he wasn't about to start now. But she was pressed up slightly against his private bits, so he let his right leg roll toward the floor some more, leaving him mostly on his back—he preferring to sleep on his side—but at least he felt the situation was a little more platonic this way.

"Thanks," she whispered in the dark, her body trembling in genuine fear as the gunfire continued outside.

"Get some sleep," he said, closing his eyes and trying to shut out the racket from their captors. He had noticed some of them eyeing Reese earlier, their lust-filled stares mentally undressing the southern belle, the only other woman, the androgynous looking Chinese observer apparently not catching their eye.

No wonder she's terrified. She probably thinks she's going to be gang raped at any moment.

The gunfire died quickly when someone yelled at those outside, the words eliciting a few snickers from within the room, some of his fellow captives' Arabic better than his. Laura was the fluent Arabic speaker in the duo, his progressively getting better, but not good enough to understand a Sudanese dialect.

Reese seemed to sense his curiosity. "Someone told them to stop shooting otherwise they'd give their position away since no one else in town had anything to celebrate."

More snickers as the translation was heard.

"Let's just hope someone *is* out there to have witnessed the idiocy," commented the British observer whose name Acton had never heard. In fact, he had heard hardly any of the names of his companions and most seemed content to keep it that way, probably due to their "day jobs".

Murmurs of assent filled the room as Acton's thoughts drifted to Laura. She would know by now that the plane was missing, and with the message he had left her, which he could only hope she had received, they would know it was a hijacking and not a crash—even though that was how it ended. He had no idea how far off course they were. He assumed they would have stayed on course until they left Eritrean airspace, then after that they had been in the air less than an hour. He didn't know what the top speed of the Antonov was, but he had to assume it was around 500mph, which meant that in that hour they could have gone at least that distance.

"How far off course do you think we were?" he finally asked the room, his voice low, his head turned toward Niner.

"The cruising speed of an Antonov Ruslan is about eight-hundred kilometers per hour," came a whispered, heavily French accented voice.

"And they wouldn't have changed course until we were below radar," added one of the Italians, causing Acton's heart to leap in hope, realizing that very little of their journey was low to the ground.

"We have to assume they didn't change course until we leveled out after the decompression," added Niner.

"We travelled for no more than half an hour after that," said Lee Fang.

Acton sighed. "So we could be as much as four hundred kilometers away from where they'd start looking." He felt Reese push closer to him, her trembling obvious again.

"Assuming they've started looking, it could take days for them to find the wreck," said the British observer. "And that's assuming they're looking."

"Wh-why wouldn't they?" asked Reese, her voice trembling.

"This is the Sudan," replied the Brit. "If they know about the gold, they'll want it for themselves, so they could simply refuse to allow other search aircraft over their airspace and search themselves. If they don't know about the gold, I can't see any reason why the skies haven't been filled with search aircraft, especially with a carrier nearby."

"I could see them refusing the US military from participating," said Lee Fang. "Sudan isn't exactly on friendly terms with America."

A Russian accent responded. "America isn't exactly on friendly terms with most of the world."

"Shut the hell up, Rooskie!" snapped Niner. "If it wasn't for you and your buddies, we wouldn't be in this situation."

Acton had almost forgot that their two prisoners had been cut loose by the Sudanese and lumped in with the rest of them. It was clear from the lack of questioning that their new captors had no clue about the gold and seemed simply thrilled at the prospect of getting ransom for their release.

One of their captors threw open the door to the room. "No talking!" he screamed, then slammed the door again, leaving an uncomfortable silence for several moments.

"I'm really going to hate killing those guys," said Niner, his voice low.

"True," agreed the Brit. "They seem a lovely bunch of lads."

Somebody snickered and was joined by another and within moments the entire room was laughing including Reese, her shoulders shaking against Acton's chest. Somebody pounded on the wall, Arabic spat, and the moment of nervous tension breaking waned, the room quieting down as people adjusted themselves once again for sleep.

And with Reese's trembling gone, Acton was pleased to feel her rhythmic breathing beside him as he drifted off to sleep moments after her, wondering what Laura was doing this very second.

Westin Excelsior, Rome, Italy

Laura Palmer bolted upright in bed, looking about her hotel suite to see what had woken her. Light was lining the fringes of the blackout curtains indicating it was far later in the day than she had planned to awaken, and a glance at the alarm clock confirmed it.

7:03am

Grabbing her phone, she double-checked the time and noted that the alarm she had set on the phone had been turned off over an hour ago, something that was known to happen occasionally, especially if she was exhausted.

And she was—or at least had been.

A knock at the door and she leapt out of bed, grabbing her robe, realizing what had woken her in the first place. A quick look through the peephole and she smiled, recognizing four faces of men who just might be able to help her. A quick check to make sure she was decent and she unlocked then opened the door.

"Miss Palmer," said Red, nodding with a smile as she held out her arm, inviting them inside. Jimmy, Spock and Atlas followed, all shaking her hand, the massive Atlas' "ma'am" rumbling through her being, his voice impossibly deep.

She glanced up and down the hallway, seeing no one, then closed the door, locking it. She pointed to the living area of the suite, essentially a one-bedroom apartment with kitchenette, then knocked on the door to the adjoining room. "Hugh, we've got company!"

She heard a grumble from the other side, Reading having arrived around one in the morning. They had discussed the situation for some time before she realized she had no memory of the conversation ending. She blushed slightly as she realized she must have passed out and Reading had put her to bed then retired himself.

"Make yourselves at home, gentlemen. Feel free to order some breakfast if you haven't eaten. Your *vacation* is on me." She headed toward the bedroom. "I'm going to get washed up and dressed." She pointed toward the adjoining room. "And don't shoot whoever comes through that door, he's a friendly," she said with a wink.

Atlas laughed, as did the others, though they were easily drowned out by his foghorn.

Laura ran through the shower quickly, feeling completely safe for the first time in days. She trusted these men, though their introduction had been less than stellar. They had saved her life numerous times, as well as that of her fiancée, James, and she would be eternally grateful.

Dressing, she tied her still damp hair back in a ponytail then joined the others. "Good morning," greeted Reading, sitting in one of the easy chairs, the others spread about the room.

"Good morning," she replied, grabbing a cup of coffee from the kitchenette, somebody having brewed a pot while she was in the shower. "Where do we stand?"

Red, who she knew was Bravo Team's second-in-command, handed her an iPad with satellite photos. "These came in about an hour ago from a friend."

Laura's eyebrows narrowed as she noted the Russian Cyrillic writing. "Are these Russian?"

Red nodded. "Yes, from a specially tasked satellite."

"What do you mean?"

"It means that the Russians took one of their spy satellites and changed its course so that it would be over this location at this day and time."

"And what am I looking at?" To her it simply looked like a shot of pretty much anywhere in the world from tens of thousands of feet.

"Flip through them. They zoom in."

She flicked her finger across the screen, the next photo zooming in, each additional photo getting closer and closer to the ground. It soon became clear it was an arid area, then she gasped as the next photo appeared and she realized she was looking at an airstrip.

With the smoking wreckage of a large aircraft.

Her hand darted to her mouth as her eyes threatened to erupt with tears. "Oh my God," she gasped, dropping into the chair offered her by Atlas.

"Keep flipping," said Red, curiously not upset by this discovery.

She flipped through several more photos and then she stopped. "There's a second plane."

"Yes," agreed Red. "And if you notice, the smoke is coming from a broken off wing, not the main body of the Antonov the Professor and our guys were on."

"So…"

"These photos show the plane landed, though roughly, and that most likely those on board survived."

"How can you conclude that?" asked Reading.

"You don't fall out of the sky and land on a runway where your getaway plane is waiting for you."

Reading's head bobbed in agreement as he made eye contact with Laura, hope restored for both of them. Laura wiped her eyes dry with the back of her hands and handed the iPad back to Red. "So you think they're alive?"

"I think at least *some* people survived the crash. How many and who, I have no idea. We know BD is dead, but if there's any chance Niner and the Professor are alive, I think we have a duty to go in there and find out."

"I agree," said Laura. "What do you need from me?"

"I suggest another hundred grand be placed into the account I sent you just in case we need to do some real palm greasing or if we get ourselves into some real shit down there and need a fast extraction. The unexpected always costs more."

Laura nodded, sending an encrypted text to her banker to move the money as Red continued to brief her.

"We've already got a plane chartered that leaves in two hours. We'll be over Sudanese airspace in five hours on our way to Kenya. Over our target zone we'll do a HALO jump—"

"What's that?" interrupted Laura.

"High Altitude-Low Opening skydive," boomed Atlas. "Seriously fun shit."

"And dangerous," added Red. "By jumping from a high altitude our charter simply continues on its way as if nothing happened. By opening low, we minimize our time in the air so there's less chance of us being spotted."

"So what you're telling me is that we"—Laura motioned between herself and Reading—"aren't qualified to do that jump."

A series of flustered half words burst from Reading's mouth as he tried to figure out a dignified way of suggesting there was no bloody way in hell he'd even consider it, qualified or not.

He failed, ending with a "bah!"

Red shook his head. "No, I need you two to remain on board. You're going to Kenya. If the plane showed up with no passengers, it would look pretty suspicious. Once there, you'll establish satellite communications with us from your hotel—I've already booked the best for you and all of the equipment you'll need will be in your room waiting for you—and we'll keep you posted on our progress."

Laura pulled at her hair. "Why not just bring what we need with us?"

"You might be searched. I want nothing on board that might suggest a problem."

Reading leaned forward in his chair. "Won't they be suspicious when the flight manifest has six passengers and only two get off?"

"One of our guys back home will modify everything that's necessary once we're in the air."

"Seems like you've thought of everything," said Laura, impressed. "What about weapons?"

"Everything is already on the plane."

"What now?"

"You two pack, then we'll head to the airport using whatever method you normally would, get on our chartered plane, and leave Italian airspace as quickly as possible."

Laura stood, picking up the hotel phone. "I'll call for a stretch to meet us out front in fifteen minutes." She was about to make the call when she stopped. "Wait a minute." She turned to Red. "You said you got the satellite images from the Russians."

"From a contact there, yes. Definitely not through official channels."

"And they had to retask the satellite."

"Yes."

"And that's a big deal."

"Yes."

"So the Russians knew."

"Absolutely."

Laura felt her blood start to boil and could feel her cheeks burning red as she looked at Reading who appeared as equally pissed.

"Goddamned Russians!" finally erupted from her as she stormed into the bedroom, hammering the keys on the phone as if shoving pins into a Vladimir Putin doll.

POMPEII'S GHOSTS

Hamashkoraib, Sudan

Acton awoke with a gentle moan, giving Laura a squeeze as he rolled into her, wrapping his arms around her body. She moaned too and as he felt her lips press against his neck, he suddenly froze and opened his eyes.

Reese!

He pushed away and saw Reese staring at him with a smile on her face. "Good morning," she whispered, her flirtatious self back it seemed.

"Um, good morning." Acton completely extricated himself from her, sitting up on his blanket and saw most of the room was already awake, Niner and the Brit in one corner, both grinning at him. He gave them a look which had them both laughing at his expense as he stood. Still a gentleman, he offered Reese his hand and pulled her to her feet when she accepted.

"I hope they let us go to the bathroom soon," winced Reese as she danced from foot to foot.

Acton nodded in agreement, he too in desperate need of facilities.

"Here they come," whispered the Brit from the window he was standing near. The entire room went silent and Acton saw two men walk by the windows, looking in as they did so, their tough looks almost amateurish, these "men" barely boys by the standards of the soldiers in this room.

In a fair fight those bastards wouldn't stand a chance.

But the chances of a fair fight were slim to none, yet Acton wasn't worried. He knew they were worth more alive than dead. His only worries were for Reese being raped, and one or more of them being used as "examples" to force the ransom being paid.

"They're gone," whispered Niner from the other side of the window frame.

Acton walked over to Niner, Reese at his side. "Who would these guys contact to demand ransom?"

"My guess is they've sent somebody to the American embassy in Khartoum," said Reese. "They're probably assuming we're all Americans so they'd want to talk to somebody at the embassy and demand payment in exchange for our release."

"How much?" asked the Brit.

"Probably ten or twenty million, then they'll negotiate rapidly down."

"They better," muttered the Brit. "I've got about sixty quid in the bank, and my wife's probably already earmarked that for something more important than me."

"Laura will cover whatever it takes," said Acton. "Assuming she's brought into the loop."

"Wangari should be in Rome with her. *He'll* definitely be in the loop," said Reese.

Niner looked at her and frowned. "We need to tone you down and fast."

"What do you mean?"

"With all due respect, ma'am, you're too hot," replied Niner, causing Reese to blush. "We need you to stand out a lot less than you do now, otherwise one of the young gentlemen holding us might take a liking to you."

Reese blanched, her hand reaching out for Acton's arm and closing around it like a vice as she steadied herself.

"Suggestions?" asked Acton, taking over for Reese.

Lee Fang stepped over, removing her jacket, revealing a tight fitting black undershirt. Her small chest size compared to Reese would definitely not attract as much attention, but the exposure of that much skin might.

Acton shook his head. "No, you're at risk as well."

Lee Fang frowned. "I assure you I can take care of myself."

"I have no doubt you could one on one, hell, probably five on one. But there's at least a dozen of them, and they all have guns."

Lee nodded then put her jacket back on as the surviving French observer came over with his own jacket. He was small framed, slight, and when Reese slipped into the jacket, she smiled, it almost looking like a natural fit.

Lee pointed at the exposed neck. "You should button up your shirt and zip up the jacket. The less skin the better." She pointed at Reese's skirt. It's too bad we don't have pants for you."

One of the Italians threw his shirt over. "Tie this around your waist."

Reese smiled thankfully, wrapping the shirt around her and tying off the sleeves.

"My bigger concern is her hair," said Niner. "She's blonde in a brown and black world."

Reese reached up and tied her hair back with a tie she had removed from around her wrist. It helped, but not enough.

"We need a head scarf," said Acton. "Laura wears them all the time when she's on Middle Eastern digs. He looked about and his eyes settled on his blanket.

"She'll die from heat exhaustion if she wears that," said Lee, Reese nodding in concurrence. Lee removed her jacket again then removed her undershirt, leaving nothing but a sport bra and ripped abs to see as the room spun to give her privacy. She tossed the undershirt to Reese as she put her jacket back on, zipping it up.

Reese quickly fashioned a headdress out of it that covered her blonde locks, and with the shirt being plain black, it muted her beauty significantly. Lee dropped to the earthen floor, scraping some of the dirt up with her fingers, then lightly smeared it over Reese's face, neck, hands and exposed legs.

"Hopefully they won't find a dirty woman appealing," explained Lee as she finished up, spreading the remainder on her own exposed skin.

Acton wasn't sure, but being accustomed to seeing Laura covered in mud, dirt and sweat at dig sites, and finding her still irresistible, had him wondering if Lee had just made them both more attractive. Reese turned to look at him.

"What do you think?" she asked, twirling.

"Ugly as sin," he said, deadpan followed quickly with a wink.

"Perfect."

The door flew open and a big pot of rice was carried into the center of the room along with a bunch of flat bread and a bucket of water of questionable purity. The door was about to be closed when Acton stepped forward.

"Some of us need to go to the bathroom," he said, the Brit repeating it in Arabic.

The man nodded and left, returning a few minutes later with an empty bucket. He pointed at it. "You go there!"

Acton thought better of reminding the man that there were women present, and simply kept his mouth shut. He turned to the group. "I suggest we eat as much as we can, ration the water, and designate one corner the latrine. Perhaps we can figure out a way to hang some of the blankets for privacy."

Everyone nodded and the Frenchman took up position by the food, quickly counting out the flatbreads. "There's enough here for everyone to have at least one," he said. He found a ladle at the bottom of the bucket of water and used it to pour some water on his hands, washing them as best he could, then wiping them on his relatively clean shirt. "If no one minds, I'll serve?"

There were no objections and he soon began handing out the bread with a fistful of rice in the center. Within minutes they were all eating, the water bucket being handed around. Acton finished all he could eat and turned his attention to the ceiling. It was a simple design, corrugated steel nailed into wood framing, the entire guts exposed.

Leaving plenty of places to hang blankets from.

He pointed to one corner. "I suggest we make our latrine there. We can hang some blankets from the ceiling, and when needed, just empty it out the window. If they don't like it, they'll get the hint quick enough to give us a better option." He looked at Niner. "What's outside the window?"

"Just a back alleyway. I wouldn't be surprised if everyone dumps their shit out there."

"Good. Wanna give me a hand?"

Niner nodded. "It's a shit job, but someone has to do it."

Overlooking Hamashkoraib, Sudan

Dawson chowed down on another handful of Cap'n Crunch, took a swig of water, then popped a chunk of Jack Link's Sweet & Hot Beef Jerky into his mouth, chewing on one of his favorite high-protein snacks. The back of Camel Man's van had turned into a treasure trove of Western decadence from food to electronics. Pretty much everything except a working phone.

Though he did find a windup emergency charger and cable.

He had spent the better part of the morning taking a few minutes here and there to charge the phone he had found and it was now at a full charge. He had transferred the photos to a laptop he had found in the van—a brand new Dell XPS—and had used the built-in software to zoom in on the shots from last night. Using the light of day and the laptop, he had pinpointed the exact location of the celebrations and, using a telephoto lens adapter for the phone—one of those simple ones that just stuck on the phone—he had set up camp, sitting on the floor of the opened van, videotaping the houses in that area then playing the video back on the laptop for the larger screen.

Armed men were circling one house in groups of two, and he spotted three jeeps that looked damned familiar parked in a nearby alley. He had counted at least twelve distinct guards, but hadn't seen any of the hostages. He had no way of knowing for certain whether or not the hostages were even there, but why guard the building if they weren't? There were much more impressive houses in the city that he could see from his vantage point, suggesting anyone worth protecting would be in a finer abode than the hovel he was staking out.

He dragged his finger along the touchpad, backing up the video. He hit play again and saw a bucket being emptied out one of the windows of the house being guarded, arms briefly visible. Watching the same few seconds over and over, he couldn't tell if it was his mind playing tricks on him, wishful thinking, or whether what he thought he was seeing was real, but it appeared to him that the hands were white.

He pushed the notebook away in frustration.

There's no way to know from this distance.

He picked up the phone again and held it up, trying to get a steady shot of the house.

And cursed as he dropped the phone out of sight, too late.

Hamashkoraib, Sudan

Samir stretched hard, it having been a late night of celebration. As he surveyed the surroundings he froze, his eyes catching sight of something shiny on the surrounding hillside. *We're being watched!* His heart leapt into his throat and he immediately spun to warn the others, then stopped.

He took another look but the reflection was gone. If it was binoculars like he was thinking, then they might be aware he saw them. He leaned against the wall, fishing some khat out of his pocket and slowly began to chew. He had his head turned slightly away from the hillside, but his eyes never budged from their careful watch.

And still they saw nothing.

No reflections, no puffs of dust, no movement.

Nothing.

Which meant either there had been nothing there, or there was, and they knew they had been made.

And that meant checking it out would be dangerous.

He grinned.

Inwardly.

What better way to possibly eliminate some of my "partners"?

He turned and walked around to the front of the house, the hill now at his back, and entered. "Jalal! Abdul!" he shouted, "Come out front!"

He stepped back outside and waited for the two men, normally his rivals, whom he had been forced to partner with in this venture.

"What is it?" asked Jalal as he stepped outside, squinting, his eyes already red from a constant khat habit and too much alcohol the night before. Abdul didn't look much better, though he never partook in the drinking, his strict adherence to his Muslim faith forbidding it. Abdul had personally spoken to all of the hostages to make sure none were Muslim and in need of being set free. None were, thankfully, otherwise their payout might be less, and with three shares now involved, things were tight enough without giving away hostages for free.

"I think someone is watching us from the hillside," said Samir, motioning with his chin toward the hill behind the house.

Abdul rounded the corner, looking up at the hill. "What makes you say that?"

"Don't make it so obvious, you fool!" cried Samir.

Abdul spun on his heel and stormed toward Samir, anger etched across his face, his eyes narrowed in hatred. "How dare you call me a fool!"

Jalal stepped between the two nonchalantly, holding up a bottle of water to his lips and taking a long, drawn out swig, his arm raised high to block Samir's view of Abdul, and Abdul's of him. It gave Samir an opportunity to defuse the situation—the last thing he wanted was a confrontation here. He wanted it out on the hillside where there'd be no witnesses.

"I'm going to go check it out," he said, his voice calm. "I need more men, just in case. Which one of you will come with me?"

Jalal finished his drink. "Perhaps I should—"

"No!" interrupted Abdul. "I'll go." He yelled for his men to bring their vehicle around and Samir did the same, moments later the two vehicles arriving, Abit at the wheel of his Toyota.

"Where to?"

"The back road, up the hill. I saw something."

Abit nodded, flooring the gas as the two vehicles raced for the outskirts of town. Samir glanced back and could see Abdul's truck right on their tail, none too happy to be in the rear.

Samir leaned forward so no one would see his lips move. "Miss a shift."

Abit downshifted as they approached a rise, but instead of dropping to second, he dropped to fourth, gutting their momentum. Abdul's vehicle roared by, Abdul giving a satisfied sneer at Samir and his men, as if he were superior in some way.

"Okay, keep up with him, but not too close."

Abit nodded and they quickly sped up. Samir turned to talk to his four men in the back. "When we get there, everyone get out, pretend you're searching with them, then when they head for their vehicle, shoot them all."

Already khat-widened eyes nearly burst from their foreheads, fear written across their faces. Samir understood why. Abdul was a terrifying force in the town, and he had a lot of followers. But his death would scatter them to the wind, increase his cut from one third to one half, and eliminate a rival.

And it would all be blamed on whoever was hiding up here in the hills.

"Don't worry," he said, grinning. "We'll say they were ambushed."

This didn't seem to reassure the men, but as they were nearly at the location where he thought he had seen the reflection, he had no time for further handholding. He pointed to an outcropping of rock.

"Honk your horn."

Abit honked several times as Samir leaned out the window, pointing to the location. Abdul's vehicle jerked to the right then shuddered to a halt as his men jumped out. Abit pulled up behind them, Samir and the others jumping out.

"Spread out!" he ordered, his own weapon at the ready as he surveyed the area.

"Look!" shouted Abit, pointing at the ground. Samir looked and saw the distinct pattern of fresh tread marks in the dirt.

Someone was definitely here!

He felt the hair on the back of his neck rise as he realized there was genuine danger here and his plan, already underway, would only add to it. He turned and saw that Abdul and his men were all clustered together as they followed the tire tracks.

He raised his weapon, as did his men. His finger shook over the trigger and he felt its cool touch as he slowly squeezed. His men were looking back and forth between him and Abdul's group, he knew wondering why he hadn't opened fire.

Suddenly one of Abdul's men noticed what was going on and shouted, spinning around with his weapon raised at waist height.

"What the hell are you doing?" screamed Abdul as he raised his own handgun, pointing it at Samir. "You dare point your weapon at me?"

Samir's eyes darted to the ground, almost ashamed for not having the balls to take this golden opportunity to take out one of his enemies. He looked up. "I wasn't," he said, his voice a pathetic whisper. Which enraged him. *Why are you such a woman? Be a man!* "I wasn't!" he repeated, louder and with more authority, sounding much more like the badass he thought of himself as. "I was simply going to tell you that we should get back. I don't trust Jalal with the hostages alone."

Abdul lowered his weapon, albeit slightly. "I don't trust him either." He motioned to his men to return to their vehicle. "Let's go."

Suddenly a shot rang out and Abdul's eyes bulged in shock and pain, blood trickling from his mouth as he dropped to his knees. He raised his weapon toward Samir, his finger slowly squeezing on the trigger, a race taking place between how long the strength would remain in his hand and how long the oxygen would keep getting to his brain.

Samir fired, ending the competition, and in less than a second eleven weapons were firing, one taken out of the duel before it had even begun.

Leaving Samir to wonder who had fired the thirteenth weapon.

Overlooking Hamashkoraib, Sudan

Dawson sat behind a large group of rocks. He knew he had been made and cursed himself for it, but without the proper equipment such as anti-reflective binoculars, he had to take risks and make do with what he had at his disposal. Fortunately he had been prepared for this and first thing in the morning had scouted a fallback position.

His phone was propped up, hidden between two stones, giving him a full view of the area. He had moved the van from its original hiding place, farther back up the road, then swept clear the tire treads with some loose brush. He couldn't risk losing the vehicle or having it damaged by stray gunfire, and instead had decided to make his stand, should it be necessary, at the original location where he had been spotted.

All of his available weapons were laid out and fully loaded. He regretted having tossed the body armor yesterday, but at the time it had been the right decision, and going back to get it now was not. He was hoping for a small group and the element of surprise, along with his training, to even the odds considerably—part of him even hoped they would discover the van gone and return to the village, but he usually wasn't that lucky.

It didn't take long before the sounds of multiple engines had his hopes of a small party fading and minutes later two technicals rounded the bend and pulled up to where he had been parked earlier. A dozen men jumped out, spreading out to cover the area until someone noticed the tire treads. The first group gathered around their leader, pointing at the ground and how the treads led back to the road.

Which was when he noticed the second group, spread out, their leader raising his AK-47 and pointing it at the other group, his men following his lead moments later.

Now this could get interesting.

Somebody in the first group spotted the move and a showdown quickly ensued, guns and voices raised, but it was quickly put to rest, leaving Dawson frowning.

And unable to let the opportunity pass.

He took aim with his Beretta and squeezed off a single round, hitting the leader of the first group between the shoulder blades, he having little doubt the man's heart had just been pierced. His target dropped to his knees, and immediately the two groups opened fire on each other.

Dawson ducked down, smiling, as the herd he had to deal with thinned each other out, at this moment apparently none the wiser as to who had started the firefight. The distinctive sounds of the AK-47s echoed off the rock walls of the hills, the ground shaking as stray rounds tore into the hard soil, and as the number of weapons waned, the screams and shouts abated, he poked his head up to take another look. Only three were still standing, all from the second group, including their leader. The man walked over to the bodies of their enemy, kicking each, putting a bullet into the backs of two who still moved.

Then they ran to the vehicles, taking both, leaving nine bodies behind for nature to reclaim.

And if any of the three were to realize the firefight had been started by someone else, they might very well move the hostages.

Dawson grabbed his gear and sprinted toward his van's new hiding place, determined to get closer to town should it become necessary to follow them.

He just hoped they didn't take out their anger or fear on any of the hostages.

POMPEII'S GHOSTS

Over Hamashkoraib, Sudan

Red looked back at his men, all giving the thumbs up. They were on oxygen now, including the handpicked crew as well as Professor Palmer and Special Agent Reading. The luggage had been moved from the compartment they were now all huddled in and into the main cabin just in case some of it decided to join them on their HALO jump. With them now over the drop zone, the plane had been depressurized to allow the rear baggage door to be opened.

At the moment the plane, a Gulf-V, was at about thirty five thousand feet, it normally at over fifty thousand. They had reduced altitude with Air Traffic Control approval due to imaginary turbulence. Red turned to Reading, speaking to everyone through the comm built into the headgear they now wore.

"Remember, as soon as we're clear, close this door like I showed you, then tell the pilot he's 'a go'. He'll repressurize and return you to altitude. We'll contact you in three hours. That should give you time to get to your hotel where your equipment is ready. Understood?"

Reading nodded, giving a thumbs-up. "Understood!"

"Good, now double-check your harness!"

Reading yanked at the red harness hooked around his waist, then at the other end attached to the fuselage, and gave another thumbs-up. "Checked!"

"Opening rear-hatch now!" yelled Red as everyone grabbed onto something. The emergency systems to prevent exactly this had been bypassed as soon as they had reached altitude, so opening the door was relatively easy, and its design, to open inward, meant they weren't dealing with a door that might rip away from the fuselage if exposed to the outside stresses from the wind.

The massive portside engine roared at them, its intake only feet away, but essentially even with them so as not to be a risk at sucking them in. But only so by inches. Red positioned himself in the small doorway then signaled the pilot. "Ready for jump on your mark, over!"

The pilot's voice came over the comm. "Khartoum ATC, Gulf Five 329, request to climb to flight level five-zero-zero, over."

There was a pause as the pilot waited for a reply to his request to go to 50,000 feet. A burst of static and accented English was heard. "Gulf Five 329, Khartoum ATC. Climb to flight level five-zero-zero and maintain, over."

"Khartoum ATC, Gulf Five 329, climbing to flight level five-zero-zero, over." The comm squelched a couple of times then the pilot's voice was heard once again. "Powering down now, jump on my mark."

Red could hear the sound of the engines change, their high-pitched whine dropping slightly as the pilot slowed the aircraft as quickly as he could without losing altitude, the idea that their relative airspeed would drop on the radar as they pushed to climb, hopefully hiding the fact they were slowing down dramatically to make the jump safer.

Less than a minute passed before his voice returned. "Jump in five… four… three… two… one… Execute!"

Red stepped out from the doorway, the wind grabbing him and tossing him down the length of the fuselage without any contact being made, and in a split second he was clear of the aircraft, arching his back to gain control, his Heads-Up-Display showing his location and altitude, as well as the rest of his team as they cleared the aircraft.

"Jumper One away clean, over," he said, waiting for the replies of the others, it not always obvious during the start of a HALO jump whether or not the team had exited cleanly. One smack of the head against the fuselage and a man could be out cold or disoriented, a spinning blip on the display and a completely controlled blip looking identical.

"Jumper Two away clean, over," came Atlas' deep bass, the comm speakers not doing it justice.

Spock was next. "Jumper Three away clean, over."

There was a pause, a little longer than Red was expecting and he was about to prompt Jimmy when his voice finally burst through the silence. "Jumper Four's exit was a Charlie-Foxtrot but I'm feeling much better now, thank you."

Red shook his head with a smile. He could hear it in Jimmy's voice that he was more embarrassed than hurt, but he had to be certain. He moved his arms slightly and slowly turned enough for him to turn his helmet and see the other three jumpers above him, staggered about a mile apart each. He could see Jimmy was fine, though a little lower than Spock, suggesting he hadn't achieved his arch as quickly as he should.

"Jumper Four, confirm your status, over?"

"I'm fine, just caught my foot on the doorframe, sent me into a spin that took me a minute to recover from, over."

"Roger that. Everyone tighten up and follow me, over."

He turned back to face their target, a blip on his display below them as they dropped at over 100 miles per hour toward the ground in broad daylight. He would have preferred a night drop but that would have wasted at least twelve hours that they didn't have. If there were survivors, and they were being moved, their trail would go cold extremely quickly.

And that assumed they hadn't been taken on the second plane or simply murdered when they had hit the ground. Even if they had been shot, recovering their bodies was still something he felt was a necessity, especially after everything he had been through with BD and Niner. And even the professor.

"Jumper One, Jumper Three. I'm seeing ground activity, over."

Red activated the zoom on the HUD and spotted what Spock was talking about. The airfield was clearly visible below them, the crashed plane large on the enhanced display, but what looked like ants now were rapidly growing into humans, dozens if not more scrambling over the wreckage, along with a couple of dozen vehicles including transport trucks.

"Looks military to me," said Jimmy. "Must be the Sudanese."

"Looks like someone was hoping to collect some pay dirt," observed Atlas, "otherwise they'd have reported finding the aircraft."

Red had to agree. "If our people are down there, they're in Sudanese hands now unless they were moved."

"I'm not sure which I prefer." It was Spock who voiced all their concerns.

Suddenly Atlas pointed out the obvious. "The second plane is gone!"

"That's good," said Red. "That means the gold is almost definitely gone, so the Sudanese will have no reason to kill any survivors. They'll be able to claim it was a rescue mission." He surveyed the area surrounding their target. "Let's land north-west of the target so the sun is in their eyes." He glanced at his altimeter that was rapidly counting down to two thousand feet. "Deploy in three… two… one… Deploy!"

He pulled the cord, deploying his chute and felt his entire body jerk upward, the sensation merely an illusion as he was still dropping though far more slowly, terminal velocity no longer in the equation. He checked for a good chute then grabbed his toggles, orienting himself with his chosen landing zone. He looked around and found the others dangling under good chutes, all angling toward him.

His altimeter was already showing less than one thousand feet, still dropping rapidly though now at a survivable speed. A glance over his shoulder showed the airfield in the distance, far enough away that he hoped no one would spot them, but not too far so they wouldn't have to walk for several hours to get there.

His HUD beeped and he returned his attention to the ground as it rushed toward him. Flaring his chute, he killed his forward momentum and hit the ground, collapsing his knees and rolling onto his side. Quickly gaining his balance, he pulled in his chute as quickly as he could, it now too easy to spot. In less than a minute he was rushing toward their target, the others following him as they stripped off their jump gear. Dropping at the side of a low hill, they all began digging, burying their equipment. Red wasn't too concerned about it being found, as long as it was after they had departed. It was all civilian gear, none of it traceable.

"Everyone good?" he asked the others.

Nods and grunts from the rest confirmed their status as he pulled out his phone, launching the map application. He pointed out their heading. "We're about three klicks from the airport. Let's move!"

As they jumped to their feet, Red suddenly stopped, holding up his fist. He cocked an ear. "Weapons fire," he whispered as he tried to get a bearing on it.

Atlas pointed left of their intended destination by a good forty-five degrees. "Sounds like it's coming from over there."

Red zoomed in on the satellite shots of the area. "There's a town that way, but too far to hear gunfire from. There's a pretty shitty looking road though that goes around that hill. It splits off from the main road."

Jimmy was leaning in, eyeing the screen. "Looks like the main road is pretty shitty as well."

"If I were moving hostages, I'd take them in the back way," said Spock.

Red nodded. "We can't ignore it." He pointed to Atlas and Jimmy. "You two head for the airport, see if any of our people are there. We'll see if we can track down that gunfire."

They split off, Red and Spock sprinting toward what could be nothing, and with the looks of the hard landscape that surrounded them, possibly in the completely wrong direction.

And as they ran, a question nagged at him.

If the hijackers left on the other plane, then who has the survivors?

Part of him wanted to ease up, to head for the safer bet of the airport, it not making any sense that the survivors, if there were any, would be transported somewhere else.

Then a plausible explanation popped in his head, sending a surge of speed to his legs.

What if they escaped during the chaos after the crash?

POMPEII'S GHOSTS

Hamashkoraib, Sudan

Acton stepped out from behind the curtain, relief attained. Niner was at the window with the Brit, one on either side, continuing to observe the guards. There had been a commotion outside almost an hour ago and the sounds of at least two vehicles departing had been heard. What it meant, they had no idea, but the behavior of their guards had changed. The disciplined rounds they had been making had slowed then eventually stopped, with a group of them now huddled nearby, talking in whispers.

"Did he just say what I think he said?" asked the Brit.

Niner nodded. "I think so." He turned to the room, specifically Reese. "It looks like they're planning on taking the women."

Reese immediately paled, looking at Acton. The Chinese observer, Lee Fang showed no emotion, but Acton was sure she must be terrified at the prospect, the stories of what happened to women in this part of the world well known he was sure to all of them.

He just thanked God Laura wasn't here.

He held out his hand for Reese and she walked toward him, taking it. He put himself between her and the door. "We can't let this happen," he said.

"Agreed," said Niner. He pointed at Reese and Lee. "Get to the back corner." Lee moved reluctantly, her partner pushing her toward Reese and Acton who had already retreated behind the curtain. "We need two men on the door. Pull the first gun in, shut the door on the rest, disarm the first, and maybe we've got a fighting chance. Let them come in after we've got a weapon, take out as many as we can, and maybe we get lucky. If we can at least stall them until their leadership gets back, that might be enough."

"You're sure they're gone?" asked Acton.

Niner shook his head. "No, but when those vehicles left, the guys left behind immediately slacked off. I'm guessing whoever is here now doesn't hold any sway over them, or just doesn't care."

"Here they come," whispered the Brit, still at the window. The two Italians took up positions on either side of the door, the Frenchman and Niner on either wall, ready to pounce, the rest forming a human shield around the two women.

Acton was still holding Reese's hand, her grip viselike, her body shaking noticeably. The sound of the door being unlocked from the outside caused Reese to yelp. He glanced at her then positioned himself directly in front of her, using his free hand to gently move Lee Fang farther out of sight, the proud warrior not happy about having to be protected like this, but even her fierce demeanor seemed shaken, cooperating completely with Acton's attempt to shield her.

The door was kicked open, one of the guards stepping in boldly, grinning gums revealed as his AK-47 led the way into the room. The Italian behind the door reached forward, grabbing the butt of the rifle and shoving it toward the floor, the barrel flipping harmlessly toward the ceiling as he then proceeded to bear hug the man, pulling him back behind the door as the Frenchman rushed forward, shoving the door closed. The Brit stepped forward, wrenching the weapon from the startled man's hands then tossed it to Niner who immediately checked the weapon and dropped to a knee, aiming at the door.

The Italian let his arms slide up and within moments he had the man's head trapped in his arms, squeezing hard. He pushed the man's head down, knocked his feet out from under him, and the snap of the spine almost seemed to echo through the room. The Italian tossed the body into the corner as the Frenchman holding the door let it open. Shots erupted from the liberated AK-47, tearing new holes in the first two men through the door. The second Italian grabbed one of the bodies, yanking it through the door, liberating him of his weapon and tossing it to the Chinese observer who dropped and opened fire. Several shots were fired randomly into the room, most hitting the ceiling, others tearing through the wood door, then nothing, shouts of what Acton assumed were "Retreat!" filling the air.

The bodies were quickly pulled inside and disarmed then searched, several weapons and magazines liberated when the sound of vehicles arriving outside caused Acton to suddenly have hope.

Something hit the ground, rolling into the center of the room from outside. Acton's eyes immediately focused on it but for a moment his brain refused to accept what it was.

"Grenade!" yelled the Brit as he spun from the window. The Frenchman jumped forward, diving on the grenade, covering it with his body as the Brit did the same, landing squarely on top of the Frenchman. Acton spun, shoving Reese to the floor as Lee Fang's partner did the same to her, both men jumping on top of the women to protect them from the blast.

The delay was interminable, time slowing with the adrenaline rush, to the point where Acton began to wonder if it were a dud or if the idiot outside had forgotten to pull the pin. He turned his head to look at the human shield protecting them, his mind thinking they would be okay, when there was a muted explosion, both bodies lifting from the floor several inches, the dirt floor vibrating horribly.

Reese screamed in horror as the Brit rolled off the Frenchman, moaning in pain, but alive, at least for now.

The Frenchman however wasn't moving, and judging by the massive amount of blood spreading out from under him, he was mercifully dead.

Niner pointed at the bodies of their enemy. "We need to block the window!" One of the Italians and Niner grabbed the body of one of the dead captors and shoved him into the window frame, ass first, effectively blocking the window from any free throws from outside, but not a carefully pushed through weapon. The liberated weapons were trained on the door and the window as shouting outside erupted then suddenly silence.

"Americans!"

The voice was from the other side of the door. It sounded like it was a good distance from the now shredded wood, as if the owner didn't trust he wouldn't be shot.

He repeated his shout. "Americans! I want to talk!"

The Brit, still lying on his back, blood seeping through his shirt, turned his head to Niner. "I think he's talking to you, mate."

Niner frowned, approaching the door but staying out of the line of fire from both sides. "What do you want?"

"It's over! If you do not surrender, we will kill you all!"

Niner looked around the room, his eyebrows climbing slightly. "Are you the one in charge?"

"Yes."

"You don't seem to be."

There was a pause. "I was gone when my men attacked you."

"So you're *back* in control?"

"Yes."

Niner looked around the room, his eyes resting on Reese and Lee. "You know why we resisted?"

"Yes, they were after your women."

"And you guarantee their safety as a man of honor?" Niner shrugged as the words came out, his expression one of "worth a try".

"Yes, I swear to Allah himself."

"Are we seriously considering this?" asked one of the Italians, his voice a harsh whisper.

Niner shook his head, lowering his own voice. "They just have to toss one grenade against that door, then another half dozen will follow and we're all dead. Hopefully this guy takes his god seriously." He looked about. "I don't see that we have many options here, but I'm open to suggestions."

It was Reese that stepped forward. "I don't want anyone else dying because of me," she said, her voice cracking as her eyes darted between the pool of blood surrounding the dead Frenchman, and the wounds on the Brit. "No one."

"I agree," said Lee Fang, stepping out into the open once again. "No one should die because I am a woman."

Niner's head bobbed as he sucked in a breath, his admiration for their decision clear. "Very well." He raised his voice. "We're going to open the door and toss our weapons out!"

"Slowly!"

He removed a knife with a six inch blade he had liberated from one of their now dead captors and threw it, the blade burying itself in the dirt at Acton's feet. Niner motioned with his eyes at their makeshift bathroom and Acton knew what he meant. He picked up the knife and stepped behind the blanket, gouging a groove in the dirt floor with his boot then placing the knife in it. He kicked the dirt back over the knife then placed the bucket overtop. Stepping out from behind the screen he nodded to Niner, who then motioned toward the Italian still at the door. He opened it slowly, keeping to the side should anyone get trigger happy, and Niner tossed his weapon through, as did the others. Everyone stepped back against the walls.

"Okay, we're unarmed!"

Several of their hostage takers cautiously entered the room, their weapons held high as they nervously looked over everyone. Another strode in behind them that Acton recognized as one of the men giving orders the day before. A few bursts of Arabic from him had the bodies from both sides being dragged out, along with the weapons. He remained in the middle of the room with two of his men.

"We will be moving you in a few minutes."

"Why?" asked Niner, his tone curious but not challenging.

"There has been an incident. You are no longer safe here."

"Where are you taking us?"

"To a more secure location." The man left the room with his guards, leaving the hostages alone.

Niner shook his head. "A more secure location? That's all we need."

"I think things just went from bad to worse," said Acton. "Now what do we do?"

Niner looked out the window. "We keep our heads down, gather as much intel as we can, and hope that whoever has these guys scared is on our side."

Acton frowned. "Somehow I don't think we're that lucky."

Outside abandoned 250 Sudan Squadron Royal Air Force Airfield

Atlas was slower than the much lither Jimmy, so used to taking up the rear, but his cardio fitness was ridiculous, able to keep going and going like a juggernaut, and as he cleared a small rise he was surprised to almost trip over his partner.

Jimmy, sprawled across the sand of the next rise, was lying on his stomach, binoculars out. Atlas hit the dirt beside him, pulling out his own binoculars. He pushed himself up the hill a little more to get a clear line of sight of the airfield when he heard an engine roar and Jimmy yell, "Shit!"

Atlas pushed the binoculars against his eyes just as Jimmy began to roll away and his heart leapt into his throat as he saw the underbelly of a vehicle leaping over a dune mere feet away. He dropped his binoculars and rolled to his left, away from Jimmy and the path of the oncoming vehicle. Drawing his Glock he kept rolling, spotting Jimmy doing the same. The vehicle continued to roar toward them and Atlas realized after finally having a chance to think that through the binoculars it appeared like it was right on top of them. In reality it was still a good hundred yards away but closing fast, giving them time to prepare.

"Suppressors!" he yelled as he pulled the "silencer" from one of his pockets, screwing it into the barrel. Suddenly the vehicle crested the rise they were on. Atlas pushed to his knee, aimed and squeezed off several rounds, taking out the passenger seat occupant and two men in the back on the passenger side. The vehicle stalled out as the driver's dead foot slipped off the gas, Jimmy having finished off the other side.

Atlas leapt forward, his weapon still trained on the vehicle and spotted Jimmy approaching from the other side. He adjusted his position so Jimmy wouldn't be in his line of fire in case he had to shoot, and within moments they had confirmed everyone was dead.

"That probably wasn't a good move," observed Jimmy. "These are Sudanese regulars."

Atlas turned and trained his binoculars on the airfield and shook his head as he saw somebody staring back at him, directing men to their vehicles. "You know it was going to be them or us. They hadn't reported the find up to the point we jumped which means they don't want anyone to know. There was no way they were going to let us live." He dropped his binoculars around his neck and began yanking bodies out of the jeep. "Besides, we're about to have company within a few minutes."

Jimmy had already cleared his side of the vehicle, jumping in the driver's seat and restarting the vehicle. The engine roared to life and Atlas jumped in, the shocks sinking noticeably on his side. Jimmy gunned the motor and popped the clutch, sending them racing forward. He slowed and turned right, heading north-east to where Red and Spock should be and soon gained hard ground which eliminated their dust trail. He poured on the speed as they travelled behind a berm, blocking their view from the Sudanese. But that didn't seem to stop the Sudanese from firing blindly, their intentions no longer in doubt.

Atlas activated his comm.

"Bravo Two, this is Bravo Seven. We're coming in hot. ETA your position five minutes, over."

POMPEII'S GHOSTS

al-Sadiq Compound, Hamashkoraib, Sudan

The small convoy of half a dozen vehicles pulled up to the gates of Ali al-Sadiq's compound at the northern edge of town, it the largest of all the houses in the area. A ten foot high wall surrounded the entire complex, easily a couple of acres in size, guard towers spaced every sixty feet with lights that would flood the entire area at night every ten feet along the wall.

It was the most secure house Samir knew of, and if al-Sadiq would grant them asylum, they would be protected against Abdul's men, who he knew were coming after them in force, Jalal not believing the story of what had happened, instead fleeing with his men to tell of Abdul's murder. Fortunately al-Sadiq and Abdul were never friends, and in fact were sworn enemies, which played in Samir's favor. He had sent a messenger ahead to explain the situation and this was the moment of truth.

Would the gates open for them?

Samir's vehicle came to a stop in front of the massive metal gates, still closed. He could see guards inside, glaring at him, their weapons held tight as if they were expecting to use them at any moment.

Samir stepped out. "I am Samir. I sent someone ahead to speak to the great Ali al-Sadiq. Will he grant us entry?"

There was a pause, no response given, then suddenly someone barked some orders from the house in the distance and two men jumped forward, slinging their weapons. They unlocked the gate then pulled it open, another man urging the convoy forward, pointing to where they should park. Within two minutes they were all safely inside, the gates closed, and for the first time since an unknown gunman had shot Abdul in the back, he actually felt safe.

Now as long as al-Sadiq doesn't kill me, we should be okay.

As he stepped out of his vehicle he saw Ali al-Sadiq himself step out onto the stone entranceway, his arms held out wide, his face occupied by a magnanimous smile, leaving Samir wondering just what the man had up his sleeve. Samir plastered his own smile on, tossing his weapon to one of his men, not daring to approach their host armed. The two men embraced and Ali led him inside after the customary pleasantries of their culture were exchanged.

Ali motioned to a chair, one more comfortable than anything Samir had sat in his entire life, then took his own seat, an opulent affair that appeared gold plated yet plush.

"What is it you have brought me, Samir? Hostages?"

"*Western* hostages, from a plane crash at the old airport."

Ali's head bobbed, a smile on his face as his eyes drifted skyward. "I suspected something was happening when the first plane arrived, then knew it after the second. I had figured that whatever there was of value had left on the first plane, but you have proven me wrong." He leaned toward Samir, jabbing the space between them with a cigar. "And I don't like to be wrong."

Samir felt himself begin to go slack when suddenly Ali laughed, tossing his head back. "You should see your face, my friend!" He batted the air. "Don't worry. You proved me wrong and yet brought me the prize. What was your plan?"

"I sent a man to the American embassy in Khartoum. I have asked for twenty million American dollars for their release."

Ali nodded, his lips shoved out. "A good starting number. It shows we are serious, that we know what we have. We shall of course negotiate down, perhaps to a couple of hundred thousand dollars, something that private money can easily raise." He paused, looking back at Samir. "And just what cut am *I* expected to receive?"

Samir's eyes darted around the room, a room filled with more opulence than he could have ever imagined before this moment, and spat out a word he immediately regretted. "Half."

Ali roared with laughter, repeating the offer again and again, laughing louder each time.

Then he stopped, all congeniality wiped from his face as he rose and pointed at Samir.

"You bring me these hostages because you killed Abdul, making an enemy of his men."

"I didn't kill—"

Ali's finger jabbed upward. "Wait! I do not need to hear your lies." He glared at Samir who bit his tongue, keeping his mouth shut. "Now you expect me to defend you and your men, for you would surely die if you faced Abdul's forces alone. And you offer me fifty percent?" He wagged his finger. "How do you expect me to feel about such an offer?"

Samir decided a hint of honesty with a healthy dose of obvious bullshit and contrition was needed. "I would be insulted, sir. What I meant to say was that half would be far less than you deserve for offering us your hospitality and protection." Samir paused, searching for a new figure, then smiled. "Perhaps you had a figure in mind?"

Ali smiled, sitting back in his chair. "Ninety percent." Samir's jaw dropped and before he could make his instinctive protest, his life was saved by Ali's finger rising once more to silence him. "And in addition to the ten percent you will get to keep, I also offer you your life. For it would be far easier for me to simply kill you now and toss your body out the gate for Adbul's men to tear apart, but I've always liked you Samir. You try hard, you have big dreams, but you just never seem to succeed, almost always late for the big score.

"But today you have impressed me. Greatly. It took courage to do what you did. And to kill Abdul for his share? I never thought you had it in you." Ali rose and extended his hand to Samir. Samir jumped up, taking the man's hand in his. "You have earned my respect, which has earned you your life. Do you accept it?"

Samir's head rapidly bobbed up and down, his eyes wide, as he realized that the thirteenth shooter had just saved his life, whoever he was.

POMPEII'S GHOSTS

Outside Hamashkoraib, Sudan

Gunfire in the distance had Dawson pausing outside of the van. He slowly turned, his trained ear trying to determine the direction. He stopped then raised his phone, zooming in, slowly scanning the landscape toward the airport. The abandoned station was out of sight, so if the firefight was at the airport, he wouldn't be able to see it. He saw some puffs of dust in the distance, but could make out little, the display simply too small.

Suddenly he saw two figures crest a rise then disappear again. He steadied the phone on the hood of the van and took a rapid series of shots as the two figures popped into view again. He zoomed in on the shots and saw two men in desert gear, civilian camo pattern, not military, hoofing it hard.

And if he didn't know any better, the man on the right was Red, the shaved dome obvious.

But he couldn't be sure, and he couldn't wait. Going to pick them up then returning here would take too long, and he needed to see where the hostages were going to be moved.

But if it were his men, he couldn't leave them hanging.

He found a good set of tire tracks, drew an arrow in the sand then wrote 'BD' beside it. Then, jumping in the van, he spun the wheels, generating a large cloud of dust that he knew any of his men would spot and zero in on. And if they didn't find his message, then they weren't his men.

If they were his men, he doubted they were here on a sanctioned mission. As he raced toward the town on the meager trail, his mind searched for an explanation and he could only come up with one.

Laura Palmer.

She'd have the money to put together a rescue mission, and she'd stop at nothing until she knew what had happened to Acton.

And if he knew Colonel Clancy, at least some of his men would have been granted some time off.

Please let my little fantasy be reality!

He slowed to a halt, easing on the brakes so as not to create a cloud of dust, hiding the vehicle behind some rocks much closer to town this time, but still a good enough distance that he should be able to outrun any pursuit launched against him.

He climbed out of the van and looked down upon the town. From this vantage point he could see clearly enough without the phone's zoom lens to see several vehicles leaving the house the hostages had been held in until a few moments ago. He held up the phone, recording their progress until they arrived at a huge complex to the north of the town. He took several snaps of the new location, frowning as he saw the fortifications and the dozens of men manning the walls.

Things just became a whole lot harder.

al-Sadiq Compound, Hamashkoraib, Sudan

Acton stumbled forward, one of the guards having shoved him hard from behind. Niner caught him before he could hit the floor and redirected him to an upward position before letting go. Acton spun, glaring at the man who simply raised his weapon at him and mouthed what he assumed were Arabic expletives at him.

One of the guards, provided by their new captor, grabbed Lee Fang by the arm and dragged her toward the door, another reaching for Reese who jumped back, avoiding the man's grasp. Acton stepped forward, placing his body between Reese and the others as the Brit, still weakened from his wounds, his arm around one of the Italians, lurched forward.

"Leave the women alone, you bloody bastards!"

Two shots rang out and the Brit hit the ground, silent, still. Reese cried out, trying to shove past Acton as all weapons were trained on the men who began to back off. Acton grabbed Reese by the wrist and Niner came up behind her, grabbing the back of her skirt, which Acton thought odd.

Then the Delta operator slipped the knife Acton had hidden earlier in their makeshift latrine into the elastic band of the skirt, letting the blade slide down, the hilt catching on the waistline. He then pulled her donated jacket out to cover the knife, letting go of her arm. To her credit she had managed to keep the startled expression on her face to a minimum, and she nodded her okay to Acton as he let go of her arm, there no longer any option.

As the two women were led out the door, the guards backed out with them, closing then locking the door. Niner stuck his head up to the small barred window. "I want to talk to the man who was in charge before we got here!" he yelled. "We had a deal!"

A gun poked through the bars, the barrel jabbing Niner on the forehead. He stepped back, wincing slightly, then glared through the bars for a moment before turning away.

As the guards retreated down the hall, Reese whimpering the entire way, Lee Fang silent, the entire room turned somber as the Brit's body still occupied the center of their cell, and two of their own had been taken, most likely to be raped.

"If we don't find a way out soon, it will be too late for them," said Niner, the room nodding its agreement.

"But how?" asked Acton, the only one voicing the obvious.

"Next time that door opens, we take out the guards and advance rather than hold." He looked around the room. "Agreed?"

A chorus of "Agreed" endorsed the plan.

A plan that would most likely get them all killed.

Overlooking Hamashkoraib, Sudan

"There!" shouted Red, pointing to some markings on the dirt as he and Spock came to a halt. "I'm pretty sure this is where that dust was tossed up," he said, kneeling down and examining the tread marks. He pointed to several deep grooves where tires had spun, then the dispersal pattern from the drive wheels. "This is definitely it."

Spock surveyed the area then suddenly strode to the left of where the vehicle would have been. "Look!" he exclaimed, dropping to a knee and waving Red over. "He's alive!"

"Who?" Red rounded his friend and his jaw dropped. Next to a tread mark was an arrow with the letters BD scratched into the dirt. And there was no doubting what it meant.

Big Dog is alive!

Red stood, pointing at the message. "Take photos then get rid of it. Make sure you get the tread, he obviously wants us to follow it."

Spock nodded, pulling out his phone and taking a series of shots as Red activated his comm. "Bravo Seven, Bravo Two. Good news, we've confirmed BD is alive, over."

"Bravo Two, Bravo Seven. I never believed he was dead." There was a pause for a moment as Spock wiped away the message with his boot, then a burst of static. "We should be on your asses in less than sixty seconds by my estimate. Prepare to jump in, this vehicle doesn't make stops, over!"

"Roger that, we'll be ready, out."

Red motioned with his head for Spock to get on the other side of the trail they had discovered and within moments they could hear an engine battling up the rise then the hood of a Toyota technical rounded the corner with Jimmy at the wheel, Atlas riding shot gun. Jimmy skidded to a halt as Red and Spock swung into the back, then hammered on the gas, regaining their lost momentum in seconds.

"Status?"

Atlas turned to Red, sliding the window open between the cabin and the truck bed. "They're about five minutes behind us, we figure. We need to ditch this vehicle and lose them. I'm thinking in town." Atlas looked between Red and Spock. "And where the hell is BD?"

"He's somewhere ahead of us. We've got his tire tracks on camera, but just follow this trail for now. If we see an opportunity to ditch and evade, we'll take it. Until then let's keep after BD."

"Roger that!" yelled Jimmy from the front.

"Stop!" yelled Spock, pointing toward a group of rocks. Jimmy's training told him to listen without asking questions and he hammered on the brakes, bringing them to a sliding halt, ABS a future feature for this vehicle.

"What is it?" asked Atlas.

"Back us up behind those rocks, quick!" yelled Red, having already spotted what Spock had, and knowing exactly what he was thinking. As Jimmy gunned them in reverse and off the path, he too saw what the others had and cranked the wheel, positioning them beside the find.

They all jumped out and eyed the nine bodies lying freshly shot on the ground.

"How long you figure?" asked Atlas.

"Today for sure," replied Spock as he felt the skin on one of the corpses.

"What are you thinking?" asked Jimmy.

Red pointed at the downslope in front of them. "That looks pretty smooth. Do you think you can jury rig her to drive down that on her own?"

Jimmy nodded with a grin. "Absolutely."

"Get to it."

Jimmy dove into the cab as Red pointed to some jerry cans in the back of the truck. "Check if those have gas in them. If they do, fill the back with a good layer. We want this seen for miles."

Atlas swung into the back as Red grabbed the legs of one of the corpses. "One in the passenger seat, one in the driver seat," he said as Spock grabbed the man under the shoulders. "Let's have them thinking they caught you guys, at least for a few minutes. That should give us time to hoof it out of here a good distance."

"I like the way you think," grunted Spock as he lifted the dead weight.

"Yeah, exactly like you."

"Got gas," said Atlas, the chug-chug already filling their ears and nostrils as the flammable liquid was spread across the bed of the truck. Red and Spock shoved the body in the passenger side, Jimmy reaching over and pulling off the man's belt, jury-rigging the steering wheel.

They grabbed another body as Atlas jumped down, his job done. The engine roared to life, and Jimmy climbed out, making room for the second body.

"You ready?" asked Red.

Jimmy nodded.

Red pointed to Atlas. "Light it."

Atlas tossed a match and with a whoosh the entire back end of the truck erupted in flames, black smoke rising. Jimmy leaned in and yanked a pry bar out that was holding in the clutch, then jumped back. The truck lurched forward but didn't stall, instead picking up speed as the engine roared in protest, demanding to be shifted to a higher gear, its protests ignored by the corpse at the wheel. They watched the Toyota speed down the hill, a thick trail of smoke in its wake, then quickly dragged the remaining bodies out of sight.

"Now let's get the hell out of here," said Red, pointing at the road. "That's BD's tread mark right there."

The four of them sprinted down the trail, the slight downgrade as it sloped into town helping dramatically, and as they came around a bend, they were able to look over their left shoulders and see their handiwork continue to rush down the hill and out into the flatland beyond, and in the distance, a convoy of Sudanese vehicles broke off the trail, taking the bait.

"Yee haw," muttered Atlas under his breath. "How much farther to this town?"

Red held up his phone, looking at the map. "About five klicks. But I'm thinking BD is holed up somewhere a lot closer than that."

"And you'd be right!" shouted a voice from behind them.

Red skidded to a halt, spinning around to confirm what his ears had already told him. A huge grin broke out on his face as he saw his best friend leaning against a large rock, a smile on his face as he held a Beretta on them.

"Bang, bang, bang, bang," said Dawson, as he pretended to shoot each of them. "You need to learn how to run much quieter."

His men surrounded him, hugs, back thumps, fist bumps and every other form of greeting known to men of combat being exchanged. Red couldn't remember the last time he had been so happy to see anyone. As things settled down, Dawson had them follow him around the rock.

"What the hell is this?" asked Spock, his eyebrow climbing his forehead. "Here we thought you were dead, and instead you've got wheels, computers, the works!"

Dawson laughed. "Not quite the works, but I got lucky. I'll explain later." Suddenly he was serious. "Sit rep?"

Red gave him the run down on what they knew so far, Dawson updating them from his side. He pointed at the comm gear. "We better get a sit rep in to the Professor so it can be passed on. With the Sudanese on our tails, we need them to know the world knows."

"Roger that," said Red, activating the comm.

Nairobi Serena Hotel, Nairobi, Kenya

Laura Palmer lay on one of the two double beds, Reading the other, both splayed out, basking in the minimum amount of clothing dignity would allow, a ceiling fan and fantastic air conditioning helping with the cool down. Reading was snoring, sometimes gently, sometimes fiercely, but Laura was too wired to let herself drift.

And she couldn't stop checking the comm gear set up on the table nearby, all the equipment that had been promised in place when they had arrived an hour ago.

Something squawked.

Reading bolted upright in bed. "What the bloody hell was that?"

Laura was already rushing toward the table, grabbing the nearest headgear and putting it on. She grabbed the mic as Reading put his own gear on.

"Dragon Fish, Bravo Two, come in, over."

Laura grinned at Reading then keyed her mic. "Bravo Two, this is Dragon Fish, go ahead, over."

"Dragon Fish, Bravo Two. Are you ready to receive sit rep, over?"

Reading held up his pen, the pad already in front of him.

"Roger that, go ahead, over."

"Sit rep is as follows. We have found Bravo One, he is unharmed. Approximately one dozen survived the crash including Bravo One-One and Juliett-Alfa. They have been taken by local hostiles and are currently held in a large walled compound to the north of the town of Hamashkoraib. Sudan regulars were at the airport and are now in pursuit of us. We have lost them for the moment. The gold was transported by the hijackers, a group of

Russians, on a pre-positioned Shaanxi Y-8 that left about fifteen minutes after the initial crash. Bravo One said he recognized one of the hijackers as ex-Spetsnaz.

"Here are your instructions. One. Contact whoever is necessary to make sure the Sudanese know that we know they found the wreck, that the gold is gone and they didn't take it, and that we expect their cooperation in rescuing the hostages. Don't tell them where the hostages are, they're liable to get them killed. Two. Use the number I gave you to contact Bravo One-Two. Give him the plane type and have him track it. Got that, over?"

Reading nodded.

"Affirmative, over," replied Laura.

"Good. We will contact you again in three hours. Bravo Two, out."

Laura pulled the comm gear off and leaned forward, dropping her head on the table as she slowly sobbed in relief.

James is alive!

al-Sadiq Compound, Hamashkoraib, Sudan

Samir stood alone in the shadows at the rear of the compound. It was quiet, dinner having finished an hour ago, his few men milling about, chewing their khat and wondering what was next. He hadn't told them that his share had been reduced to ten percent, meaning the benefit they might gain could be minimal. Then again, if they did receive one hundred thousand dollars or more like Ali had suggested, his share would be several thousand for sure.

At least he assumed so.

Any math beyond what could be done on his fingers and toes was beyond him. It was times like these that had him questioning his father's strict Muslim upbringing, calling education a Western scourge, he having survived with no education whatsoever, so why should his children need any.

His mother disagreed, but never dared contradict her husband. It was only when he would leave for the day to work another more educated man's fields would she gather the children around and try to teach them to read and write.

He had failed miserably, treating his mother with little respect and threatening to tell Father if she should try to force him.

I was a little shit.

His parents were dead now from some disease and his two sisters had left for Khartoum years ago and he had never heard from them since. It didn't surprise him—he had never treated them with respect either. He saw how some of the townsfolk were with each other, big families, big gatherings, happiness. Husbands and wives, brothers and sisters, all getting along.

That wasn't his family, nor was it that of his men. All were essentially outcasts with no one to go home to. They were each other's families. They were his brothers. And they deserved more than what he was going to be getting them.

If anything.

Samir had a sinking feeling that he would be dead before the sun rose tomorrow. If Abdul's men did indeed arrive and demand he be handed over, Ali might just do it. Samir was of zero worth to him now that he had the hostages under his own lock and key.

What a fool I was to come here!

But it had been his only choice. Abdul's men were too numerous for his small cadre to take on alone.

But who shot him?

He was pretty sure that was a question he'd go to his grave having no answer to.

Footsteps behind him had him spinning. One of Ali's men walked up to him. "The prisoners are demanding to see you," he said. "Shut them up." The man pointed to a doorway a dozen yards away. "Down the stairs, straight through two sets of doors, the room at the end."

Samir nodded and hurried off, glad to be useful for the first time since he arrived. If he could do this, if he could keep the prisoners quiet, Ali might see some value in keeping him around.

Night suddenly turned into day as every light on the compound turned on. Shouts could be heard as guards rushed toward the front of the complex along with the sounds of engines revving as what he was certain was Abdul's men arrived, seeking revenge.

Samir decided the best place for him was out of sight, so he continued on task, descending the stairs and through the first of two heavy metal doors, the guards manning them nodding as he passed. He heard a woman cry out that sounded American and he paused. Stepping back a few paces, he looked through the small barred window and gasped. The Asian looking woman was naked, tied onto a table by the wrists at one end, her legs dangling over the other edge of the table, one of Ali's men undoing his belt, a lecherous leer on his face as his tongue flicked in and out of his mouth in anticipation.

In the far corner the blonde American was huddled, her hands over her head, trying to protect herself from what was happening, the two men paying her no mind at the moment, more interested in their prize already laid out for them.

He had to admit he felt a stirring in his own loins, a naked woman something he could count on three fingers the number of times he had seen one. And this one was far more attractive than the cows he had paid to be with.

But he had never raped a woman, nor would he. Pay? Yes. Why not? But rape? No. Real men didn't rape, no matter what the reason. He had made a commitment to that Asian man that their women wouldn't be touched, and he was a man of his word. Usually. He had given Abdul his word, which was why he had hesitated to shoot the man.

Who fired that damned shot?

He opened the door, stepping into the room unarmed, and grabbed the man about to rape the Asian woman by the shoulder, yanking him back. "What do you think you're doing?" he yelled. "These women are under my protection! If you soil them they won't be worth anything!"

"Go mind your own business, coward!" yelled the man, wrenching himself free and returning his attention to his target. Samir grabbed him again but this time the man shoved him back toward the door in a rage, turning to face him as he put his wagging member back in his pants. The other guard simply turned toward Samir and pumped two rounds of lead into his stomach.

Samir grabbed his stomach, immediately feeling the warm fluid rush over his hands as he bled out, slipping down the door as he quickly weakened.

Then a scream of rage brought him back to his senses. The blonde woman erupted from the corner, a knife held high in her hand. She plunged it into the shooter's back, yanking the blade out as the man dropped to his knees, then thrust forward, burying the blade deep into the second man's kidney as he turned to retrieve his gun, now sitting in the corner of the room.

She pulled the knife from the would-be rapist then with a flurry stabbed the shooter at least a dozen more times in the back, the frenzied attack bringing him down hard, then finally silencing his cries. The rapist was crawling toward his gun. The blonde woman, now covered in blood, leapt like a tiger onto his back. She raised the knife high, two handed, then plunged it down, the blade sinking to the hilt, probably piercing the man's heart as he stopped moving almost instantly. She withdrew the knife and plunged it in again, over and over, screaming the entire time.

"Stop!"

She froze, the knife in mid-air, ready for its next blow. It was the Asian woman who had given the order.

"Cut me loose!"

The blonde woman jumped to her feet, quickly complying with the instruction, slicing the bonds holding the Asian woman's wrists to the table legs. The woman immediately sat up and looked about the room. In a corner sat a pile of clothing that she quickly donned, then, taking the knife from the blonde, she stepped toward Samir, dropped to one knee and jammed the knife deep into his throat, twisting the blade.

His head dropped onto his chest as she withdrew the blade and kicked his body aside. And as the last few coherent thoughts flashed through his dying brain, he realized he had led a life entirely wasted until now. He had saved these women, of that he was sure, and his death at their hands was a fitting justice for all he had done to this point.

His eyes closed for the last time and his lips murmured his last words.

"I'm sorry."

US Embassy, Khartoum, Sudan

Laura Palmer was sporting a female power suit that exuded wealth. It was a way she hated to dress, but found it very effective when dealing with bureaucrats, especially in the Third World. They respected money, power and penises. As a woman, she had plenty of the first, which gave her the second, and according to James, she had more balls than most men he knew.

And this evening all three were on display, Reading helping contribute to the third criteria. They had contacted Wangari immediately after hearing from Red and the IMF representative promised action but Laura had zero faith in the United Nations or the International Monetary Fund. Instead, since she knew James and the others were alive and definitely still in Sudan, they had checked out and flown to the Sudanese capital of Khartoum within the hour.

And now they sat at the US Embassy, in the ambassador's office with several aides and a Sudanese general, in full dress regalia, promising he knew nothing of what they were speaking of.

Reading was almost purple, ready to blow a gasket, and Laura's toe was tapping in concert with her knuckles on the arm of the chair she sat in. The ambassador was dancing around the issue in political-speak, getting nowhere.

Finally Laura blew, standing up and placing herself to the side of the ambassador's desk, perching on the corner and leaning toward the general.

"Do you know who I am?" she asked, her tone firm with a touch of rudeness and a soupcon of arrogance.

The man looked up at her with a pleasant expression as if he had been through these dances thousands of times before, and was quite content to do so another thousand times. "Yes. You are Professor Laura Palmer."

"It might interest you to know that I am quite wealthy."

"Extremely," interjected Reading. "Filthy rich, in fact."

"I was not aware of that," said the man, shifting in his seat as if she were suddenly of more interest than the public servant he was facing.

"Which means I have options available to me that the general public do not."

"Of course you would."

"Which means that I can take out an advertisement in every newspaper and magazine in the world describing either how the Sudanese government cooperated fully with the effort to retrieve the innocent victims of this hijacking, or of how they refused to cooperate."

The General opened his mouth and Laura held up her finger, Reading smirking in the background at this side of her she knew he had never seen, as few had.

"So here's what I'm going to do. *I* know *you* know that you found the plane crash site. *I* know *you* know that the gold is gone. Now here's what I'm going to *pretend* you don't know, so that you can thank me in a moment for being so helpful to your government. *I* know a second plane left with the gold and the hijackers aboard. *I* know that almost a dozen people survived that crash and were left behind. *I* know that locals—whether you want to call them rebels, militants, terrorists or just plain criminals, I don't care—but let's agree 'people not representative of your government', took these survivors to a nearby town. *I* know exactly where they are, and will inform you of that location when it is necessary." She paused, looking about the room then settling on the General. "Are we all clear on the facts so far?"

The man nodded, his lips pressed together tightly, clearly pissed at being spoken to in such a way, and probably more pissed that it was by a woman.

To hell with him and his sexist culture.

She knew very well that the way she was dressed would earn her forty lashes as a Sudanese woman under article 152 of the penal code. She could just imagine what would happen to a woman who dared to wear shorts and a t-shirt in public like she regularly did on her dig sites.

To his credit, however, the General did manage to hide his disdain, his position probably exposing him to all manner of Western women whether he liked it or not.

But he had nodded. Though not a verbal acknowledgement of what she said, it was an acknowledgement nonetheless.

"So, now that we've agreed on the facts, and I've informed you of several things that you were not aware of minutes before, I have no doubt that you will now want to cooperate fully in the international effort to retrieve these innocent United Nations representatives."

"Of course." The response was curt, clipped, almost forced. But she didn't care.

"Excellent. Here's what we will need to proceed."

Outside al-Sadiq Compound, Hamashkoraib, Sudan

"You wanted a diversion, I'd say you've got it," said Spock as they all watched the assault now taking place on the compound. About half a dozen technicals with fifties mounted in the rear were taking turns strafing the front of the compound while several dozen hostiles on foot had taken cover all along the street, firing at any target of opportunity that might pop their head up to take a shot.

And in classic amateur style, they had left the rear completely open for escape.

Or in this case, entry.

The lights were quickly being taken out by the attacking forces and several RPG's had hit the gate which was being heavily defended.

"Now or never," Dawson said, motioning for them to move forward. As they raced through the flatlands surrounding the north of the town, the sun behind them and low, they managed to close the distance in less than ten minutes, coming to a rest behind some heavy shrubbery. Dawson surveyed the situation once again, the sun now set behind them. "It looks like they've only got one guard in each of the towers, everyone else is up front. Let's take out the corner tower lights, wait sixty for him to tell his buddies he's okay, then take him out, enter over the wall, then find someone for a friendly chat. Questions?"

Four head shakes and they repositioned closer to the two-three corner outside the north-west of the compound. "Take out the lights," ordered Dawson. Atlas and Jimmy took aim with their suppressed Glocks, Atlas shooting from the left, Jimmy the right, eliminating the four lights in just as many shots, leaving the corner in near complete darkness.

Then they waited.

"Hasni, are you okay?" came the shout within seconds.

"Yeah, they just hit the lights!"

"Too bad Hasni's about to die," muttered Atlas. "Say goodbye, boys."

Dawson continued his mental countdown, listening for the chatter between the guard posts to stop. As predicted, it did with ten seconds to spare. He raised his own Glock with suppressor, provided by Red earlier. "Bye bye, Hasni." He fired, the body dropping to the floor of the guard tower.

They listened.

"It would appear nobody noticed," said Atlas. "Poor Hasni."

They rushed forward, Red tossing a rope with hook over the wall then holding it tight as Dawson then the others scaled the ten feet. Dawson swung over the lip then dropped to the ground below, immediately scanning their surroundings. As he turned he fired his weapon into the stomach of a surprised guard who had apparently been making rounds alone. As the man grabbed at his stomach Dawson raced forward, shoving his hand over the man's mouth and pushing him to the ground. Moments later the rest of the team was covering him.

Dawson looked down at the man, his face barely visible in the dark.

"Where are the hostages?"

The man shook his head. Dawson pushed his knee into the man's stomach. His muffled cry did nothing to hide the pain he was in.

"I'll ask *once* more. Where are the hostages?"

The man's eyes darted toward the back of the building. Dawson removed his hand, leaving about an inch of space should the man decide to cry out. "Through the door, down the stairs."

"Thank you." Dawson pistol whipped him into unconsciousness, the man at least now dying with no more pain, a stomach wound a hideous way to go. They reached the building unscathed, the firefight out front still intense, the light from fires now flickering across the entire area as grenades and RPGs continued to be exchanged. Dawson found the door and tried it.

Locked.

He pointed at the door and Jimmy placed a charge on the lock, blasting it with a small explosion that merely mixed in with the background noise as the door swung open. The lights were on inside revealing two guards at the bottom of the stairs. Two quick shots and both were out of the game as Dawson rushed down toward them. There were four doors, two on either side, all with small barred windows. He looked inside the first to his left and gasped.

Inside were at least a dozen women lying on the floor in near darkness. He slid the lock across and pushed open the door. The stench was unbelievable, clearly latrine facilities not provided.

"Oh my God!" gasped Jimmy as he stepped inside. "What the hell is this?"

"Slaves," boomed Atlas. "Modern day slaves."

Dawson felt his stomach hollow out as the women slid across the floor toward the back wall, clearly terrified. Dawson holstered his weapon, raising his hands. "Does anybody speak English?"

A girl, no older than ten, raised her hand, it shaking in fear. Dawson almost felt himself crack. "I do," came the whispered voice as gunfire continued to crackle outside.

Dawson knelt down. "My name is Burt. What's yours?"

"Aliya."

Dawson smiled at her. "That's a pretty name."

Her head dropped, but her wide eyes still met his.

"We are American soldiers. We are here to help you," said Dawson, praying to God he wasn't about to give these poor women false hope and just get them killed. "Do you understand?"

She cried out in Arabic what he had just said then leapt into his arms, hugging him as hard as he had ever been hugged as the other women, most just girls, rose and surrounded them, hugging the soldiers and thanking them.

"We've got three more cells just like this," said Red from behind him. "What the hell are we going to do, BD?"

"We can't leave them here," said Dawson as the mass of once hopeless women continued to surround him.

For the love of God we can't leave them here!

al-Sadiq Compound, Hamashkoraib, Sudan

"It's getting pretty intense out there," said Niner.

"I wonder whose attacking?" asked Acton.

Niner shrugged. "Dunno, but I don't think we can count on them being friendly."

Several bursts of gunfire outside their cell door silenced the room, everyone spreading to the sides and away from the line of fire. The bolt on the door slid aside and the door swung open. Acton tensed himself up, ready to leap into action, they having all agreed to fight the next time they had an opportunity.

When the person he least expected burst through the door.

"It's us!" cried Reese, covered in blood and dirt and still barefoot. She was quickly followed by Lee Fang who looked her usual stoic self, but her eyes revealed something different, and Acton prayed that she hadn't been raped.

"What the hell happened?" asked Niner as he stepped forward.

Reese tossed him the gun then pulled out the knife he had slipped her earlier. "I killed them!" she cried, clearly still wired from the adrenaline rush as she bounced around the room. "Me! Who would have thought? Little old me! Little old me!" Her eyes met Acton's and she threw herself in his arms, suddenly sobbing. He embraced her, patting her head as the realization of whatever horrors she had had to commit to escape sank in. That the alternative would have been far worse he had no doubt, but he said nothing, realizing words weren't what she needed right now.

The others said nothing, instead pulling the bodies of the guards inside and closing the door over as they assessed their newly acquired weapons.

POMPEII'S GHOSTS

They now had four AK-47s and half a dozen extra magazines, along with one well-used knife.

"Let's move out. We'll clear this level room by room," said Niner, taking point. The door was pulled aside and he stepped out in the hall, the entire group advancing, Niner covering the front while Lee Fang covered the rear, the Italians opening each cell door as they moved, all thankfully empty. At the end of the hall there was another door, and through that Acton knew were the stairs that led up to the rear of the compound, the same way they had been led in here. Unless one of these doors led to another set of stairs, it was the only way out he knew of.

The rooms cleared, Niner opened the door at the end of the hall, all four of their weapons now facing forward.

"Hold your fire!" he yelled, his fist shooting up in the air as he stood straight, a huge grin on his face. "We've got company!"

Acton couldn't see what was going on from his position at the back, Reese still clinging to him, but the joy in Niner's voice was obvious.

"We thought you were dead!" cried Niner.

And then Acton knew. It had to be Dawson. He pushed himself up on his toes and felt a sense of relief wash over him as he spotted several of the Bravo Team members on the other side of the door. He lowered his head and whispered in Reese's ear. "Everything's going to be okay now, help is here."

Red stepped through the crowd and tossed a satellite phone to Acton. "Speed dial #1," he winked. "Why don't you give them a sit rep?"

Acton's eyes narrowed and he held in the #1 button. It dialed.

"Hello?" asked the voice he would recognize no matter how bad the connection.

"Hi hon, it's me," he almost whispered, his voice cracking as the pressure of the past two days began to lift."

285

"James! Oh thank god you're alive!"

"We didn't all make it, I'm sorry to say, but Dawson and Niner are okay, and so am I. Reese is good along with four of the observers. We've also got two of the hijackers here. I'm afraid we took some casualties though."

"Where are you?" asked Reading's voice as Laura obviously switched them to speaker phone.

"Hi Hugh, good to hear your voice. We're still in the basement of the compound. We've cleared this level but there's a heavy gunfight happening outside." He looked down the hallway, through the doors, and saw the faces of scared women begin to appear in the hall from several of the rooms. "Oh my God," he whispered as he realized what they had stumbled upon.

"What is it?" asked Laura, her voice filled with concern.

"I think we just found a human trafficking ring." He felt Reese's fingers dig into his arm at his words as she witnessed her possible future. "We're going to need some serious help."

"Hold your position, we'll be there soon with the Sudanese army, ETA ten minutes," said Hugh.

Dawson saw Acton with the phone and smiled as he watched his friend speak to his fiancée. It made him want to call Maggie, which surprised him.

Maybe there's something real there after all?

Dawson stepped through the crowd toward Acton. "Situation?"

"They're on their way with the Sudanese army. ETA ten minutes."

Dawson wasn't sure he was overly happy with it being the Sudanese coming to the rescue, but at the moment he had no choice. "Very well," he said. He and Red pushed through the crowd and reached the steps, Niner with them. "What's the layout, Sergeant?"

"Half a dozen cells beyond the door, all empty save a few bodies including one of our own." He nodded toward the stairs. "This appears to be the only way in or out."

"Okay, then this is what we have to defend," replied Dawson. "Have all the civilians moved as far back as we can, into the rooms with the doors closed. We don't want anybody getting hit by strays. First line of defense will be upstairs at the door. Shoot anything that approaches. This is fallback position number one, the second set of doors is number two. If we lose that, we lose the fight." He motioned to Atlas and Jimmy. "You two take point."

Both men rushed up the stairs and took up position on either side of the door. Dawson followed them up and shattered the light bulb with his Glock sinking the entire stairwell into complete darkness. He peeked out the door, satisfied no one had yet discovered the true situation. The air was thick with smoke now, and his trained ear suggested there was gunfire being exchanged from within the compound now, the attackers apparently having broken through the gate.

Suddenly his comm squawked, as did the others.

"Bravo One, Defiant Leader. Identify your location, over."

Dawson's eyebrows popped as he activated his comm, Red punching him in the shoulder with joy. "Defiant Leader, Bravo One. Identify yourself, over."

"Bravo One, Defiant Leader. We are here courtesy Mr. Grey. ETA on your location in sixty seconds. Please identify location of friendlies, over."

Dawson sent a silent thank you to Colonel Clancy, aka Mr. Grey at times. "Defiant Leader, Bravo One. If it's above ground, it isn't friendly. We are in the basement of the compound. Be advised Sudanese regulars are approaching location along with at least one helicopter. I will try to get them to hold, over."

"Roger that, Bravo One. Keep your heads down until the rain stops, over!"

Dawson rushed down the stairs with the others, being near the above ground doors no longer a wise move. "Phone!" he yelled to Acton who turned and said something to whoever he was talking to then tossed it to him. Dawson caught it. "To whom am I speaking?"

"Laura Palmer and Special Agent Reading," replied the professor's excited voice.

"This is Dawson. Under no circumstances have the Sudanese enter this zone, I repeat, under no circumstances. I will contact you shortly." He ended the call and tossed the phone back to Red.

"Let's button this place up, the cavalry's arriving!"

POMPEII'S GHOSTS

Approaching al-Sadiq Compound, Hamashkoraib, Sudan

"He said to hold your troops!" yelled Laura, the General none too pleased to be given orders from some unknown on the ground.

"Look!" yelled Reading, pointing out the open side door of the chopper they were in with the American Ambassador and the General.

Laura gasped as at least a dozen helicopters raced toward them. Muzzle flashes lit up the area surrounding the compound, much of the main building on fire, the gate blown open but blocked by several destroyed technicals. The scene was utter chaos and as the General spotted the approaching strike force he yelled into his comm. Reading pointed below at a column of Sudanese military vehicles as they raced toward the firefight then suddenly stopped, several vehicles turning around, a hasty retreat underway.

Missiles streaked from the weapons pods of the helicopters, the guard towers ringing the compound erupting in flames. A series of rockets quickly eliminated much of the forces outside the compound, removing their cover within seconds, then turning the exposed hostiles into ground beef as their cannons opened up on the startled attackers.

From their vantage point through the open door it was like a movie screen, the horror almost lost at times as the action in the distance played itself out, dozens upon dozens dying, never seeing their attackers, and as the heavy resistance faded, several large Black Hawks positioned themselves over the compound, their cargo leaping out the sides as dozens of Marines slid down ropes.

As the troops split into coordinated teams, the compound was quickly subdued, the firefight moving into the large house. Gunfire continued to be heard, muzzle flashes lighting up the night through open windows, the occasional explosion as a grenade was tossed.

And then it was over.

They continued to hover as they watched the compound being secured, several of the choppers now landing.

"Look!" Laura pointed to the rear of the compound as a large group of people began to file out. "That must be them!" She turned to the General. "We need to land! Now!"

Acton stepped outside, the gunfire silent, the shouts of dozens of American soldiers and the thumping of helicopters filling their ears instead. He and Dawson led Reese toward the command chopper, a full-bird Colonel standing near it on his comm giving a situation report to somebody. As he saw them approach he ended his conversation.

"Mr. White, I presume?" he said to Dawson.

Dawson nodded. He motioned toward Reese. "This is Miss Reese. She's the ranking UN official."

"Glad you made it out of this alive," said the Colonel, nodding toward the large group of women that had been liberated. "All in all it looks like a lot of good was done here tonight."

"We lost a lot of good people," replied Reese, still covered in blood from head to toe, her story still a mystery to Acton. "Too many died, but every single one of them died a hero in my books."

"Agreed," said Acton. "There was one French soldier who threw himself on a grenade and saved us all. It was the most heroic thing I've ever seen. When we're situated I think we'd all like to make sure that those who died get some sort of special recognition from their governments for what they did."

The Colonel nodded. "You'll all be debriefed on the carrier."

Dawson pointed at the two Russians they had captured earlier. "Those two are hostiles, part of the team that hijacked our transport."

The Colonel pointed to two of his men. "You two! Take those two into custody!" he ordered, indicating the Russians. He motioned toward the freed sex slaves. "What are we going to do about them?"

"We take them with us, of course," replied Reese, her tone indicating how shocked she was at the question.

"It's not part of my mission parameters," said the Colonel, who held up a finger cutting off Reese before she could respond, *"however,* they are clearly victims in a hostile environment, and didn't you say one of them claimed to be American?"

Acton smiled. "Yeah, that was me. I can't remember which one though. And I had the distinct impression there may have been more than one."

The Colonel motioned to one of his men. "Some of those women might be American citizens. Load them all on the choppers and we'll sort it out on the carrier."

"Yes, sir!" The Lieutenant rushed off to coordinate the evacuation as Reese beamed her appreciation to the Colonel and then Acton, hugging him hard.

"Thank you!" she whispered in his ear.

"James!"

Acton spun around and saw Laura, dressed to the nines, and Reading jogging toward them. Acton let go of Reese, who seemed to not want to release her grip on him for a moment, then finally capitulated as he started to pull away. He ran over to the love of his life and grabbed her in his arms, picking her up over his head then kissing her hard. He had been sure he was going to die at so many points during this ordeal, he had almost written off any hope of seeing her again.

When their lips finally parted he stuck a hand out to greet Reading, who took his friend's hand in his and pumped hard, clearly relieved he was okay. Acton stepped back, still holding Laura. "What's with the outfit?"

"I had to play millionaire," she said, twirling with one hand over her head. "You like?"

"Very becoming," grinned Acton. "Anything I need to know?"

Reading laughed. "Only that she intimidated the medals right off a Sudanese general who wasn't cooperating."

"That's my girl!"

The Bravo Team members waved a greeting as they approached, Laura giving Niner and Dawson hugs, expressing her relief they were okay.

"In no small part thanks to you, I hear," said Dawson. "Red tells me you funded their little enterprise?"

She batted the words away with her hand. "It was nothing; I did what I had to do. It was you guys"—she nodded toward Red and the others—"that put together the plan and got the job done, and I thank you for it." She squeezed Acton by the waist again. "I have you to thank for getting him back for me."

"And Niner to thank once again for keeping me alive," added Acton with a slight bow to the man.

"Nothin' doin', Doc."

Several soldiers jogged up to them. "Please follow us, we're evacuating immediately."

Acton and the others followed and they were split into several groups, Acton, Laura, Reading and Reese, the four civilians, loaded onto one Black Hawk, it immediately lifting off. Acton looked down at the still smoldering compound and shook his head. He leaned back and closed his eyes as he wondered what had happened to the gold, and whether or not it would ever be recovered, and those responsible brought to justice.

"Why were you sorry?"

"Huh?" He opened his eyes and turned to look at Laura.

"In your message, you were cut off. You started to say you were sorry."

Acton had to think back on what he had said, then he suddenly remembered. "Oh!" He turned and took her hands in his, his finger rotating her engagement ring back and forth. "What I was going to say, was 'I'm sorry I didn't get to marry you'."

A smile spread across Laura's face as she leaned in to kiss him. After pressing her lips against his for several blissful seconds, her mouth migrated up his cheek to his ear.

"Perhaps we should take care of that sooner rather than later."

Rijeka, Croatia
Two days later

Major Anatoly Kaminski picked up one of the large gold bars, this one much heavier than its predecessor, the old gold being melted down and re-poured into standard 400 Troy ounce bars, over twelve kilos each, or twelve times as heavy as the ancient Roman bars were.

And these were stamped with nothing indicating their true origins. They would be spread around the world, sold at private dealers, cleaned through questionable banks and jewelers, with the proceeds going to fund Omega Team operations aimed at restoring the Soviet Union. A quarter was supposed to go back to the Eritrean generals that had allowed their mission to succeed, but Kaminski had been informed that part of the deal would never be honored, there no way the Eritreans would dare protest lest they lose the two billion the IMF and UN had agreed to pay.

He slowly turned the alluring metal, his own reflection now showing in its lustrous surface, when he paused. There was something on his chest. He dropped his chin and looked down to find a red dot bouncing up and down in the center of his shirt. His mouth opened wide as his head popped up to find the source.

But it was too late.

His chest tore open with a momentary, horrendous pain, then he dropped to the floor, dead.

Dawson moved his sight to the next target, squeezing the trigger as he cleared his zone of hostiles, the rest of the team doing the same. It hadn't been hard to find the Russians. They were able to pull the registration number off the Russian satellite photos, and eventually trace it back to Croatia, which wasn't a surprise. He knew they wouldn't take it anywhere near Russia, they wouldn't want it being traced back to them, but he also knew they had to take it somewhere fairly civilized, but whose ties weren't that strong to the West.

And there was little doubt the Russians were involved what with the retasking of their satellite. And once this mission was completed, a plain manila envelope with the satellite photos would be placed in a location along with the two uncooperative prisoners such that the Russian leadership would get the message.

We know.

The all clears sounded over his comm, the building lightly defended by less than a dozen men. They clearly hadn't been expecting company but Dawson couldn't risk them not having squeezed off an SOS. He activated his comm. "Open the doors, send in the transports."

He was situated above the smelting plant, on the catwalk that ringed the activity below. The gold had only arrived here earlier that day so he was hoping most of it hadn't been converted yet but from his vantage point there appeared to be a fairly substantial stack of bars much larger than he remembered.

The doc is going to be pissed.

Large doors at the loading dock opened and several civilian trucks pulled in as he descended the stairs to the main floor. Niner jogged up to him. "We've got about eight pallet's worth. Looks like they had to break things up into smaller batches from the plane which is good for us. They should fit in our trucks no problem. Five of them look like the old stuff, the other three the new stuff."

"Anything in the smelter itself?"

"Negative. Looks like they were just about to start loading another batch when we hit them."

"Anything too hot to handle?"

Niner pointed to a batch of large bars on cooling racks. "Those would be the hottest. Want me to hose 'em down?"

"Do it."

Niner walked over to the wall and picked up a hose off the floor, moments later spraying the hot metal bars, a burst of steam revealing how hot they truly were. A forklift was lowered from the back of one of the trucks and it immediately raced toward one of the pallets, Jimmy at the controls. The first pallet was raised and transported to the first truck. Lifted inside, the pallet was lowered onto rollers then pushed to the rear of the truck by Atlas and Mickey.

Red walked up, waving his phone. "I've got photos of all the kills. I've already sent them to Control."

"Good, but I've got little doubt it will just confirm what we already know."

"Agreed."

They both watched as a second pallet was loaded into the back of the truck. Minutes later the third pallet was loaded and the truck pulled up to the now closed loading dock doors, Atlas and Mickey securing everything so no one could see inside, then climbing into the cab of the truck, readying for the next leg of the mission.

Niner turned off the water, tentatively touching the soaked gold with his fingers then grinning a thumbs up to Dawson as he tossed the hose aside. It took another ten minutes for the rest of the gold to be loaded into the other two vehicles, and in less than fifteen minutes from the first shot being fired, they rolled out of the loading dock and into the large paved area of the quiet industrial zone of the port city of Rijeka.

Niner closed the doors behind them and sprinted to the third truck, jumping in the back with a helping hand from Sweets. Dawson was in the lead truck with Atlas and Mickey as they rolled through the empty streets toward the port. Dawson activated his comm. "Topcat, Bravo One, ETA six minutes, over."

"Bravo One, Topcat, six minutes, acknowledged, out."

A traffic light changed to red and Atlas stopped the truck, the other two lining up behind them. As they waited for the lights to cycle, a police vehicle pulled up at the opposing light, facing them. Dawson activated his comm to warn the others.

"We've got local police, standby."

The light changed and Atlas eased out the clutch, the truck roaring forward, its heavy cargo straining the engines. The police car pulled forward as well as Atlas focused on changing the gears, ignoring them as Dawson laughed, ribbing Mickey in the sides as the two pretended to be having an animated conversation. They rolled through the intersection, now less than three minutes from the docks when Atlas cursed.

"They've turned around."

"Keep moving," replied Dawson as he activated the comm. "Topcat, Bravo One, we're about to have local law enforcement trouble. Request some assistance, over."

"Bravo One, Topcat, help is on its way, over."

"Okay boys, just keep moving forward like we're doing nothing wrong, rear vehicle how about you drive like an asshole."

"Roger that," came Red's voice over the comm. Dawson looked at the passenger side mirror and saw the rear vehicle disappear as it swung into the center of the road, taking up both lanes as the cop car closed the gap with the small convoy.

"There's the docks," said Atlas as he continued to pour on the gas, the laws of physics fighting back as the truck barely passed 40kph on the speedometer. Flashing lights followed immediately by a siren had them all cursing at once as they saw the open gates of the docks start to close in response.

"Go through them," ordered Dawson as he pulled his Taser and activated his comm. "Non-lethal force only, gentlemen."

"Going through!" yelled Atlas as he braced his arms, the bumper slamming into the chain link gate, tearing it from its track and hurtling it to the side. He cranked the wheel to the right as he geared down then gave it gas again as he raced for the small cargo ship at the end of one the piers.

"They're still in pursuit!" informed Red over the comm.

"Bravo One, Topcat. Heads down boys, over."

Suddenly two Apache gunships appeared to their left, over the water, angled down as they raced toward their position. The first crossed their path, banking hard to the right to face the opposite direction, the other banking on their left side, the two helicopters taking up position on either side of the road leading to their ship. The three transport trucks blew past the helicopters then just as Red's truck cleared, they threw on all of their lights, blinding the driver of the cop car who cranked his wheel to the left and into the water.

Atlas turned left and rushed to the end of the dock, a ramp leading into the side of the ship already down, three forklifts already in position. Atlas hit the brakes just after clearing the first forklift and killed the engine as they all leapt out. Several dozen men burst from the hold of the ship, immediately lowering the gates on the arriving trucks and climbing inside, pushing the first pallets toward the waiting forklifts. The entire process took less than five minutes and the ship was steaming for the Adriatic Sea and international waters, the Apache gunships escorting them.

Dawson walked over to one of the pallets and pulled an old Roman bar of gold from the pile, stuffing it in his pocket.

Red walked up beside him, surveying the gold. "Who's that for?"

Dawson knew Red trusted him implicitly and it would never occur to him that he had taken it for himself. "I owe somebody."

Red nodded then looked up as an announcement came over the PA system.

"Mission accomplished. We are now in international waters!"

Cheers erupted from the throngs of soldiers that had taken part. Dawson felt the ship roll slightly as they turned south, their final destination Italy, the gold of Emperor Vespasian, the charge of Plinius, and the testament to the heroism of Valerius and his men, finally returning home, to join the remains already awaiting their arrival.

The ghosts of Pompeii finally able to rest.

St. Paul, Maryland
Two weeks later

"Stop fidgeting!"

"Hey, you try standing here while someone who claims they know how to tie a bowtie fails miserably at it."

"Sorry, but as somebody who mastered this simple task when he was a boy, I refuse to be belittled because I never learned how to do it facing someone else!"

Acton slapped his best friend's hands out of the way. Gregory Milton, Dean of Acton's university, winced, but not from the slap. Acton immediately became serious and walked over to the other side of the room, grabbing Milton's wheelchair. He pushed it over to his friend. "Sit now before you over do it."

Milton dropped into the chair and sighed. "You're right, I need to save it for the ceremony."

"Why don't you just sit in the chair? Nobody would care. I certainly wouldn't."

"No effin' way. I don't want that chair in a single wedding photo. Years from now I want to look back on the day my best friend *finally* tied the knot and not have to remember almost becoming a cripple."

Acton understood his friend's desire, especially since when Milton had been shot the doctors had proclaimed he'd never walk again. But here he was, standing at the mirror trying to help his friend put on a bowtie.

"I've got an idea," said Milton, spreading his legs as wide as he could. "Sit here," he said, patting the tiny piece of exposed chair.

"Hey, I'm almost a married man."

"Don't flatter yourself, you're too flat chested to be my type."

Acton laughed and parked it right between Milton's legs. He leaned back and Milton forward and watched in the mirror as the bowtie was finally done to perfection.

"There you go, see, I told you I knew how."

The door burst open, Reading poking his head inside. "You about ready—oooh, a little rumpy pumpy while you're still single, Jim?"

Acton shook his head, roaring with laughter as he pushed himself up from the chair, Milton smacking him on the ass.

He turned to his friend, his eyes starting to glisten.

"Let's go get me married."

Hamashkoraib, Sudan
Three weeks later

Kerieme stretched, looking in the mirror at his graying beard. He swore he had aged another ten years while waiting for the American to email him where the van had been left. True to his word, the email had arrived and he had found it, all locked up and in good working order, except for a chunk of the deliveries being used or missing. He had cursed the man countless times, but eventually forgave him when he realized it was the American and others like him that had helped rid their town of at least three militias and apparently freed a large group of slave women.

And he had kept his word.

Clearly the American was a good man, and though an infidel, Kerieme had never bought into the entire 'us versus them' mentality that seemed to consume so many of his faith. Was the person a good person? Then he didn't care what religion they were.

"A package arrived for you a little while ago."

It was his wife's voice calling from the kitchen that had his eyebrows jump. *A package?* He couldn't recall the last time a package had arrived at his house, if ever. He always had to drive to Khartoum for his pickups and deliveries. For something to actually be delivered to him personally was unheard of.

"What is it?"

"I don't know, it's a box."

He entered the kitchen, pecked his wife's cheek, then sat down at the table, picking up the package. It had a decent heft to it for its size. He pulled out his knife and cut through the string, then the brown paper revealing a small, plain box. He sliced open the tape and folded open the top. Inside was a cloth wrapped around something rectangular. He picked it up, again surprised at the weight and placed it on the table, his wife now sitting beside him, her own curiosity piqued. Unwrapping the cloth, they both gasped at what was revealed.

A gold bar, glistening in the sunlight that poured through the window, and a handwritten note.

Thanks for the loaner.

THE END

ACKNOWLEDGEMENTS

Many current events have inspired this book. No, Vesuvius didn't blow its top again, but I've always been fascinated by Pompeii and it is one of those bucket list destinations that I hope to visit some day. The history is fascinating and Pliny the Younger's accounts riveting reading in themselves. Many of the details including the time lines were taken directly from his letters to add authenticity to the story. Any inaccuracies I will plead artistic license rather than error!

Eritrea, Ethiopia and Sudan aren't even remotely close to being on the list, especially after reading the way their women are treated. Though it took place in Nigeria, the plight of the poor, mostly Christian school girls kidnapped by Boko Haram—whose name, translated into English, literally means "Western education is a sin", says it all—heavily influenced this book in ways I hadn't anticipated, a theme developing of women as the victims, then in the end, it being the women in Pompeii who save themselves from the predators, and the two women of the UN group that actually free the others.

At the time of this writing at least 200 of these girls are still missing, and there are new reports of fresh kidnappings of women by the same group. The fact that this type of activity goes on is disgusting. The fact that these types of groups actually receive funding from people educated or successful enough to have money to give, is even more so.

As a father of a daughter I find these events chilling, but what I find even more so is the fact that according to the FBI, more than 100,000 children are sold for sex in the U.S. each year. That's right. 100,000 children in the United States. Sold for sex. Each year. The numbers are similar for other Western nations.

If that were the premise of a book, I don't think most readers would believe it.

Another inspiration for this book, and its incorporation was entirely intentional, was the Malaysian Airlines crash. The idea that in today's society our most expensive machines can't actually be tracked in real time, yet we can track every cell phone to within a few feet, I found incredible. What caused the Malaysian Airlines flight to *crash* is anybody's guess for now, and I hope answers will come soon so the families can find peace, but the completely botched initial search and coordination is inexcusable, and the press coverage giving so much false hope to the families despicable. This style coverage was hinted at when Laura returns to Rome.

As James Acton often says, there's just not enough news in the day for a 24 hour news channel.

News becomes opinion.

And eventually fiction.

From inspirations to assisters, there were as always people who helped me with this book. My father as usual with the research, and Brent Richards for some weapons info, Brent again, along with Ian Kennedy for some terminology (army slang), and Chris "Goldfinger" Leroux for some gold info, including letting me experience holding the real thing in my hand. I think my quote was, "Holy shit, this stuff really *is* heavy!"

And one final thing, a "plug" if you will. Niner's Immortal t-shirt is actually a real thing! A buddy of mine, Ian Dandrade, who I've known for over ten years and haven't seen in as many since he moved to California, is an entrepreneur who has a line of clothing that is growing in popularity. Check it out at www.ImmortalClothing.com, especially if you're into MMA and extreme sports.

And as per usual, one final thing as a reminder to those who have not already done so, please visit my website at www.jrobertkennedy.com then sign up for the Insiders Club. You'll get emails about new book releases, new collections, sales, etc. Only an email or two a month tops, I promise! And don't forget to join me on Facebook, Twitter and Goodreads.

And as always, to my wife, daughter, parents and friends, thank you once again for your support. And to you the readers, thank you! You've all made this possible.

ABOUT THE AUTHOR

J. Robert Kennedy is the author of over one dozen international best sellers, including the smash hit James Acton Thrillers series, the first installment of which, The Protocol, has been on the best sellers list since its release, including a three month run at number one. In addition to the other novels from this series, Brass Monkey, Broken Dove, The Templar's Relic (also a number one best seller), Flags of Sin, The Arab Fall (also #1), The Circle of Eight (also #1) and The Venice Code (also #1), he has written the international best sellers Rogue Operator, Containment Failure, Cold Warriors, Depraved Difference, Tick Tock, The Redeemer and The Turned. Robert spends his time in Ontario, Canada with his family.

Visit Robert's website at www.jrobertkennedy.com for the latest news and contact information.

POMPEII'S GHOSTS

The Protocol
A James Acton Thriller, Book #1

For two thousand years the Triarii have protected us, influencing history from the crusades to the discovery of America. Descendent from the Roman Empire, they pervade every level of society, and are now in a race with our own government to retrieve an ancient artifact thought to have been lost forever.

Caught in the middle is archaeology professor James Acton, relentlessly hunted by the elite Delta Force, under orders to stop at nothing to possess what he has found, and the Triarii, equally determined to prevent the discovery from falling into the wrong hands.

With his students and friends dying around him, Acton flees to find the one person who might be able to help him, but little does he know he may actually be racing directly into the hands of an organization he knows nothing about...

POMPEII'S GHOSTS

Brass Monkey
A James Acton Thriller, Book #2

A nuclear missile, lost during the Cold War, is now in play--the most public spy swap in history, with a gorgeous agent the center of international attention, triggers the end-game of a corrupt Soviet Colonel's twenty five year plan. Pursued across the globe by the Russian authorities, including a brutal Spetsnaz unit, those involved will stop at nothing to deliver their weapon, and ensure their pay day, regardless of the terrifying consequences.

When Laura Palmer confronts a UNICEF group for trespassing on her Egyptian archaeological dig site, she unwittingly stumbles upon the ultimate weapons deal, and becomes entangled in an international conspiracy that sends her lover, archeology Professor James Acton, racing to Egypt with the most unlikely of allies, not only to rescue her, but to prevent the start of a holy war that could result in Islam and Christianity wiping each other out.

From the bestselling author of Depraved Difference and The Protocol comes Brass Monkey, a thriller international in scope, certain to offend some, and stimulate debate in others. Brass Monkey pulls no punches in confronting the conflict between two of the world's most powerful, and divergent, religions, and the terrifying possibilities the future may hold if left unchecked.

J. ROBERT KENNEDY

Broken Dove

A James Acton Thriller, Book #3

With the Triarii in control of the Roman Catholic Church, an organization founded by Saint Peter himself takes action, murdering one of the new Pope's operatives. Detective Chaney, called in by the Pope to investigate, disappears, and, to the horror of the Papal staff sent to inform His Holiness, they find him missing too, the only clue a secret chest, presented to each new pope on the eve of their election, since the beginning of the Church.

Interpol Agent Reading, determined to find his friend, calls Professors James Acton and Laura Palmer to Rome to examine the chest and its forbidden contents, but before they can arrive, they are intercepted by an organization older than the Church, demanding the professors retrieve an item stolen in ancient Judea in exchange for the lives of their friends.

All of your favorite characters from The Protocol return to solve the most infamous kidnapping in history, against the backdrop of a two thousand year old battle pitting ancient foes with diametrically opposed agendas.

From the internationally bestselling author of Depraved Difference and The Protocol comes Broken Dove, the third entry in the smash hit James Acton Thrillers series, where J. Robert Kennedy reveals a secret concealed by the Church for almost 1200 years, and a fascinating interpretation of what the real reason behind the denials might be.

The Templar's Relic

A James Acton Thriller, Book #4

THE CHURCH HELPED DESTROY THE TEMPLARS. WILL A TWIST OF FATE LET THEM GET THEIR REVENGE 700 YEARS LATER?

The Vault must be sealed, but a construction accident leads to a miraculous discovery--an ancient tomb containing four Templar Knights, long forgotten, on the grounds of the Vatican. Not knowing who they can trust, the Vatican requests Professors James Acton and Laura Palmer examine the find, but what they discover, a precious Islamic relic, lost during the Crusades, triggers a set of events that shake the entire world, pitting the two greatest religions against each other.

Join Professors James Acton and Laura Palmer, INTERPOL Agent Hugh Reading, Scotland Yard DI Martin Chaney, and the Delta Force Bravo Team as they race against time to defuse a worldwide crisis that could quickly devolve into all-out war.

At risk is nothing less than the Vatican itself, and the rock upon which it was built.

From J. Robert Kennedy, the author of six international bestsellers including Depraved Difference and The Protocol, comes The Templar's Relic, the fourth entry in the smash hit James Acton Thrillers series, where once again Kennedy takes history and twists it to his own ends, resulting in a heart pounding thrill ride filled with action, suspense, humor and heartbreak.

J. ROBERT KENNEDY

Flags of Sin
A James Acton Thriller, Book #5

Archaeology Professor James Acton simply wants to get away from everything, and relax. A trip to China seems just the answer, and he and his fiancée, Professor Laura Palmer, are soon on a flight to Beijing.

But while boarding, they bump into an old friend, Delta Force Command Sergeant Major Burt Dawson, who surreptitiously delivers a message that they must meet the next day, for Dawson knows something they don't.

China is about to erupt into chaos.

Foreign tourists and diplomats are being targeted by unknown forces, and if they don't get out of China in time, they could be caught up in events no one had seen coming.

J. Robert Kennedy, the author of eight international best sellers, including the smash hit James Acton Thrillers, takes history once again and turns it on its head, sending his reluctant heroes James Acton and Laura Palmer into harm's way, to not only save themselves, but to try and save a country from a century old conspiracy it knew nothing about.

POMPEII'S GHOSTS

The Arab Fall

A James Acton Thriller, Book #6

THE GREATEST ARCHEOLOGICAL DISCOVERY SINCE KING TUT'S TOMB IS ABOUT TO BE DESTROYED!

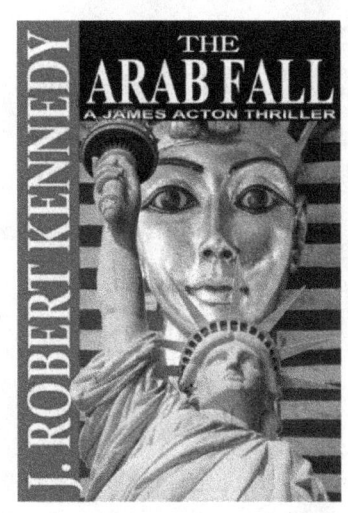

The Arab Spring has happened and Egypt has yet to calm down, but with the dig site on the edge of the Nubian Desert, a thousand miles from the excitement, Professor Laura Palmer and her fiancé Professor James Acton return with a group of students, and two friends: Interpol Special Agent Hugh Reading, and Scotland Yard DI Martin Chaney.

But an accidental find by Chaney may lead to the greatest archaeological discovery since the tomb of King Tutankhamen, perhaps even greater. And when news of it spreads, it reaches the ears of a group hell-bent on the destruction of all idols and icons, their mere existence considered blasphemous to Islam.

As chaos hits the major cities of the world in a coordinated attack, unbeknownst to the professors, students and friends, they are about to be faced with one of the most difficult decisions of their lives. Stay and protect the greatest archaeological find of our times, or save themselves and their students from harm, leaving the find to be destroyed by fanatics determined to wipe it from the history books.

From J. Robert Kennedy, the author of eleven international bestsellers including Rogue Operator and The Protocol, comes The Arab Fall, the sixth entry in the smash hit James Acton Thrillers series, where Kennedy once again takes events from history and today's headlines, and twists them into a heart pounding adventure filled with humor and heartbreak, as one of their own is left severely wounded, fighting for their life.

J. ROBERT KENNEDY

The Circle of Eight

A James Acton Thriller, Book #7

ABANDONED BY THEIR GOVERNMENT, DELTA TEAM BRAVO FIGHTS TO NOT ONLY SAVE THEMSELVES AND THEIR FAMILIES, BUT HUMANITY AS WELL.

The Bravo Team is targeted by a madman after one of their own intervenes in a rape. Little do they know this internationally well-respected banker is also a senior member of an organization long thought extinct, whose stated goals for a reshaped world are not only terrifying, but with today's globalization, totally achievable.

As the Bravo Team fights for its very survival, they are suspended, left adrift without their support network. To save themselves and their families, markers are called in, former members volunteer their services, favors are asked for past services, and the expertise of two professors, James Acton and his fiancée Laura Palmer, is requested.

It is a race around the globe to save what remains of the Bravo Team, abandoned by their government, alone in their mission, with only their friends to rely upon, as an organization over six centuries old works in the background to destroy them and all who help them, as it moves forward with plans that could see the world population decimated in an attempt to recreate Eden.

In The Circle of Eight J. Robert Kennedy, author of over a dozen international best sellers, is at his best, weaving a tale spanning centuries and delivering a taut thriller that will keep you on the edge of your seat from page one until the breathtaking conclusion.

J. ROBERT KENNEDY

The Venice Code

A James Acton Thriller, Book #8

A SEVEN HUNDRED YEAR OLD MYSTERY IS ABOUT TO BE SOLVED.

BUT HOW MANY MUST DIE FIRST?

A former President's son is kidnapped in a brazen attack on the streets of Potomac by the very ancient organization that murdered his father, convinced he knows the location of an item stolen from them by the late president.

A close friend awakes from a coma with a message for archeology Professor James Acton from the same organization, sending him along with his fiancée Professor Laura Palmer on a quest to find an object only rumored to exist, while trying desperately to keep one step ahead of a foe hell-bent on possessing it.

And seven hundred years ago, the Mongol Empire threatens to fracture into civil war as the northern capital devolves into idol worship, the Khan sending in a trusted family to save the empire--two brothers and a son, Marco Polo, whose actions have ramifications that resonate to this day.

From J. Robert Kennedy, the author of fourteen international best sellers comes The Venice Code, the latest installment of the hit James Acton Thrillers series. Join James Acton and his friends, including Delta Team Bravo and CIA Special Agent Dylan Kane in their greatest adventure yet, an adventure seven hundred years in the making.

Pompeii's Ghosts

A James Acton Thriller, Book #9

POMPEII IS ABOUT TO CLAIM ITS FINAL VICTIMS—TWO THOUSAND YEARS LATER!

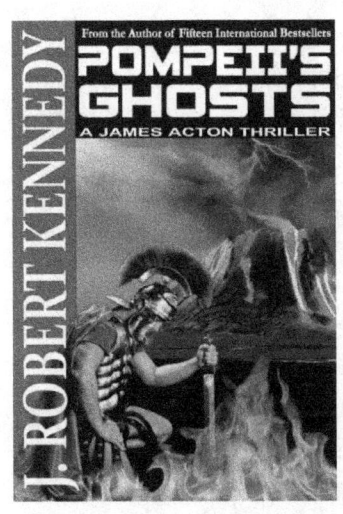

Two thousand years ago Roman Emperor Vespasian tries to preserve an empire by hiding a massive treasure in the quiet town of Pompeii should someone challenge his throne. Unbeknownst to him nature is about to unleash its wrath upon the Empire during which the best and worst of Rome's citizens will be revealed during a time when duty and honor were more than words, they were ideals worth dying for.

Professor James Acton has just arrived in Egypt to visit his fiancée Professor Laura Palmer at her dig site when a United Nations helicopter arrives carrying representatives with an urgent demand that they come to Eritrea to authenticate an odd find that threatens to start a war—an ancient Roman vessel with over one billion dollars of gold in its hold.

It is a massive amount of wealth found in the world's poorest region, and everyone wants it. Nobody can be trusted, not even closest friends or even family. Greed, lust and heroism are the orders of the day as the citizens of Pompeii try to survive nature's fury, and James Acton tries to survive man's greed while risking his own life to protect those around him.

Pompeii's Ghosts delivers the historical drama and modern day action that best selling author J. Robert Kennedy's fans have come to expect. Pompeii's Ghosts opens with a shocker that will keep you on the edge of your seat until the thrilling conclusion in a story torn from the headlines.

J. ROBERT KENNEDY

Rogue Operator

A Special Agent Dylan Kane Thriller, Book #1

TO SAVE THE COUNTRY HE LOVES, SPECIAL AGENT DYLAN KANE MIGHT HAVE TO BETRAY IT.

Three top secret research scientists are presumed dead in a boating accident, but the kidnapping of their families the same day raises questions the FBI and local police can't answer, leaving them waiting for a ransom demand that will never come.

Central Intelligence Agency Analyst Chris Leroux stumbles upon the story, and finds a phone conversation that was never supposed to happen. When he reports it to his boss, the National Clandestine Services Chief, he is uncharacteristically reprimanded for conducting an unauthorized investigation and told to leave it to the FBI.

But he can't let it go.

For he knows something the FBI doesn't.

One of the scientists is alive.

Chris makes a call to his childhood friend, CIA Special Agent Dylan Kane, leading to a race across the globe to stop a conspiracy reaching the highest levels of political and corporate America, that if not stopped, could lead to war with an enemy armed with a weapon far worse than anything in the American arsenal, with the potential to not only destroy the world, but consume it.

J. Robert Kennedy, the author of nine international best sellers, including the smash hit James Acton Thrillers, introduces Rogue Operator, the first installment of his newest series, The Special Agent Dylan Kane Thrillers, promising to bring all of the action and intrigue of the James Acton Thrillers with a hero who lives below the radar, waiting for his country to call when it most desperately needs him.

Containment Failure

A Special Agent Dylan Kane Thriller, Book #2

THE BLACK DEATH KILLED ALMOST HALF OF EUROPE'S POPULATION. THIS TIME BILLIONS ARE AT RISK.

New Orleans has been quarantined, an unknown virus sweeping the city, killing one hundred percent of those infected. The Centers for Disease Control, desperate to find a cure, is approached by BioDyne Pharma who reveal a former employee has turned a cutting edge medical treatment capable of targeting specific genetic sequences into a weapon, and released it.

CIA Special Agent Dylan Kane has been given one guideline from his boss: consider yourself unleashed, leaving Kane and New Orleans Police Detective Isabelle Laprise battling to stay alive as an insidious disease and terrified mobs spread through the city while they desperately seek those behind the greatest crime ever perpetrated.

The stakes have never been higher as Kane battles to save not only his friends and the country he loves, but all of mankind.

In Containment Failure, eleven times internationally bestselling author J. Robert Kennedy delivers a terrifying tale of what could happen when science goes mad, with enough sorrow, heartbreak, laughs and passion to keep readers on the edge of their seats until the chilling conclusion.

J. ROBERT KENNEDY

Cold Warriors

A Special Agent Dylan Kane Thriller, Book #3

THE COUNTRY'S BEST HOPE IN DEFEATING A FORGOTTEN SOVIET WEAPON LIES WITH DYLAN KANE AND THE COLD WARRIORS WHO ORIGINALLY DISCOVERED IT.

While in Chechnya CIA Special Agent Dylan Kane stumbles upon a meeting between a known Chechen drug lord and a retired General once responsible for the entire Soviet nuclear arsenal. Money is exchanged for a data stick and the resulting transmission begins a race across the globe to discover just what was sold, the only clue a reference to a top secret Soviet weapon called Crimson Rush.

Unknown to Kane, this isn't the first time America has faced this threat and he soon receives a mysterious message, relayed through his friend and CIA analyst Chris Leroux, arranging a meeting with perhaps the one man alive today who can help answer the questions the nation's entire intelligence apparatus is asking--the Cold Warrior who had discovered the threat the first time.

Over thirty years ago.

In Cold Warriors, the third installment of the hit Special Agent Dylan Kane Thrillers series, J. Robert Kennedy, the author of thirteen international bestsellers including The Protocol and Rogue Operator, weaves a tale spanning two generations and three continents with all the heart pounding, edge of your seat action his readers have come to expect. Take a journey back in time as the unsung heroes of a war forgotten try to protect our way of life against our greatest enemy, and see how their war never really ended, the horrors of decades ago still a very real threat today.

The Turned

Zander Varga, Vampire Detective, Book #1

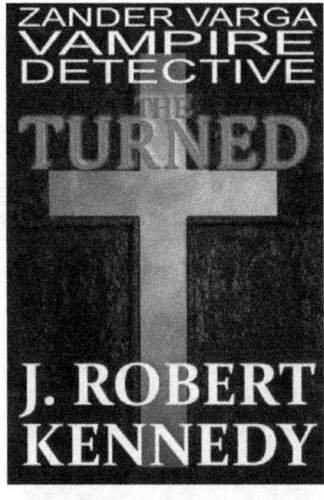

Zander has relived his wife's death at the hands of vampires every day for almost three hundred years, his perfect memory a curse of becoming one of The Turned—infecting him their final heinous act after her murder.

Nineteen year-old Sydney Winter knows Zander's secret, a secret preserved by the women in her family for four generations. But with her mother in a coma, she's thrust into the front lines, ahead of her time, to fight side-by-side with Zander.

And she wouldn't change a thing. She loves the excitement, she loves the danger. And she loves Zander. But it's a love that will have to go unrequited, because Zander has only one thing on his mind. And it's been the same thing for over two hundred years. Revenge.

But today, revenge will have to wait, because Zander Varga, Private Detective, has a new case. A woman's husband is missing. The police aren't interested. But Zander is. Something doesn't smell right, and he's determined to find out why.

From J. Robert Kennedy, the internationally bestselling author of The Protocol and Depraved Difference, comes his sixth novel, The Turned, a terrifying story that in true Kennedy fashion takes a completely new twist on the origin of vampires, tying it directly to a well-known moment in history. Told from the perspective of Zander Varga and his assistant, Sydney Winter, The Turned is loaded with action, humor, terror and a centuries long love that must eventually be let go.

Depraved Difference

A Detective Shakespeare Mystery, Book #1

WOULD YOU HELP, WOULD YOU RUN,
OR WOULD YOU JUST WATCH?

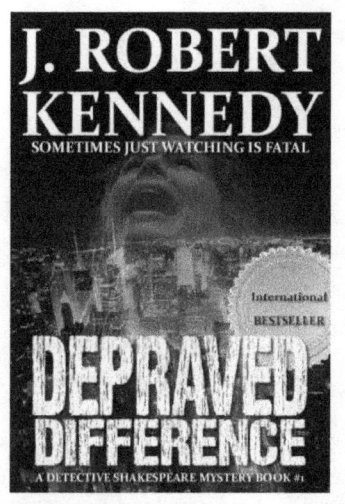

When a young woman is brutally assaulted by two men on the subway, her cries for help fall on the deaf ears of onlookers too terrified to get involved, her misery ended with the crushing stomp of a steel-toed boot. A cellphone video of her vicious murder, callously released on the Internet, its popularity a testament to today's depraved society, serves as a trigger, pulled a year later, for a killer.

Emailed a video documenting the final moments of a woman's life, entertainment reporter Aynslee Kai, rather than ask why the killer chose her to tell the story, decides to capitalize on the opportunity to further her career. Assigned to the case is Hayden Eldridge, a detective left to learn the ropes by a disgraced partner, and as videos continue to follow victims, he discovers they were all witnesses to the vicious subway murder a year earlier, proving sometimes just watching is fatal.

From the author of The Protocol and Brass Monkey, Depraved Difference is a fast-paced murder suspense novel with enough laughs, heartbreak, terror and twists to keep you on the edge of your seat, then knock you flat on the floor with an ending so shocking, you'll read it again just to pick up the clues.

Tick Tock

A Detective Shakespeare Mystery, Book #2
SOMETIMES HELL IS OTHER PEOPLE

Crime Scene tech Frank Brata digs deep and finds the courage to ask his colleague, Sarah, out for coffee after work. Their good time turns into a nightmare when Frank wakes up the next morning covered in blood, with no recollection of what happened, and Sarah's body floating in the tub.

Billionaire Richard Tate is the toast of the town, loved by everyone but his wife. His plans for a romantic weekend with his mistress ends in disaster, waking the next morning to find her murdered, floating in the tub. After fleeing in a panic, he returns to find the hotel room spotless, and no sign of the body. An envelope found at the scene contains not the expected blackmail note, but something far more sinister.

Two murders, with the same MO, targeting both the average working man, and the richest of society, sets a rejuvenated Detective Shakespeare, and his new reluctant partner, Amber Trace, after a murderer whose motivations are a mystery, and who appears to be aided by the very people they would least expect—their own.

Tick Tock, Book #2 in the internationally bestselling Detective Shakespeare Mysteries series, picks up right where Depraved Difference left off, and asks a simple question: What would you do? What would you do if you couldn't prove your innocence, but knew you weren't capable of murder? Would you hide the very evidence that might clear you, or would you turn yourself in and trust the system to work?

J. ROBERT KENNEDY

The Redeemer

A Detective Shakespeare Mystery, Book #3

SOMETIMES LIFE GIVES MURDER A SECOND CHANCE

It was the case that destroyed Detective Justin Shakespeare's career, beginning a downward spiral of self-loathing and self-destruction lasting half a decade. And today things are only going to get worse. The Widow Rapist is free on a technicality, and it is up to Detective Shakespeare and his partner Amber Trace to find the evidence, five years cold, to put him back in prison before he strikes again.

But Shakespeare and Trace aren't alone in their desire for justice. The Seven are the survivors, avowed to not let the memories of their loved ones be forgotten. And with the release of the Widow Rapist, they are determined to take justice into their own hands, restoring balance to a flawed system.

At stake is a second chance, a chance at redemption, a chance to salvage a career destroyed, a reputation tarnished, and a life diminished.

A chance brought to Detective Shakespeare whether he wants it or not.

A chance brought to him by The Redeemer.

From J. Robert Kennedy, the author of seven international bestsellers including Depraved Difference and The Protocol, comes the third entry in the acclaimed Detective Shakespeare Mysteries series, The Redeemer, a dark tale exploring the psyches of the serial killer, the victim, and the police, as they all try to achieve the same goals.

Balance. And redemption.

CPSIA information can be obtained
at www.ICGtesting.com
Printed in the USA
LVHW111315181120
672034LV00026B/110